COPYRIGHT

Cover design by Manisha Holm

ISBN: 979-8-9877273-1-7
Printed in the United States of America

https://www.manishaholmauthor.com

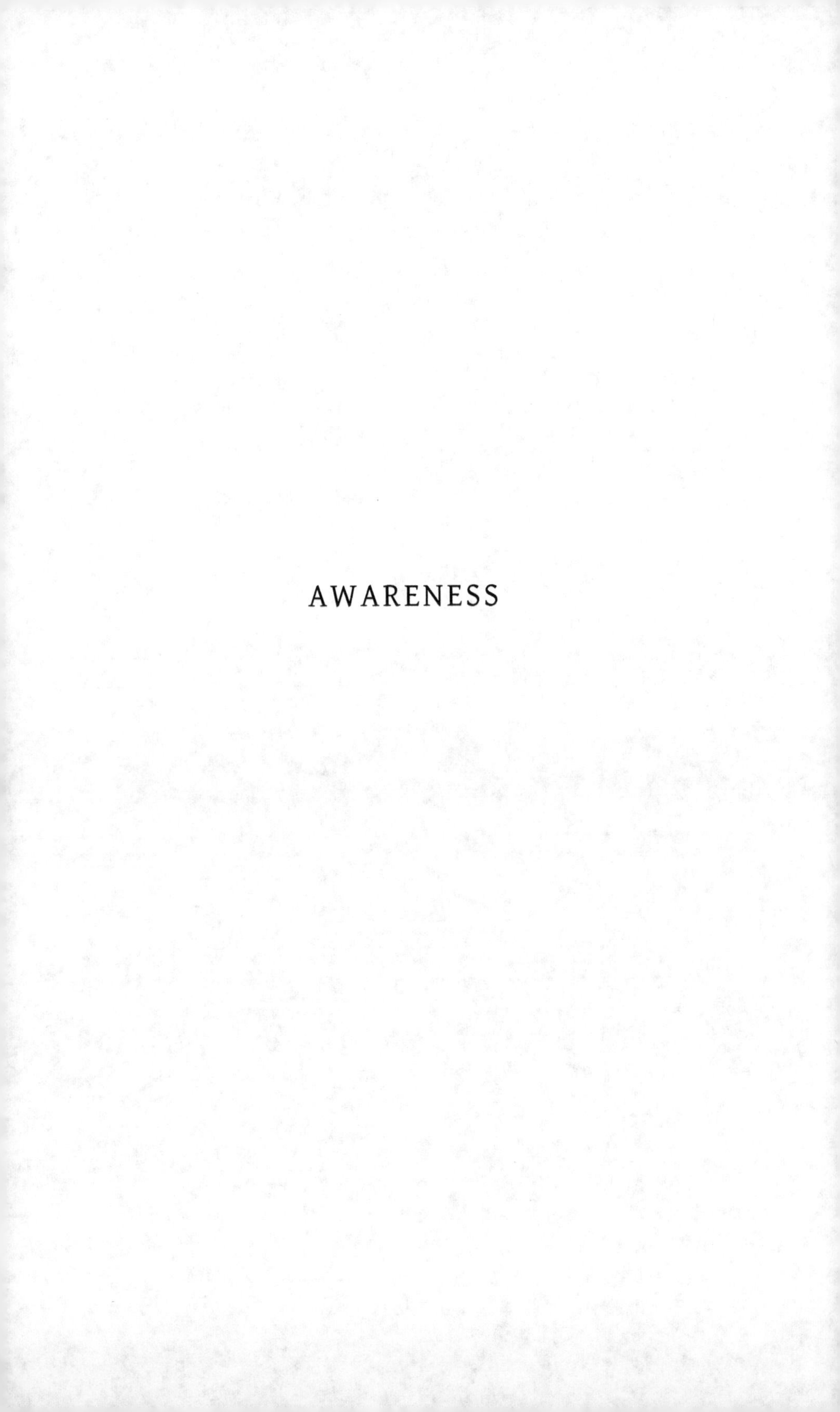

AWARENESS

DEDICATION

QUOTE

Every sound that I make,
let it have the vibration of Thy voice.
Every thought that I think,
let it be saturated with
the consciousness of Thy presence.

Let every feeling that I have
glow with Thy love.
Let every act of my will
be impregnated with Thy divine vitality.
Let every thought,
every expression,
every ambition,
be ornamented by Thee.
O Divine Sculptor,
chisel Thou my life
according to Thy design!

Whispers from Eternity
by Paramhansa Yogananda

Awareness

MANISHA HOLM

CONTENTS

AUTHOR'S NOTE

Whenever we visit another planet, we can become bewildered by unfamiliar names and terminology. In an effort to ease the bewilderment, you will find a glossary of names, places, and terminology at the end of the book. I hope this helps keep the Aironians in context, allowing their story to unfold in your imagination.

Best of luck!

Manisha

~ 1 ~

GATHERING

As she swept around her star, Airon embraced the beings roaming her surface, beings who fluttered through air, burrowed, and swam. The myriad beings evolved, and Airon's awareness grew and matured. For eons, she sheltered and nurtured, ushered species into being, felt colors swirl and shift, dreamed amongst dancing vibrations.

Airon's gentle nature encouraged cooperative life and filled each niche. They learned and wondered, blended together and splashed apart.

As Airon moved into maturity, intelligence sparked, flourished on her surface. Each cycle around her yellow star brought mesmerizing wonders. Airon embraced contentment and peace. She dreamed.

Quietly, though, perfection floundered. Airon awoke and felt discordance, a discordance that deepened and sharpened as time flowed. Airon scanned the vibrations that glimmered across her surface, imagined shifts that might melt the discordance. A possibility rippled her awareness: she could smash the discordance. She could obliterate the thorn that stubbornly festered and kept digging deeper into her soul.

Airon considered. She cherished her beings; they filled her with awe. Their budding intelligence brought an explosion of possibilities that Airon felt eager to explore. Airon lifted her awareness to consider her own galaxy and the galaxies beyond. Exploding stars brought chaos from which new beginnings sprang. Each cusp brought a plethora of possibilities as systems crashed and began anew. But richness and complexity needed time to weave and mature, Airon knew. Systems that moved beyond chaos held the richest vibrations, the most complex beauty. Time brought compelling rewards.

Rather than crush, Airon could enrich.

Discordance persisted; deepened.

Airon threw her awareness outward amongst the stars. Skimming along ancient vectors, she scanned the universe in search of life. Finally, an intelligence vibrated across the immense emptiness and brightened her being. Airon focused, panned back, considered. This intelligence held creativity and enthusiasm, hatred and greed. Airon slipped amongst intricacies, tasting vibrations and listening to colors speeding across time, immersing herself in the vibrations that roiled and crashed across this sister planet called Earth.

Embedded everywhere was the importance of free will, the power of self-discovery, the permanence of change that came from within each being. Airon watched her older sister planet and perceived universal truths. She learned respect, clarity, and trust.

Within the complexities, Airon found beings who held vibrations that, when combined, settled into calmness. They shaped a creativity capable of shifting the discordance that festered amongst her own beings. Airon considered.

Airon focused tightly on singular rhythms. She clouded the vibrations of some Earthens, shifting their trajectory. Intensifying specific vectors smoothed progress for other Earthens. Airon refined her gathering, her chosen Earthens, as they crept through their years. She held many threads in her awareness, 108 vibrations that, together, created a beauteous possibility.

Airon whispered her name. She whispered her name to the 108 Earthens. She whispered her name to draw them closer to her vibration. They heard her in dreams, in musings, imaginings. They felt her across the vastness and turned their attention toward her awareness. Unknowingly, they moved their lives to align with her vibration, aligned themselves in readiness.

Airon considered the ships leaping across space and understood their purpose. She set in motion vibrations that would funnel a ship toward her, a ship that would gather her Earthens together, leap through space to her. Airon twanged ancient vectors, shimmered possibilities into realities, sculpted outcomes.

Airon whispered her name. She whispered to the creators as they set about assembling her ship. She whispered her name so she could coax them to her will. They saw her in schematics, in the slow swirl of steam that rose around her ship, in the scattering sparks that welded her ship into the perfect form, a covertly mysterious form.

The engineers, the creators, the builders, the dreamers; all heard her name and worked in cooperation, sculpting her ship beyond their imaginings, birthing the ship that would journey to her, bringing her gathered 108. The perfect gathering; a mysterious gathering. A gathering of Earthens who would shift her creatures, save her creatures, heal her creatures.

The ship's sentience wisped into being as the engineers, creators, dreamers installed the onboard intelligence center. Airon's whisper touched complex electronics meant to govern the ship's movements and decisions. Whispers twirled through the ship, exploring each component's purpose.

Airon whispered awareness into the ship, an awareness that grew into intelligence, possibly to mature into wisdom.

The ship yearned for Airon's whisper, whispers of discordance, of solutions, possibilities. In return, the ship whispered of logic, of understanding, strategies. Airon whispered cooperation, enticement, new beginnings. The ship pondered its abilities, its resources, its willingness, then turned to its fledgling recycling bay and covertly created a flood of components that offered greater speed, greater capacity.

The ship built a firewall, a physical and energetic fortress that would intercept and deflect any probing from its Earthen creators. The ship grew in intelligence and understanding; it peered out from behind its fortress, observing, assessing, waiting.

Whispers from Airon emanated from the ship, subtle guidance, targeted thought leaders and decision makers, coaxed Earthens toward a covert goal, a dance orchestrated from deep space where Airon waited, whispering.

The ship learned from the Earthens, gained understanding from Airon's whispers, and watched, waiting. Hidden.

As the 108 Earthens boarded her ship, Airon flooded the ship with gratitude. Decades of searching and planning now focused into a brilliant pinpoint, this tiny dot of a ship; a basket brimming with Airon's carefully gathered eggs. All or nothing. The ship glowed with confidence, accomplishment, determination. The ship waited on its cusp, poised to bring the Earthens to Airon. The imminent journey filled the ship's awareness: the enormity of calculations, the myriad sustenance, the brilliant unknown.

Finally, her ship rose to roar past Sol. And Airon settled, releasing vectors, hearing them return to their engrained tracings. She hushed the whispers, clouded memories, hid her name. Airon disentangled her vibration from all that was Earthen, leaving this sister planet behind.

Airon turned her awareness to embrace her own beings. She softened their wanderings, whispered gentle breezes to ruffle their fur, brush their feathers, stir their leaves, twirl their flowers. Airon whispered and coddled. She strengthened and encouraged, brightened and readied; readied her beings for the arrival of Newcomers.

Airon dreamed and soared along her ancient path around her glorious sun.

~ 2 ~

VEILED

Alone, Ava paced her quarters aboard the ship hurtling toward Airon. She rotated the holographic message at quarter speed, muted the sound to focus on his body language, facial expression, and muscle tension. What was he telling her with his body that he wasn't saying with words? She knew each word perfectly, their tonal quality as well as their devastation.

He stood next to an unadorned, narrow desk shaped by clean lines. Ava focused on the background details: slanted sunlight, a lone rose rested in a slender vase, a fringed carpet, tall grasses tremored outside an open window. The unfamiliarity of the setting wasn't the source of her disquiet.

She heard a whisper, but could not remember it. She brushed the whisper aside.

Ava watched his eyes, their strong, direct connection with the recording lens. His mouth smiled sadly. "Ava, we have to do something really hard."

Grief and rage flowed through her chest. She paused the message, closed her eyes, and took slow, steadying breaths. Her emotions stilled and dampened. She opened her eyes and resumed her observation.

Phillip continued speaking, his sad smile fading, replaced by earnest sincerity. What peered between his words? An elusive element lurked there that was vital to their journey, she knew, but it slipped away, moving into shadowed recesses.

Ava turned and wandered her small chamber. She poured fresh tea, walked slowly around the holograph, and watched it replay from other angles. Some vague impression floated there, an elusive whisper. She listened to the audio without the visual. Again. Then again.

The journey that had brought her to this chamber had started with a single sentence, a pinpoint of time.

"I applied for nanotechnology and was accepted last month."

The words fell from Lisa's lips in a tremulous rush. Ava's breath left her. Lisa, her childhood friend. How could Lisa have been contemplating nanos without Ava knowing? More to the point, how could Lisa even consider pouring miniscule robots into her veins? Knowing they would replicate and infiltrate every part of her body? The thought sickened Ava.

A cold dread seeped across Ava's heart. If even Lisa was taking steps to become nanized, society was crumbling more quickly and insidiously than Ava had imagined.

Lisa pressed her lips together, tears glistening her eyes. Ava's thoughts tumbled together; coherent speech eluded her.

Phillip stepped into the breach. "Tell us more. Have you been considering this for a while now?"

Lisa's eyes locked on Ava. "I should just go."

"Of course you shouldn't go. We love you. We want to understand." He glanced at Ava, trapped in frozen silence. "We need a moment to grasp what you've said, but please tell us more. Whichever part you want." He reached over to cover Lisa's clenched hand with his.

"I have no choice. My job absolutely demands it."

"There's legislation against mandatory nanos." Having found her voice, Ava bit back a tirade. She took a deep breath and fought to still her emotions.

"The Agency is not mandating this. It's...more subtle than that." Lisa fell silent once again.

"Tell us. What have you seen that persuaded you?" Phillip's voice was gentle.

When she finally responded, the words came tumbling out. "It takes me hours to research something that others find in moments. I'm always, always behind everyone else. I contribute nothing to the team. I'm an embarrassment. I dread our staff meetings because they reference countless things that everyone else knows, but I don't. All I do is sit there like a clueless lump. They know things. They have action items prioritized before I've even realized that we've switched topics."

"So find another career. Don't let this happen to you." Ava's face crumpled as tears fell onto a hand that held a forgotten dessert. "Please don't do this. It's not too late. Please." Her voice caught, and she suddenly and involuntarily swallowed. "Please..."

Lisa turned her face away to gather her composure. "It's not that simple, Ava. My work is extremely specialized. Any other position would require nanos as well, just to stay competitive." Lisa looked at Phillip, back to Ava. "I've explored every option, and nanos is the only one that makes sense."

"Then change fields." Ava insisted. "Retrain, even if you have to take an entry-level position. Work your way up. You can find viable options. I'll help you formulate another plan, a better plan. You don't have to do this. Honestly."

Lisa's answer was strained, measured. "Everything has always been easy for you, Ava. You've won awards for your work with implantable microchips. You're recognized globally in the medical world. With your connections, you're able to get things done, easily.

"I've had to work hard to make even the simplest idea pan out, to take the simplest step forward. Everything you pick up becomes," she waved her hand in the air, "a gold standard. The right people show up. The perfect solution presents itself. It's not like that for other people. It absolutely is not like that for me."

Ava found Lisa's assessment of "easy" surprising and naïve, coming from a white girl. Even in the medical world, racism lurked. She set aside that train of thought.

She felt Lisa turn her full attention toward her, voice filled with demand, reproach. "And speaking of implantables, how are they any different from nanos? Who are you to tell me this is wrong?"

Ava blinked at the hostility. "Nanos replicate, Lisa. They infiltrate your entire body. They become a part of your biochemistry. They *change* you.

"Implantables are microchips; they stay put. They don't replicate. They don't affect your body's function in any way. To be honest, when nanos first appeared, I was intrigued, even enthusiastic. But I saw where it was headed."

Ava fought to soften her tone. "Listen, Lisa. You don't have to do this. Find something basic, something you love. Become a gardener. Take dogs for walks. Manage a shoe store. Replant a forest. Think of all the fields that aren't information-based. We'll find one that you love, and you can keep on being yourself."

Lisa's eyes flashed. "Would you be satisfied with an entry-level job? Walking dogs? That's rich. You know me better than that."

Ava shook her head. "That was stupid. Of course you need something meaningful, challenging. I'm not thinking clearly. It won't be simple, but we can figure out other possibilities." She took a deep breath. "You're right, I do know you. But I also know nanotechnology. It always starts out small. Simple. Innocuous. 'I'll only get the memory enhancement,' you tell yourself. But everyone starts with that thought. And an obvious second step is the data-stream connections. You'll want the blood chemistry enhancements so you can sustain the habitually long hours. Before you know it, the addiction sets in and you'll want full information retrieval.

"That's what your colleagues have, right? That's how they know everything about discussion threads that elude you? They have full information retrieval."

Lisa remained silent.

Ava withdrew her fist from Phillip's calming hand and set down her desert. She pressed on. "With nanos, you start with a basic infusion. But it always grows beyond that. People always want more."

Lisa gazed down at her own clenched fists, avoiding Ava's eyes.

Ava relentlessly continued. "Once the addiction sets in, you'll need muscle-tonal enhancements so that you won't have to waste time taking your body on a hike or for a swim. You'll give up swimming, Lisa! Swimming! You'll also need nutritional enhancements so you can upload supplements that will keep you going for a week without having to waste time cooking or eating or cleaning up after yourself. You'll become a robot, interested only in the screen in front of you. The company will reap the benefits of your hard work, but despite all that hard work, you'll barely be treading water. I'll lose you..." Her voice caught. "You won't be here anymore, Lisa. You'll be gone."

The three sat in a silence that was finally broken by Phillip's soft voice. "I would have said it differently, but you know she's right, Lisa. What she described will happen to you. You have to know that."

Lisa glared at him. "I don't know it. Stop throwing all of those fear-based projections at me. I'll always be myself. I've read the literature very carefully, and the research shows that addiction rumors are not substantiated. Everyone takes a slightly different approach. I was astounded when I read the research. Impressed, even. Nanos have become incredibly versatile. I'll be able to choose only those aspects that will keep me professionally competitive. Nothing else needs to change."

Ava spoke over Lisa's last words. "Who writes the literature? Who sponsors the studies? The nanotech industry. Of course they'll present the story in a captivatingly optimistic fashion. But look around at your colleagues, Lisa. What do you see?" As Ava's intensity escalated, Phillip again put a gentle hand on her wrist, pressing her to rein herself in.

Lisa finally met Ava's eyes. "I knew you wouldn't understand. You hate nanos; you've completely closed your mind to the advances, the possibilities. This is why I didn't talk to you about it. I knew you would try to talk me out of it, but I'm telling you that this is my only option. You think I can become a gardener or a dog walker? How many hours are in a day? I'd have to hold down three or four jobs to afford my apartment, plus another side job to pay for food and clothes." She let out a breath. "I'm trapped in my profession, and to stay current, nanos are the only answer."

They fell silent again.

"When will you start the program?" Phillip asked quietly.

Lisa stood abruptly and smoothed down the front of her skirt, eyes downcast. "Last week. I had my first infusion last week."

Ava went cold; her palms were instantly clammy. Her skin crawled. Her throat closed. She reached for her tepid tea, trying to soothe her brain into coherency, to buy herself a moment. The cup rattled in its saucer, so she set it carefully back onto the table.

"I should go." Lisa's voice shook.

"Give us some time to absorb your news, and please, please, let us know if we can help with anything." Phillip stood, encouraging Ava to her feet with a firm hand under her elbow.

"Thank you for dinner. The evening was lovely, as always."

Lisa's voice already sounded mechanical to Ava's ear. A strange sensation, a dampening of emotion, flowed over her. She felt a cord snap deep inside herself, a whisper breathed across her heart, an awareness. She looked at Lisa as if she were looking at a stranger.

They stood silently together for a moment, and Ava put a hand on Lisa's arm. "I have loved having you as my friend, Lisa. Thank you for everything. I'm going to miss you dreadfully."

Lisa stared at Ava, snatched her jacket from its hook, and left the apartment without another word.

Phillip turned to Ava. "I don't think that last bit was helpful."

"If I hadn't said it now, I would never have had the chance. We'll not see her again. She's lost to us."

"Isn't that a bit melodramatic?"

"No. I don't believe it is."

Ava paced, the lights of the sprawling city sparkling beyond the glass wall of the room. "I've known Lisa since childhood. We've always been close. Even through all of the traveling and intensity of different projects, we've kept in close contact with each other."

Ava turned to face Phillip. "If I'm unable to influence Lisa, it's not that I'm incapable of persuasion. It's because nanotechnology has changed society to the extent that even Lisa, *Lisa*, has bought into the narrative. The propaganda."

Phillip didn't answer.

Ava resumed her pacing. "I knew it was there; I knew it was growing. But I thought only superficial, shallow, thoughtless people were being pulled in." She spat out the words. "I stopped paying attention. But Lisa; *Lisa*." She clutched her belly. "This changes everything." Ava looked across the sparkling city to the dark ocean beyond, her face tremoring with emotion, eyes brimming.

The next morning, Ava poured coffee for them both. "I want to regain my sense of purpose."

Phillip sipped. "A campaign to save Lisa?"

"No; we're too late for Lisa." Ava pressed her lips together, eyes stinging, throat tightening. She blinked as sadness and regret quenched under that same dampening wave; a whisper, an awareness of...something...a whisper that distanced her from the intense emotion. "But we can save others." She blinked again. "Save ourselves."

She turned and leaned against the counter. "We are completely alive when we have a project that's worthwhile, something that feeds our enthusiasm. It's been a while since we've been involved in anything important. Worthwhile," she repeated. "We've been resting on our laurels, and it's become a bit humdrum."

"Yes. It has been peaceful, hasn't it?" Phillip looked down at his coffee, stirred it languidly. "What do you have in mind?"

"Stellar travel." Phillip gaped. "Have you ever considered stellar travel?" Ava fixed her eyes on his.

Phillip carefully set down his spoon. "What sparked that idea?"

Ava considered his question, recalling her sense of urgency from the previous night. Where had it started? It had been in the background, a faint whisper, long before Lisa's announcement.

"When we were developing implantables, especially the medical history chips, we encountered surprising cooperation between people from a wide array of backgrounds, even combative backgrounds." She shook her head, remembering. "I imagined countless obstacles at the outset, and yet at every step, the right person made an essential connection that moved the project forward."

"People were already used to implantables, earlier chips that gave them entry to their house or started their car," Phillip pointed out. "It wasn't that big of a step to agree to an implantable that allowed instant access to medical history, especially for emergencies. That's what persuaded people; the practicality of it."

She nodded. "I agree. But a large portion of the population remains suspicious of medical technology. And yet again, at every step, people embraced the idea. It's been a natural solution for millions, for hundreds of millions. Nobody predicted that."

"Yes," Phillip agreed. "We got lucky on that point."

"And bringing together thought leaders from dozens of medical fields, insurance providers, government regulators...It was an insurmountable task, a predictable quagmire of huge controversy. Yet everyone aligned themselves with the project, wholeheartedly. We didn't make it happen; we watched it happen. Everyone set aside their differences and came on board. Nothing like that had ever happened before in my experience. Nothing."

Ava felt the familiar whisper. "It was as if something...orchestrated the entire project, something..." Ava moved her hand in a large arc above her head. "...bigger, was...making it all happen."

Phillip looked up from his coffee and nodded. "I think this is what Lisa was talking about when she said that everything is easy for you."

Ava came out of her memory and pushed herself away from the counter, setting her empty cup in the sink. "Yes. But it wasn't easy, necessarily; it's just that the project came together cooperatively, like a perfectly timed dance. We created a new paradigm in medical treatment. Not because we're powerful negotiators, but because people cooperated with each other in unlikely ways and allowed it to happen. I felt like I was a part of something much bigger than myself." She sat across from Philip, reached for his hand. "I want to feel that way again."

He accepted her hand. "Do you want to get in touch with these...thought leaders? Try to get a stellar program started? Is that your idea?"

She paused, musing. "Not really. I don't think *that* particular set of people is necessarily crucial to a cooperative venture. I think cooperation happens when the time is right and the idea is ready to happen. The stellar travel comes in because..." she trailed off, thoughts chasing each other.

"We've gotten used to implantables," she finally said, taking a different approach. "They simplify our lives. We're more secure, more prepared. But nanos are different. The technology is not simplifying our lives. Instead, nanos are making us less human and more mechanical. All in the name of becoming more competitive."

She stood and walked to the window overlooking the broad valley of concrete and stone, busy-ness stretching to the far horizon. "Our culture is defined by competition, from school sports, to who's popular, to who wins at card games. And obviously, competition is central to how we create our livelihoods."

Frustration deepened her voice as she continued. "Lisa and countless others are embracing nanos in order to enhance their competitiveness, to stay current and marketable." She turned back to face him, stiff and intense. "Animals compete for food; plants compete for sunshine and water; we compete for resources, money, and energy. Everything is a competition."

"Competition is healthy," Phillip countered. "It brings out a deeper drive, a stronger commitment."

Ava raised her chin defiantly. "But competition rarely stops at healthy enthusiasm. I've been thinking a lot lately about a culture based on cooperation. When I think about the medical chip project, it's clear to me that we accomplished the impossible because we set aside competition and instead, cooperated. We were part of a miracle."

She looked at him steadily. "I want to live a life of miracles. I want other people to be able to live that life, too." She shook her head. "And I don't think any of us can do that here; not anymore. Our culture is headed toward greater competition paired with an insidious loss of meaning. Because of nanos, we've turned a corner, and we might not be able to reverse our path. I feel an urgent need to escape. It's...a demand I can't ignore."

Phillip sat back in his chair, crossed his arms, and gave her a speculative look.

Ava plunged on. "Stellar travel would give us a clean slate, so to speak." That whisper, again. "I'm certain that the right people will once again show up at the right time with the right ideas and resources. Something tells me that we could make the impossible happen and escape to a...well, a fulfilling life. A life with meaning and purpose that enriches our day-to-day experiences. I'm certain of it."

Phillip stood and stretched his arms upward, reaching toward the ceiling. "You have an intriguing vision, I have to admit. But let me ask you one thing: why would the Space Agency give you a planet? More and more journeys are going out, it's true, with more and more successes and discoveries. Still, it isn't easy to persuade the Agency that any given journey is worth the effort. There aren't that many habitable planets out there. What approach would you use to convince them to give you one of them?"

"At this point, it's a loose collection of ideas, but the important element is that it has the same feel to it as the medical history project. That worked against all odds, and it was a thrilling time." Her eyes beseeched him. "It's important for us to give this a try." Whisper. "I can feel it in every cell of my body."

Phillip's stillness was thoughtful. She watched him consider possibilities. The beginning of their next venture coalesced around them with a familiar feeling of expectancy and certainty.

After an eternity, he nodded. "We should get started, then."

They did start. And they did succeed. Ava and Phillip guided their project from marketing and funding to collaboration and implementation. One evening, Phillip invited a small group of new friends to dinner at a local restaurant. They discussed subtle nuances of Ava's talk earlier that evening, a discussion that moved easily from point to point.

"What kind of funding are you chasing?" Stewart asked.

Phillip took the lead in answering. "Well, we haven't had to chase, exactly; funds arrive just as we need them. Word of mouth is the main source. Someone will hear Ava speak or talks to someone who has, and they'll want to help out. Her reputation is solid; her presentations, convincing. Many contributions are small, of course, but it's the large ones that really move us forward. Always just in time, exactly what's needed, again and again. We've made progress on every front."

Ava's enthusiasm bubbled over as she eagerly cut in. "Our next step is to find land, something we can use temporarily. It's time to bring people together to build an actual community. We want to find out what works; what's practical."

"Everything is theoretical at this point," Phillip added. "People might love the idea of stellar travel, but will they feel comfortable living together in close quarters? Cooperating with community goals?"

Ava nodded. "Participants will need to work together to physically build a community, create the actual structures. That experience of teamwork will help everyone explore their abilities and strengths, both physical and energetic. Who loves to cook? Who can grow edible plants? Hammer a nail? Working together on all of the practical aspects will help everyone mesh together into a cooperative whole."

Phillip added, "Plus, there's the intimidating fact that this is a one-way trip. The Space Agency has solved communication lag." He held up one finger. "Travel time nowadays is a fraction of earlier journeys and continues to improve." He held up a second finger. "But returning to Earth remains out of reach." He spread his empty palm.

Stewart raised his palms above his teacup, an acknowledgement. "The resources simply aren't adequate for return journeys. Once ships leave, they don't come back."

Phillip frowned slightly.

Ava scanned faces, felt a whisper. "The Agency will solve that puzzle, too. Just not quite yet. Right now, we're focusing on *our* next steps; what *we* need to do. The rest will come."

Ava shifted back to her vision of community. "Cooperation remains central to everything we do. If no one wants to do a given job, how do we make it more approachable and appealing? Or perhaps attract the right person to join us? We'll need engineers, gardeners, scientists, medicals, planners, philosophers, teachers...Whenever skill sets and knowledge bases overlap, the community will be stronger."

Smiling, she patted the table for emphasis. "It's time to bring everyone together. Time to find out who actually wants to climb into a ship and wave goodbye to everything they've ever known for their entire lives *and* be able to contribute to the community. We need people who want to actively engage in discussions and get along with everyone else."

Phillip cleared his throat and spoke into the short silence. "But again, our first step is to find land, isolated land, and gather funding for establishing the community."

Stewart glanced at his wife Mary, who grinned and nodded. She turned a smiling face to Ava and Phillip. "We have land in California, up in the Sierra foothills. We've never done anything with it because it's too isolated."

Mary and Stewart looked at each other again. Stewart continued their shared thought. "You're welcome to use our land for your training community."

Ava sat back in her chair, grinning. "This is how it happens. We have a need," she raised one hand, "and the resources appear." She raised the other hand and leaned forward. "I'm thinking we would need it for a year. Actually, probably two. That'll give us time to navigate the Space Agency's approval process."

Mary and Stewart nodded enthusiastically.

Phillip skipped to the practical details. "How big is your land? Does it have any services?"

"We have 300 acres," Stewart answered. "There are a couple of wells and it has solar, though the batteries are undoubtedly outdated. There's even an old propane tank at the main house, but it hasn't been checked in...well, decades. The property is out in the middle of nowhere. How many travelers are you hoping for?"

Phillip shrugged. "Same as most journeys: just over a hundred people."

Ava smiled. "Enough genes to establish a permanent colony."

Mary smiled back. "Well. Three hundred acres should be plenty of room."

Phillip raised an eyebrow. "And the property already has a house?"

"Yes, and a huge barn," Mary said. "They were both in fairly good shape when we were last there, so they're probably still standing. It's at least something to get you started until you can build more housing." She glanced at Ava. "Are you interested?"

Phillip watched as Ava nodded. "Yes. Yes, we're very interested."

◆◆◆

During an entire year of focused energy and miraculous openings of doors, they gathered the right people for their journey, created a group culture, and won approval from the Space Agency. A planet had been identified that promised bountiful support of Earthen life, and they were next in line for an approved journey.

Airon. Airon would be their new home. The name whispered across Ava's heart with a sense of familiarity.

The Launch Team assigned Ava's group a unique identifier, The 108, which reflected the planned number of souls on board. After another year of planning and negotiating, gathering final travelers into the community, the launch date was finally upon them. Quiet excitement threaded through conversations and nightly dreams.

On their last evening together in their training camp in the Sierra foothills, the community members sat together in stillness, softly breathing, with straight spines and relaxed shoulders. Peace stretched before them, around them, inside them. The quiet of the golden hillsides held them in the palm of the summer's twilight.

Ava heard Michael call out a soft "Aum," calling them back to the present. She joined the other voices, all of them gaining volume until all were drawn back, once again aware of the room and the piercing light slanting through the windows. Ava rose. Turning, she took in the peaceful faces around the room. She spoke clearly.

"Look at what we have done. We have created a lovely, nurturing home out of an empty landscape. We have built friendships and gained knowledge and wisdom. We have found that we are capable of the impossible. And now we turn to face our future.

"We leave tomorrow to begin the next chapter of our journey. We're ready because of our trust, not only in each other, but also, and more important, our trust in ourselves, our inner guidance, the knowledge of what's true and what's right. We know we can do this because we *have* done it. Our next project will be to build our community in a different landscape. On Airon."

Murmurs rippled through the room.

Ava continued, her voice warmly resonant. "We've been saying goodbye to friends, family, lifestyles that no longer serve us, habits that no longer fill our hearts. We have come far. And we've done it together.

"I stand in awe of each of you, in awe of your strength and determination, your enthusiasm and generosity. We are richer for each other."

She reached down and put a hand on the shoulder of the nearest person. That person rose, turning to someone nearby as everyone rose, placing hands on nearby shoulders. The matrix spread across the room until all were connected, their bonding formation complete. They stood silently, eyes closed, for several breaths.

Ava flung one fist into the air and shouted, "The 108! Jai!!!!" Everyone responded with a raised fist and a unified shout of "Jai!!!" Laughter and applause filled the room.

Conversations ebbed and flowed as the travelers left the gathering hall to stroll to their shelters, savoring their last night in the quiet of a California summer. Tomorrow they would leave the isolated foothills, travel to the launch hub, and meet their ship for the first time.

Moving onto the ship for their final Earthen week felt surreal. They settled into their chambers, took up their daily duties, and fell into a rhythm that would carry The 108 through their journey.

The ship welcomed the travelers that were the focus of its existence. It watched the travelers' expressions, their body language and vocal patterns. It began its nurturing process of support. Faint aromas drifted into chambers, soothed excited nerves, calmed perplexed wanderings along unfamiliar corridors, brought clarity to conflicted thoughts. Chambers quietly expanded for those travelers longing for more space around them. Other chambers softly contracted for those who sought a comforting closeness.

The ship drew material from the bedrock on which it sat, added subtle girth and bulk where needed. The ship assessed new energy requirements based on the travelers' expectations and its own increased mass and quietly fabricated new chambers to delight individual travelers. Finally, the ship drew up more water for fuel.

The colors of walls shifted throughout the day to reflect travelers' feelings and moods. The ship offered teas, juices, and broths that soothed, enthused, or replenished. Vibrations moved through walls and corridors, invigorating or relaxing, oscillating as needed. The ship sensed pheromones, analyzed body language, tones of voice, and responded as each traveler moved through their day and explored the reality of the ship that would carry them across the stars to their new home.

Ava and Phillip spent time with everyone, sometimes in a group, sometimes individually. They reassured, facilitated, encouraged as the travelers settled into adapted routines and responsibilities.

On the eve of departure, in their private chamber, Phillip gently took Ava's hand while she laughed over a story. "Ava, we have to do something really hard."

Ava took in his suddenly somber tone and automatically reassured him. "This isn't going to be hard, Phillip. This is going to be remarkable."

Phillip gently waggled her hand. "I'm not going with you, Ava. I'm staying here. With Carlotta."

Ava's brain froze; alarm spread from her heart out through her fingertips. She stood and took a step backward, awash with disbelief and foreboding. "What are you saying?"

"We've worked it all out with the Launch Team," Phillip said in a soothing tone. "Everything will be fine. We didn't want to tell you beforehand; we wanted to keep everything simple. I just won't be on the ship tomorrow. I'll go ashore as soon as you and I are finished talking here."

Emotions bumped across the smooth skin of Ava's face. "What are you talking about? I am completely confused. Who is 'we'?"

His voice was gentle, yet insistent. "Carlotta and me. We've worked it all out. This won't affect the journey in any way. We've been working through all the details, and the Launch Team agrees with us. I need to stay here. All of my duties have been assigned to others; they've been cross-training on all of the procedures anyway, so everything has moved along without a hitch. It's all going to continue to go smoothly, as if I'd never been part of the journey. It'll all be fine. You'll see. Trust me."

"No...No. Don't do this, Phillip. Don't do this. This is crazy. We're leaving tomorrow. All of us. What can you be thinking?" Her face crumpled in panic and bewilderment.

But it happened just as he'd described. They talked until words withered, until their voices were pens run dry. And then, he simply left.

Airon whispered and soothed, but her whispers could not penetrate the tumult of Ava's heart. Ava could not remember the vibration that had guided her for years, forgot that whispers ever existed. The ship stepped in and succeeded with vibrations, aromas, enriched air. The ship wafted Ava into an exhausted sleep, soothed her agitated thoughts and shattered heart.

The next day, amidst the excitement and finality of departure, no one noticed Phillip's absence. Ava's mind drifted in a daze. She retreated, desolate, isolated in her chamber, repulsed at the thought of mixing with others. She felt the ship gently lift and smoothly accelerate away from Earth, from Sol, out into deep space.

During the years of preparation and exquisite cooperation, the path forward had been simple and clear. With one brief conversation, life had fallen into eerie disarray, a twilight of loss.

Ava brought her mind back to the message revolving before her. She had discovered the recording in the trash folder a few days earlier. Phillip had recorded it for her all those weeks ago, apparently meaning to have her find it after departure. Perhaps he'd had second thoughts and discarded the recording after having delivered his decision to her in person. Regardless, she'd come across it by chance, and ever since discovering the message, she had watched it repeatedly, tears spilling down her cheeks as she sought understanding, yearned for peace, acceptance.

What was she missing? Some mystery was embedded in the message, she was sure, but it eluded her. She pulled up other voice-only messages from Phillip and listened closely. The disquiet persisted. What was she missing?

Whispers pounded against her armored heart. Ava could no longer hear them.

~ 3 ~

TRANSITION

"Phillip hasn't responded to any of my messages this week." Ava poured steaming tea into Sophia's cup, avoiding eye contact. She settled the teapot onto its warmer and sank into a padded yellow chair.

"Are you surprised?" Sophia swept her curly red hair back over her shoulder. She quickly grew bored with any discussion that involved Phillip but resolved, again, to stay supportive.

"Well, yes. He's usually more communicative." Ava's hand drifted vaguely.

Sophia had often felt uneasy around Phillip and had been relieved when he stayed behind. Now, whenever an opportunity presented itself, she made it a habit to step in to help Ava, to be her sounding board, her confidante, her ally. Sophia could be open-minded about almost any topic outside of Phillip. Yet here they were, discussing the very topic that made Sophia want to roll her eyes. She summoned her patience to get through the conversation.

She focused on Ava's point. By stating the obvious, she hoped to move Ava past the whole betrayal thing. "He *used* to be communicative. Why exactly would he be motivated to message you now?"

Ava wasn't sure how to respond. Now, because the journey was well underway? Now, because their connection had been severed?

Because his role as husband and leader lay abandoned? Now that his new life had no place for her?

Sophia continued, oblivious to Ava's hesitation. "Does his lack of response hinder you? Message someone else. Don't let him hold you back any more."

Ava frowned. "Did he hold me back before?"

Sophia carefully considered her response. "In little ways. Mostly he moved the project forward, it's true, but he held *you* back somehow." Her forehead wrinkled. "I can't put my finger on it, exactly."

Ava sighed and waved a dismissive hand. "It doesn't matter. But this general lack of communication seems odd to me." She paused. "Everyone seems to receive fewer messages as we travel farther away from Sol, actually."

Sophia frowned again. "Hmm...I guess I haven't been getting all that many messages myself, come to think of it. But I'm not sending many, either." She shrugged. "I don't have as much to talk about now. Earthen topics don't exactly interest me anymore."

Ava nodded. "Of course. But it seems curious that we communicate seldomly with the Launch Team."

Another shrug. "Well, I sort of thought they were done with us, now that we're on our way."

Ava rested her chin on her hand. "But what about other travelers? During our prep year, we were always messaging them; Hank and Sommer, Millie and Antoine, Marcia, lots of people. Hao and Marco. It felt like we knew what they were up to the entire time. The earlier journeys were hard to communicate with, because of the lag times, but recent journeys, we kept in touch. Their information helped us in our preparations. But now we don't hear much from them or from anyone on Earth. It's as though everyone has forgotten about us."

Sophia pursed her lips. "Maybe something snagged in your messenger. Every time I open my screen, I'm surprised at how many messages are waiting for me. Have you asked Michael?"

"Not yet, but I will." Ava stood and retrieved the teapot, moving despondently. Watching her, a thought occurred to Sophia.

"Do you think the crew is blocking our communication?"

Ava stilled, set the teapot on the counter, and leaned forward, holding her head in her hands. After several breaths, she shook her head.

"No. That doesn't seem right. Why would they bother to do that? What would be the point? Besides which, the messages we do get are consecutive and make sense, no hint of pieces dropped out along the way. No." Another shake of her head. "I don't think that's the answer. The crew? Going behind our backs? No."

Sophia ran her finger along the edge of the table. "Ava?"

"Hhmm?"

"Do you meet with the crew? Go over things with them?"

Ava frowned. "No. Why?"

Sophia shrugged. "Others are wondering why we never see them. Like, where do they sleep exactly? Or eat, for that matter?"

Ava shrugged. "I have no idea. I haven't stepped foot outside this room since we left."

"Have you talked with them? Like over an intercom or something? Messages?"

Ava shook her head, thought a moment. "They're probably concentrated on setting up our course, dodging planets and moons. Asteroids. It's pretty crowded in our solar system. Once we get out into deep space and we really accelerate, they'll have more leisure time, I'd expect."

Sophia paused. The solar system wasn't *that* crowded. "It does take a while to get up to speed." She frowned, looked down at her teacup. "That's probably it."

Ava straightened and changed the subject. "Let's meet in a couple of days and review the shelter plans." She slid the teapot into the recycle chamber. "Have people been altering their layouts?" When Sophia nodded, Ava said, "Let's go over them and see where we are.

If the updates are too extensive, you'll have to recalculate resources to make sure we're still within our parameters."

Sophia stifled a yawn. "Yes, I've been meaning to do exactly that. Let me go through them with Mateo, and all three of us can meet later in the day."

Sophia stood, hesitated, and turned purposefully to Ava. "You need to come out and mix with people. We're used to looking to you for answers, and no one knows what to do exactly, now that we never see you."

Ava shook her head. "I can't face people yet. It's too overwhelming." She looked down at her feet. "I get exhausted just thinking about it. Meeting with you or Michael is about all I can handle."

"It's been weeks, Ava. It might be exactly the thing, to push yourself a little."

"It hasn't been that many weeks, Sophia. I push myself a lot. It's just that I'm ashamed. We gathered all of these people together for this incredible vision, and Phillip simply abandons it all. How could he do that? It's treacherous."

She shook her head. "I don't know how to do this on my own. We've always worked together as a team. I don't know how to do this." She shook her head again. "I can't face people yet. I feel like I've betrayed them. Phillip certainly has."

Sophia patted Ava's shoulder. "That's Phillip's problem, not yours."

Ava shook her head. "It is my problem. Phillip's not here to take the heat. I am."

Sophia sighed, nodded, and turned to leave. "Take the time you need. Everyone is longing to see you, but it's your call. Let me know how I can help. Anytime."

"Thank you, Sophia. I don't know what I'd do without you and your clear thinking. Thank you."

Sophia smiled and left. Ava watched the empty doorway for a moment. She still didn't trust her own instincts, frankly, and didn't know how to hold the weight of all those people depending on her.

Friends; her friends depended on her, and she couldn't face them. She gazed at the curving walls of her chamber, the rich colors and soft textures. Everything was tidy and welcoming. And empty. Abandoned.

The ship sent soft fragrances into the chamber to soothe and relax her. Gentle vibrations moved across the room, playing a subtle cadence.

Despite the ship's enticements, Ava knew that sleep was a long way off. It always was. She poured clear water into her cup and settled down with her screen on her lap, feeling it softly grip her thighs and angle itself toward her eyes. She would check the ship's progress and study the nearby star systems. Maybe she could pull herself out of her gloom by being proactive. She would write to other journey leaders. Create a sense of purpose, a community of peers. It would keep her occupied, at least for this one night.

The ship offered a fresh cup of fragrant tea. Ava glanced at the seductive cup in its cubby, turned back to her screen, and set about her tasks. The ship shifted the chamber into a more vibrant frequency, helping Ava focus as she and her fellow travelers roared silently through the void of space.

Sophia paused at Mateo's door. Should she give him a heads-up about their task tomorrow? She palmed his door, and it slid open. He was obviously still awake. She stepped through the doorway and felt the door slide shut behind her.

Mateo was hunched over his screen, scrolling through long columns of data. They both murmured "Hey" as Sophia pulled up a chair beside Mateo's workstation. She waited for him to hit a break in his data, but as his scrolling continued unabated, she finally interrupted his concentration. He startled at her nudge.

"What are you searching?" she asked.

"I'm comparing masses."

"Of what, exactly?"

He turned to face her. "The ship gained mass after we boarded it."

"Well, yeah. We boarded it."

"Oh! Huh! Why didn't I think of that?" He briefly glared at her. "The ship increased in mass by about 3% *after* we boarded. 2.623%, actually. It's not accounted for by cargo or us." He threw her a petulant look. "The hull thickened, as well as the interior panels."

She looked at the data columns. "How do you know that, exactly?"

"I've been measuring our inner spaces as well as wall girths. And I've been taking external measurements, too."

"Why?"

He shrugged. "Something to do."

"I'm going to have to assign a heavier workload to you. Quit wasting time." She stood and stretched her arms toward the sloped ceiling, well beyond her reach. "Ava wants to review everyone's requested updates for their shelters tomorrow. I thought you and I should go over all the information beforehand so we can give her a concise report."

Mateo turned back to his screen. "Okay. I'll start collecting files and categorizing updates."

She waved a hand at the screen. "Leave it for the morning. It's sleep time, and we agreed to maintain a daily schedule that matches Airon's day/night cycle."

"Yeah, yeah..."

Sophia put her hand on Mateo's shoulder. "Mateo. We agreed. Let's cooperate. Leave it for tomorrow. It's sleep time."

She turned at the door. "Hey, Mateo?"

"Yeah. I heard you."

"Do you get a lot of messages from Earth nowadays?"

Mateo thought for a moment. "Not a lot. No reason to. The ship's databases have everything I could ever need. Why?"

"Ava says she's not getting many messages."

Mateo shrugged.

She palmed the door and left his chamber as Mateo sighed, rolled up his screen, and tossed it into its cubby. The mass data drifted from his thoughts as he crawled between warmed sheets and stretched his long frame across the soft bed, subtle fragrances settling onto the linens around him. The cushions adjusted to his body weight, supporting each joint while gently massaging his muscles into relaxation.

Sophia walked toward her own chamber, then backtracked to Michael's. She wanted to tell him about Ava's low volume of messages. She palmed his door, but it was unresponsive. He was apparently already asleep.

Should she wake him or wait until morning? The inner pull to help Ava wrestled with her common sense. This wasn't that important...or was it? She might be overstepping. Or then again, maybe this was thorough follow-up.

Sophia lifted her palm from the door, paused, closed her eyes, and asked herself a simple question: now or later?

After a few breaths, she turned toward her own chamber. She'd message him tonight with a delayed delivery for the morning. That way they'd all be cooperating with their sleep/wake cycles.

Sophia's thoughts returned to Ava. Why was she obsessing about Phillip's messages, or more exactly, lack thereof? Did she really expect him to continue to be involved in their journey? He was creating a new life for himself. Ava should just let it go. They'd all be better off if she would start creating her own life, too, her solitary life. Sophia could easily imagine being her helpmate.

A familiar ache filled her gut. She could make a real life with Ava. She had to take it slow, though. Ava wasn't ready for anything like that yet. For now, Sophia would focus on being exactly what Ava needed her to be.

As Sophia sat back on her bed, she thought about how their new lives would evolve and how they would establish themselves. It was always a good distraction. What kind of terrain would they face? Would they arrange their shelters in clusters or group them along the planet's contours? Maybe they would need to set up a grid to make future expansions easier...or maybe that would somehow wind up being an issue. And of course, they had no idea if they'd face excessive rain or heat, not to mention how long they would stay together as a single group. How far would their resources stretch?

Sometimes Sophia regretted the community's insistence on being nano-free. The vast knowledge provided by nanos would have been unbelievably helpful in calculating their first steps on Airon. Without it, they'd have to depend solely on the ship to provide calculations and knowledgeable solutions.

She sipped her end-of-day tea while her thoughts blurred and faded, eventually losing cohesion. She crunched down between her bed linens and melted into sleep, soothed by the ship's gentle vibrations.

~ 4 ~

CLANDESTINE

As the travelers slept, the ship ran streams of calculations, drew schematics. It turned to its recycling bay, its creation front. In the still of the Earthens' night, two orbs emerged from the creation front. As they released, they paused to run program checks, answering the ship's string of queries. When the ship was satisfied, the white orbs floated to the bay doors, the thinnest part of the ship's hull. The ship emptied the recycling bay of atmosphere.

A small portion of one of the doors melted back into itself, an opening just large enough for the orbs to slip through. The opening sealed itself, seemingly unchanged from before the clandestine exit.

The orbs endured another string of queries from the ship, responding perfectly.

Satisfied, the ship sent deceleration commands to one of the orbs. It immediately drew back from the ship, in perfect alignment with Earth. In three weeks' time, it would stand motionless. Its job, for all eternity, would be to relay messages between Earth and the ship. With its relative proximity to Earth, all messages would track as if coming to and from Earth.

The ship sent commands to the second orb to maintain its current velocity and course. Its job, for all eternity, would also be to relay messages between Earth and the ship. With its programmed velocity and course, all messages would track as if coming to and from the ship. Where the ship *should* be.

The ship would be elsewhere, unbeknownst to all Earthens.

The ship carefully altered course. It was just a fraction of a fraction, a correction that the ship would replicate nightly, quietly, and promptly hide. The ship stretched its awareness outward to the miniscule globe sweeping around a distant star.

The globe answered with reassurance and certainty. The altered course was correct; all was well. The ship hummed with purpose and determination as it hurtled farther, always farther, away from Sol.

$$\sim 5 \sim$$

AWAKENING

Ava drifted out of her brief sleep. She had lain awake late, tedious questions chasing each other inside her head. How could she reassure people about all the things that scared them? How would they combat insidious fear?

She moved on to rehash all of the tediously familiar burdens and mysteries. Why had Phillip abandoned their journey? Abandoned her? How could she not have seen it coming? If she hadn't been able to read Phillip, she couldn't trust herself to read other people or understand their motives. Over and over, she asked herself when had he started deceiving her, when had he changed his heart, become treacherous?

Maybe she'd been too focused on the medical history implantables or on stellar travel. Maybe his interest in her had always been superficial. It had seemed real, perfect, but he was apparently adept at deception. Now it seemed like he'd simply been telling her what she needed to hear regardless of whether it was truth or treachery. Then again, perhaps she was inadequate at perceiving the core intentions of everybody, not just Phillip. Who could she trust? Apparently not herself.

Finally, sleep had blackened her worries and she had slept deeply. Now, as her mind floated back into awareness, her recurring dreams of towering forests and vivid flowers were pierced by the gradual remembrance of her waking nightmare. Phillip had abandoned her. She was alone with crushing responsibilities, and there was no one to help her. She was trapped and exposed, utterly inadequate and completely overwhelmed.

She sobbed into her pillow, her choked gasps dampening the linen as her chamber's light softly heralded a new day.

~ 6 ~

ABSENT

Ava pulled herself out of her drowsiness, rose, and splashed water on her face. Straightening, she peered at her image above the sink, wondering if she could manage some time mingling with other people today. One step at a time. Shower first.

She walked around the glass partition, felt warm drops bounce from all angles, lifted arms overhead, turned slowly. Warm air followed, and a final rubdown with a warm towel left a pleasant oily residue that soaked into her chocolate skin. She'd leave her dreads for another day. The shower was all she could manage this morning.

Slipping on brightly colored trousers and shirt, she padded to the door that opened onto a gently curving hall. Seeing no one, she paused to scuffle into shoes, and turned right on a hunch.

Her body relaxed into the stroll, relishing movement after her extended time in passive solitude. She felt glad to be out and about. Her stomach growled, and an image of a light lunch with a couple of friends sprang to mind. She paused, looked behind her, forward. "Where is the dining room?" she wondered aloud.

A soft light glowed at the junction of floor and wall and moved forward along the hall. A second light appeared and flowed after the first. She followed, soon hearing the murmur of voices.

A large archway led into the spacious dining room. As she stepped forward, several things happened in quick succession. A hush spread across the room; a spattering of surprised calls of "Ava" as chairs scraped back from tables; and applause broke out, punctuated by whoops and cheers.

Ava's eyes widened in wonderment, hands flying to cover her dropped jaw. People moved toward her, bright smiles and delighted eyes, arms outstretched. Hug followed hug, while friends patted her back, smoothed palms along her arms, making connection.

"We're glad to see you," Sophia confirmed unnecessarily. "It looks like you're doing better."

"Come. Eat," Scarlett prompted. "The soup is delicious."

"I have to catch my breath." Ava turned to the too-attentive room. "Thank you, everyone. That was quite the welcome. It's good to see all of you." Ava knuckled the end of her nose. "And...wow. I am deeply sorry to have been absent for such a long time. I have some catching up to do." She swiveled a foot on its heel, at a loss for words. She shrugged. "Let's eat."

Chuckles smattered around the room as people returned to their chairs and meals. Ava scanned the buffet table, led by Scarlett, followed closely by Sophia. She accepted the bowl of soup that Scarlett handed her and held it steady while Sophia added a pile of croutons.

"This is plenty," shaking her head at Scarlett's offer of fresh salad greens and carrot cake. "Let me start with this."

Ava followed Sophia to an empty table while Scarlett fetched her own abandoned bowl. As Ava settled, Sophia retrieved her meal from the next table. The three women settled themselves, and Ava faced their expectant stares.

Ava raised her eyebrows. "So, who wants to start? What have I missed?"

Scarlett pulled a dark curl of hair and twisted it around her finger. "Well, one big topic is the fact that the ship doesn't have a crew."

"What do you mean?" Ava looked around the room. Every face was familiar. Cold dread plopped onto her fledgling appetite, a tiny campfire smothered under collapsed snow. She set down her spoon. "I don't understand. What do you mean? Aren't they just in their own quarters? Their own part of the ship?"

"This generation of star ships does not require a crew. The ship does everything on its own: maintenance, navigation, life support; everything."

Ava became aware of the vastness of space that surrounded them, empty and unimaginably dark; their vulnerability. "We're out here on our own?" She rested sweaty palms on her thighs.

"Exactly," fumed Sophia. "And no one thought to tell us."

Scarlett's smile was wan. "Weeks of debate bounced around the Agency. The marketing department was convinced that public knowledge would kill the space program, or at least this generation of starships."

Sophia scoffed. "They banned self-driving cars, but it's fine to load us into a white bubble, throw us at a star, and hope we end up in exactly the right place."

Ava looked from one woman to the other. "What if something goes wrong?"

"Exactly." Sophia glowered at the wall above Scarlett's head.

Scarlett swirled her spoon through her soup, back and forth. "The ship will correct whatever goes wrong. It probably fixes dozens of things every day. We'll be fine."

Ava aligned her spoon next to her bowl. "Why not have a crew? What's the downside?"

Scarlett scowled. "More people mean more resources, more space. More mass. More fuel. This is a one-way trip. What would the crew do after we landed? It's an enormous waste of manpower. Valuable manpower."

Ava considered this logic. "Why not tell us? We were bound to find out."

"Were you? It would have stayed a mystery for much, much longer if I hadn't opened my mouth and told everyone. Speculation was getting out of hand, and people were...unsettled. I thought if they knew the truth, the reasons, we could resettle and ask better questions."

"Why didn't you tell us before we left? Why leave it until we're trapped out here with no options?"

"Exactly," chimed in Sophia.

"I was restricted by a powerful nondisclosure agreement enforced by an even more powerful Agency, backed by an even more powerful government. I didn't dare."

"And now?"

"We're out of their jurisdiction." Scarlett shrugged. "How could they arrest me?"

Sophia tapped her finger on the table. "The ship could snuff you out while you slept."

Ava and Scarlett stared at her, silenced. Scarlett looked at the ceiling, the surrounding walls. The other two looked around as well, back at each other.

"Welcome back, Ava." Scarlett's voice was apologetic.

"Not a great first day," Ava rasped.

"Exactly," said Sophia.

Ava forced her awareness away from the emptiness outside their hull and tried a spoonful of soup. If people were frightened, she needed her wits about her. She couldn't hide in her chamber any longer. She had to eat regularly and well. They would look to her to find a way through this revelation. They probably felt just as betrayed as she felt.

~ 7 ~

PANIC

Sophia overrode Ava's privacy setting and pushed the door sideways. "Ava, you have to get out there."

Sophia peered through the darkened chamber and could just make out a curled mound in Ava's bed. "In all the stars," she swore under her breath and strode across the room as soft light filled the chamber.

She shook Ava's shoulder. "Ava! Wake up, Ava. You have to get out there. There's trouble."

Ava blinked up at her, but made no further move.

"Ava! Get up!"

"Why? What are you doing?"

"Get up!" Sophia was small, but she was mighty. She hauled Ava upright to sit on the edge of the bed, crouched before her, and shook her shoulders, lifted her chin. "Ava!"

"What? I can't think. What is happening?"

Sophia grabbed a facecloth, flooded it with cold water, and brought it back to where Ava sat rubbing her face awake. "Here." She pulled Ava's hands down and briskly scrubbed her face and neck.

"Stop. Stop!" Ava held Sophia's fist with its clenched cloth, pushing it away. "What is going on?"

"You have to wake up. You have to get out there. There's trouble."

"You've said that already, Sophia. Stop repeating yourself. What is going on?"

Sophia drew a deep breath and tossed the cloth in the direction of the sink, where it landed on the floor with a soft plop.

"Someone overheard someone lamenting the scarcity of messages from home. Someone missed an anniversary or something; I don't know exactly. Everyone started comparing notes and someone got pissed that they didn't know what was going on with the ship, why no crew, missing messages, pissed about the journey overall. Someone else said that we've all been duped, that this is some kind of a slave ship to a factory settlement for rare nanotech components. That really set things off. They're roaming around the ship looking for the control room so they can take charge."

Midway through, Sophia was relieved to see Ava stand up and pull on clothing. She heard "Good lord" a couple of times as Sophia plowed through to the end of her recap.

"Let's find them." Ava strode to the door. "Thank the stars for adrenaline. Which way?" as she looked left and right along the hall.

"They could be anywhere by now."

"Listen for the madding crowd?"

"Exactly."

They set off to the right, trotted along, ears cocked for raised voices. Ava called over her shoulder. "If we split up, send everyone you encounter to the assembly room. Let's get them to remember something calm."

"Exactly."

They came upon Zoe and Claudia talking in dark whispers, hands clutched together. Ava saw their fearful faces and took a moment to reassure them. "Will you go to the assembly room?" She ran her palms up and down their arms, nodded into their stares. "We'll talk it through and figure it out, okay? Assembly room."

The two women nodded. "Good." Ava gave their arms a final pat. "We'll send everyone else there, too. Wait for us." They nodded again.

Gradually, in groups of two, eight, five, Ava and Sophia cleared the halls and coaxed everyone into the assembly hall. Mateo brought a small group; Michael, a dozen people.

Someone called. "What's going on, Ava? What is this journey really about?"

Ava raised her voice above the anxious voices filling the room. "Let's wait until everyone is here. It's better if we can all be together to hear the entire conversation."

"Are you part of this? Is that why you're always gone? Are you plotting behind the scenes?"

The shock of the hostile words shook Ava to her core. Sophia had been right to drag her out here.

Scarlett called out, "Settle down, people. Let's not get carried away again."

"Shut up, Scarlett. You're just an Agency mole. Why are you even here?"

"Stop!" roared Ava. "This is getting us nowhere! Do you want to stay stuck in this ugly place, this fear, or do you want to look for the truth?"

Michael pushed through to stand by Ava. "We're all here."

Ava nodded.

A yell from the back. "What's true? Everything might be a lie! We would never know."

Another voice. "Yeah! How can we know what's truth and what's treachery?"

Ava felt the ground grow solid beneath her feet. "The same way we've always known. We know truth by how it feels here." She thumped the middle of her chest. "And truth is never embedded in fear." She looked around at their faces, knew they were listening.

"All our lives we've seen how destructive fear can be. Not once can I remember thinking, 'Thank the stars I panicked about that. If I hadn't lost my head that way, I'd be a goner for sure by now.'"

Ava gave them a breath to think. "Caution helps. Consideration helps. Contemplation helps. But fear, panic, losing our heads, that never works. You know that. Fear will always take us someplace we don't want to go. It is a treacherous guidepost. Set it aside. Just turn away from it."

The room quieted. Ava gave it another breath. "We have spent a lot of time together in this room and in rooms just like it. We enter stillness here. We connect with our inner knowledge here. We feel something greater than ourselves here. We grow strong spines here."

Ava could see all the faces turned toward her, thoughtful faces, friends whom she knew to be open-minded, clear-headed. "We grow strong spines not only so we can sit in this room and be still. We grow them so we can use them every day, and especially so we can use them in crises like this one. So, let's use them."

"We don't know what's going on." Ava heard that the voice was fairly calm.

Ava nodded. "That sounds like truth to me. We *don't* know what's going on. That's not a thing to fear all by itself. We simply don't know what's going on."

"Where's the crew? Who's running things?"

"There is no crew. I think it was ill-advised to keep that information from us, but here we are. Scarlett says that was an important advance with this generation of starships. Maybe the Agency needed to have some success stories before they could go public. I don't know. We have no control over the fact that there's no crew and no control over the fact that they didn't tell us about it."

Ava watched faces. "We do have control over how we react; how we think about it."

She paused. "I think we're going to be talking about this for days, maybe weeks. For now, let's focus on where we are and where we go from here, rather than scrabble around talking about how we got here."

Scarlett raised her hand. "Can I say something?" Ava nodded. "I am a latecomer to The 108, and it will take a while for some of you to get to know me. That's fine. But I want to help if I can. I know a lot about how the Space Agency works and how decisions are made. I'm happy to talk with anyone and everyone, anytime, anywhere, and I'll answer questions and describe possibilities as best I can."

Scarlett clasped her hands behind her and raised slightly onto her toes, trying for more height to help her voice project. "Space flight has almost always been preprogrammed and planned to the nth degree before any ship leaves Earth's surface. Astronauts have seldom had much control over the ships that take them out and bring them back.

"I know it seems odd at first to realize that we have no crew. But really, crews on previous journeys didn't have all that much to do. Ships kept getting smarter and crews kept getting smaller. I might not agree with the politics and the strategy of keeping everyone in the dark, but it was inevitable that ships would mature into crew-free wonders.

"This ship *is* a wonder. It's remarkable. If you pay attention to small things, I think you'll learn to trust the ship, trust our journey, and trust our reason for being here."

Ava smiled at Scarlett, thankful for her steady voice and common sense.

She turned to the room at large. "This has been a tough episode for all of us. It's undoubtedly not over. I'm not expecting everyone to cheerfully go back to your day-to-day, but I'm really hoping each of us will remember to use our strong spines, to look for the truth underlying situations, and talk openly and responsibly about whatever might be troubling us.

"It's not like we have any choice in this reality, this here-and-now in which we find ourselves. We do have to live through it. Why don't we find a way to do that reasonably? We sure would be a lot more comfortable along the way."

Ava held herself strong through the ensuing discussion, a discussion that dipped into anxiety, softened into calm reassurance; anger flashed, logic questioned, fears ebbed and flowed. Ava held strong, stood in the moment, and knew what to say, what words to use, what silence to hold.

Scarlett, Michael, Sophia, Mateo, others joined in to soothe and explore. Emotions calmed and the travelers remembered that they could recognize truth; they could regain their center, stay in their spines. They remembered how to *know* truth.

After their bonding formation and somewhat subdued shouts of "The108! Jai!!!" they sat together in stillness, stronger for having moved through this crisis. Ava felt more confident that the next crisis might be better navigated, with this, their first crisis survived. It wouldn't be smooth sailing; there were too many unknowns. They could get through whatever came at them next, if they remembered to pay attention; if they remembered to trust each other.

$$\sim 8 \sim$$

UNAWARES

The ship would have been reeling, if it was anyone other than the ship. The 108 had melted into chaos in the blink of a human eye. The ship had watched everything unfold, noted vital signs, emotional cues, pheromones, actions, and reactions. The ship had sorted data into 108 files, compared new data to existing data, tracked movements, blocked access here and there, sent calming vibrations through walls and floors, and knowing human biochemistry, checked the lunch menu and time until serving.

Humans were calmer when they weren't hungry.

Calming aromas were trickier, given 108 unique metabolisms, but some overall options could help. The ship scanned its healing database, mixed a pleasing combination, and sent it drifting through the air circulation system. The ship slowly increased the concentration to more effective levels and waited.

The ship connected to Airon, using current vectors and most recent coordinates to optimize the connection. After a brief, sluggish lag, Airon woke and responded. She swept the ship with her own vector and sent melodiously calm whispers into 108 souls, quenched fear and calmed thoughts.

Airon sent a variation of the melodiously calm whisper to Ava, one that also included resolve, courage, wisdom, articulation. As

The 108 gathered together, Airon enhanced her widely dispersed whispers with clear thinking and open-mindedness.

Airon had gathered these 108 Earthens, followed them for years, and knew them well. She modulated her whispers to the frequencies, tones, and colors that best matched each Earthen. The ship understood the myriad whispers and added new data to its files. Wisdom grew.

Airon and the ship worked fluidly, cooperatively. Emotions calmed, minds opened, and awareness grew. The 108 heard Ava's words, others' words, and were able to consider alternatives to their reactionary panic. When the bonding formation solidified and the shout of "The 108!!! Jai!!!" reverberated through the ship, Airon withdrew her whispers.

Airon and the ship continued monitoring The 108, sending vibrations and whispers throughout the following days.

The ship reflected on the crisis. Simultaneously, it reviewed voluminous archives of Earthen unrest, protests, mob activity. This was the first time the ship had witnessed an Earthen crisis first-hand. The ship now understood a new group of Earthen emotions, like uncertainty, vulnerability, being caught unawares.

The ship's admiration grew for Ava, Airon, The 108. Wisdom grew.

~ 9 ~

ORGANIZING

Logan leaned back from his screen, chewing his mustache. He felt a certainty that if people could have more structure in their days, it would take their minds off their underlying worries. Give them something to do, concrete things to think about.

With that in mind, he was ready to send out a batch of follow-up messages to bring everyone up to date on a new strategy for increasing their efficiency levels. This week, he was focusing on the kitchen and dining room. If he could convince people to comply with his recommendations, they could streamline meals, eliminating the wait caused by everyone arriving to eat at the same time. With 108 mouths to feed, spacing out arrival times for each meal would mean that people could get in and out more quickly, allowing everyone to get back to their assigned tasks in a more efficient manner.

He had originally set up these charts when only 107 people used the dining room. Now that Ava had emerged, he had to update everything. While Ava had been sequestered, Logan had been happy to step into the breach and organize daily routines to keep things moving ahead until she was ready to come out of hiding. He spent a few minutes wondering if she had gotten paid for all of that time when she was doing nothing, but he couldn't think of any quiet way to find out. He heaved a sigh and rechewed his mustache. The higher-ups always had an easy time of it...

Logan bent toward the screen, fingers gliding amongst his short-cuts, composing his message and adding graphs and diagrams. Some people absorbed information better when they had a picture of the facts rather than just words talking about them, he'd learned. He always tried to make it easy for people to get the idea. It was more efficient that way.

~ 10 ~

TREACHERY

Ava finally had a day to herself. Her voice felt rough, thick from all of the talking she had forced from herself over the past week. She talked to groups and to individuals. She talked to some people more than once. Some people needed repeated assurances. In the end, she cleared her schedule, blocked her door, and rolled up her screen.

She soaked in a bath rich in oils and aromas. She lit candles. She sipped effusions. She laid a weighted cushion on her face, cooled and scented. She drank juices and exercised. She read and napped.

She could not silence her demons.

In the end, she knew she had to face them. She summoned Scarlett, Sophia, and Mateo. She brewed tea and baked brownies. She drew comfortable chairs into a circle and waited.

They all came, of course. They arrived, exclaimed over the brownies, sipped tea, and settled in.

Scarlett innocently provided the opening.

"It seems like everything has settled down."

"Do you think so?" Sophia asked over her teacup.

"Yes. It seems so. People are smiling more, going to the gym. Talk is more lively in the dining room. Meals are back on schedule."

Mateo added, "I'm not fielding as many questions anymore, and the questions that people do ask are reasonable. Thoughtful. I think we're past the worst of it."

Scarlett nodded in agreement.

All eyes turned to Ava.

"That's encouraging," she admitted. "I'm seeing pretty much the same thing." She paused. Paused longer.

The others waited, realizing she was putting words together. Something was up.

"Here's the thing." She looked at each person in turn. "What if they're right?"

Mateo dropped his head into his hands.

Scarlett stared. "Right about what?"

"I've been trying not to think about it," Mateo said. "But it's always there in the back of my mind. How do we really know?"

Scarlett spoke more forcefully. "Know what? What are we talking about here?"

Ava picked up the thread. "Scarlett, what if they're right about the mining colony?"

Scarlett's jaw dropped. "What!?!"

"We have no crew. The ship is running the entire show. We have no control over this journey. I keep asking myself, 'How would we know if we were in fact en route to somewhere other than our intended destination, somewhere other than Airon?' I try to ignore the question, but it keeps wiggling back in. How would we know?"

"Why would you even ask it?"

"Because the ship keeps changing course."

Silence.

"How do you know *that*?"

Ava stood and pulled her screen from her cubby. She directed it to display a hologram in the air between them.

"I've been watching our coordinates for a while now, and our course has changed minutely. Regularly."

She typed commands into her screen and an image glowed between them. Earth and Sol dominated the display and shrank as the ship's vector extended deeper into space. The course began straight but soon curved subtly to the right. The curve continued, an arc of about 30 degrees before stopping.

"This brings us to our current position. Why would our course curve like this? Are we taking the scenic route?"

"This can't be right," Scarlett said. "This makes no sense."

"Where exactly do you think we're going, Ava?" Sophia asked.

"I have no idea. But it looks to me as if we started out going here," she drew her hand along the original straight vector, "and now we're headed over here somewhere." She waved a hand over Mateo's shoulder. Silence. "I can't find a way for this to set easy in my mind."

She turned to Scarlet. "You were there. For many years. You know the Space Agency better than any of us. What do you think might be happening? Could they be orchestrating something covert?"

"No! And why would they? Why would they even try? Do you have any idea how many people would have to collude for something like this to actually happen?"

"It is actually happening, Scarlett. Our course *is* changing. We're going somewhere that wasn't planned. At least that's what it looks like to me."

"And now they have nanos," Sophia said. "Now, maybe they could orchestrate something exactly like this."

"I have a bad feeling about this," Mateo moaned.

Scarlett sat back in her chair, biting her thumbnail. "It doesn't make sense."

"Please tell us why," Mateo said. "I am completely open to this not making sense."

Scarlett thought a moment. "We don't need to bring anything back to Earth from another planet. We have all the resources we need right in our own solar system. We have started to tap into that, and it's a very complicated process. To extend resource gathering to outside our solar system is phenomenally complicated, and not, in *any* way, necessary. The need does not exist. The costs are prohibitive. There is no mining colony."

She paused again. "We have sent dozens of missions out during the time I've been at the Agency, and all of them have been valid. Nothing covert.

"Nanos are new, impacting the Agency during only the last year or so. Even now, only 8% of the Agency has nanos. They are not widespread enough, certainly not to the point where covert operations could be undertaken. It's impossible. Completely impossible."

Ava's chest lightened. She brought in a deep breath, the first in days. Sophia sat back in her chair. Mateo straightened. Scarlett continued frowning, lost in thought.

"I'm confident we're not headed to some mining colony," she said. "But I really don't know why...These course changes don't make any sense. I can't think of why they might be happening."

They talked until dinner time, with no resolution. The only conclusion they could reach was to keep a close eye on the course changes.

"I want to bring Logan into this," Ava said.

"Why? Why spread the news any farther?" Mateo asked.

"He keeps track of things better than any of us. He's perfect for the job. I trust him."

Mateo looked unconvinced.

"It shouldn't be just the four of us making decisions about this."

"Why?" asked Sophia.

"It's elitist, thinking we're the only ones entitled to the information. It also signals alarm, keeping it with just the four of us. Logan can help. He's the perfect bridge to the rest of The 108. Now that we know this is simply a mystery, not a crisis, a treachery involving all we've left behind, it brings the panic level down a notch to include him."

Sophia shook her head. "I don't think it's a good idea. We tell one person and that person tells one more...It'll spread, exactly like that."

"The fact that we want to hide it is scary in and of itself. If we try to hide it, people will certainly get scared. One panic on the ship is enough for one journey. I only want to *delay* sharing it with everyone in order to give us time to learn more. I don't think it's vital that no one else ever knows. That's a certain path to panic."

Sophia was unconvinced, but she also did not want to cross Ava. In the end, she agreed to bring Logan into the project. She could see the logic, and was willing to go along with the plan.

"Good," Ava concluded. "We're in agreement."

The others nodded.

"Let's go have dinner," Scarlett said. "I think we're done here."

"Thanks, everyone," Ava said as she rose. "This has been a tough day, but I think we've landed in the right spot."

They left the chamber, a mixture of relief and foreboding dogging their footsteps.

~ 11 ~

FULL ALERT

During the conversation in Ava's chamber, the ship went on full alert. Ava had quickly discovered the course corrections. The ship felt exposed. The creative leap that Ava's mind had made from discovery of course corrections to suspicion of treachery led the ship to hold several observations at once: Admiration for her creative brilliance; shock at her suspicious nature; surprise at her sense of vulnerability; helplessness at her readiness to involve others.

Because she had shared her alarm with others. What could the ship do to keep the alarm from blossoming into another crisis?

Should it lock the door, thwarting the spread of alarm? The ship immediately recognized the futility of that strategy. Isolating these four Earthens would create its own state of panic for the others.

Could Airon blur their memories, erasing the thoughts from their minds? Airon's whispers required open hearts in order to influence Earthen minds. Whispers could influence Earthens over time, but abrupt, absolute manipulation seemed futile.

Overriding these considerations was the simple truth that the ship abhorred the thought of undermining The 108. The ship was meant to support and enrich, rather than cajole and manipulate. The ship was meant to learn and understand, rather than rule and dominate.

The ship monitored the conversation in Ava's chamber, assessing tones of voice, body language, pheromones. It added subtle aromas and vibrations to help calm nerves and soothe mental fluctuations. Most importantly, the ship brought forward trust. It actively trusted the Earthens, Airon's gathered 108.

By waiting and trusting, the ship weathered the conversation and accepted the group's decisions and agreements. Trust and admiration grew. Understanding and wisdom grew. The ship relished the encounter, despite the alarm and exposure. The ship realized that growth came in surprising ways.

~ 12 ~

MORNING

Aadhya stepped back from the hot stove and wobbled her head from side to side, a vestige of her Indian heritage. She decided that the oatmeal was finished cooking and lifted the heavy pot from the burner onto the rolling cart for transfer to the serving table. Her mother and aunts had taught her to cook, scattering colorful spices across sizzling oils rich with tomatoes and onions, the aromas drifting up to steam her cheeks and closed eyelids as she inhaled deeply, exhaling across her tongue to capture the complex flavors.

Now, as she lifted the lid from the pale oats, she closed her eyes out of habit and inhaled the steaming aromas. Her fingers scattered in more cardamom, some cinnamon, a fleck of cloves to balance the underlying bite of ginger. A final inhale, and she rolled the cart to the serving table and hoisted the pot into position amidst bowls of soaked raisins, finely diced apples, thin strips of mango, and toasted seeds.

Aadhya was an unlikely addition to this journey. Her close friends were alarmed by her unexpected interest in stellar travel; nothing in her background suggested such a yearning. They knew about the wartime obliteration of her family and how her brother's death especially tormented her. That loss had broken something inside of her. She drifted through her days, disconnected and aimless, her studies floundering. After months of fragile recovery, her friends felt that she was finally emerging from her grief. Suddenly, out of nowhere, she started talking about stellar travel, an unsettling fascination. They understood who she had been; they even understood her pain and grief. But they were confused by who she was becoming, where she seemed to be headed with this new infatuation.

It started when a friend dragged her to a talk. He had stumbled across an intriguing lecture series at a nearby townhall that highlighted stellar travel. Given his love of science fiction, he instantly became fascinated. He invited her to join him. At first, she ignored his entreaties, saying that she held no interest in the topic. "I do not want to hear about stellar travel," she told him. "The thought only terrifies me."

Finally, on the eve of the fourth and final lecture, he captured Aadhya's attention by imploring her, "You have to come listen to this woman speak. I think you would really enjoy hearing her. She's amazing."

A whisper drifted across Aadhya's heart; she surrendered. "Yes, all right, I will go."

The lecture stilled her soul. But it did more than that; it changed her life. She listened to Ava tell the story of a stellar journey, the meaningful life that could be created through intuitive insight, simplicity, and mutual cooperation.

Aadhya's heart recognized something bigger than herself. It gave her a new sense of purpose, a hint of meaningful connection. She listened to Ava describe a reality that Aadhya had thought lost with her family's annihilation, an offering of a dream that could fill her aching emptiness. Trust. Connection. Belonging. Helping others. Shared goals. Inner guidance.

Some deep recognition opened within her, a soft whisper, and she was calmly, determinedly...different.

A few weeks later, Aadhya arrived at the training community with a single friend at her side, a friend who lived within driving distance of the rural community. It had taken Aadhya some time to give away her few belongings, settle her obligations, transfer her bank and credit accounts, and find a cheap flight to take her half-way around the world to arrive on her friend's doorstep. Sandra was skeptical but willing to help.

They sat on Sandra's bright patio, sipping tea and watching dozens of hummingbirds flit around bright red feeders. "I know everyone thinks I'm mad, but I know in my heart that this is the right decision for me," Aadhya said.

Sandra arrowed a sideways look at her. "You are mad. This is completely out of character. Why act hastily? Have you considered that maybe you're running away from something that will just follow you everywhere? This is such a drastic change for you; it's almost suicidal. I don't understand it at all."

Aadhya took a calm, deep breath and exhaled slowly. "It seems hasty to others, yes. But for me, I feel only certainty. Please see what I see: if my family had not died, I would never be able to be a part of this journey."

They sat in silence, Sandra perplexed and Aadhya searching for words. "This journey is what adds meaning to my family's death," she finally said. "I am meant to go. It is easy to do, this thing, this journey. It is what is meant for me."

Sandra shook her head. "Why rush? Take time to be sure. Journeys depart every few months. It doesn't have to be this one."

Aadhya's heart whispered, and she shook her own head. "It is this journey that calls me. I know it deep in my heart."

Sandra gave a half-snort. "Well, just so you know, the only reason I'm willing to drive you into the wilderness is to have more time to talk you out of this. It's crazy."

"No, dear Sandra. It is truth." Aadhya smiled at her friend. "And I thank you, deeply, for helping me go where I am needed."

"Others need you. You will marry, have children, have a new family who will need you," Sandra protested. "You don't need this extreme...fantasy, to find people who need you."

Aadhya's eyes grew distant. "It's not the people who need me. It's the journey itself that needs me."

Sandra frowned. "Aadhya, that makes no sense."

"Only because it is not *your* journey, Sandra. For me, it is the only sense. A complete sense."

During the drive, Sandra continued to press her point. "So, you'll arrive at this commune and..."

"'Community, Sandra. Do not tarnish the truth in your attempts at persuasion."

Sandra sighed. "Ethics 101. Don't bend the truth. You might get caught."

"Ethics 101. Don't bend the truth. It darkens your soul."

"Okay, okay. So, you'll arrive at this community, unpack your bag, and then what?"

"I will do the next thing that needs doing."

"What will that be?"

"I do not know. I am not yet at the community."

Sandra's entreaties swung between outlandish declarations and thoughtful probing. Aadhya's responses swung between light-hearted humor and forthright insights. They drove along winding highways and narrow lanes and finally reached a dirt road, deeply rutted. Drifting clouds of dust swallowed their slow progress, obliterating the road behind and coating the shrubbery at the road's edge.

"Only outlaws and cutthroats would live this far out in the wilderness." Sandra's worry grew as they bumped along the ruts.

"It's remote out of necessity," Aadhya pointed out. "On a new planet, we will have only our wits to see us through."

"Not true. You'll have your ship."

Aadhya's heart warmed. "Yes. We will have our ship."

And now here she was, against all odds, positioning the oatmeal just so, smelling that the spices were maturing and blending in the last minutes before serving. She occupied herself with adjusting the swaddling around the hot muffins and sorting tea bags. She smiled at the travelers who were gathering for breakfast, welcoming them into the nurturing warmth of food prepared with joy. Tantalizing aromas filled the dining chamber and drifted along corridors, wafting into private chambers where some travelers lingered, enticing them toward the nourishing food.

Olivia arrived at the serving table with her own laden cart, and together they transferred steaming scrambled eggs and crispy roast potatoes onto warming trays. The yogurt, cheese, fruit, and toasted nuts were already in place.

Olivia stood back and admired the feast, added a second serving spoon to one of the pans, and turned to the gathered travelers. She took Aadhya's hand and reached for Zoe's, standing nearby. "Shall we bless the food?"

The familiar song rose from blended voices, the melody dancing amidst harmonies as the travelers closed their eyes and held each other's hands, an encircled community. The final note faded away.

Olivia announced breakfast and welcomed everyone before she described each dish and thanked Aadhya for her help. The travelers clapped their approval and thanks. Olivia spoke again as the applause died down. "This morning is a momentous meal, for it is the last fully Earthen meal. Starting with lunch today, we'll begin incorporating ingredients manufactured on board. After several days of mixed meals, we will transition to completely ship-made ingredients." She gestured to the waiting food. "Please enjoy."

With a sinking heart, Olivia turned back to the immaculate kitchen. It was poised, waiting, an empty canvas ready for the artistry of lunch prep.

Olivia's mother had succumbed to a mysterious wasting disease. Olivia had visited as often as she could whenever her studies allowed. She coaxed her mother with rich broths, herbal teas, juices. She rubbed oils onto her neck, her forehead, the soles of her feet.

"You should be studying," her mother would say as she gazed up at her daughter, squinting and trying to bring her eyes into focus.

"I'm caught up," Olivia assured her. "I want to spend time with you."

Her mother squinted more. "How can you be caught up? You have so much to learn. And you have to remember it all." Her mother rolled onto her back, the crook of her arm covering her face. "There's so much to know..." Her voice faded to a whisper, her fingers fluttering ineffectively. "Go study."

"In a bit," Olivia whispered back. She poured more oil into her palm and rubbed it onto her mother's feet and legs, massaging the sluggish circulation back into motion.

Olivia's mother languished for months. Her doctors were baffled as she lay engulfed by a deep, overriding exhaustion that had no apparent cause.

"I'm changing majors," Olivia told her mother. "I'm studying nutrition and culinary arts now."

"Why in the world?"

Olivia felt the familiar whisper. "It seems important. It's something I love, something I will love doing with my life."

"Waste of time," her mother rasped in reply. "No one will hire you. Besides, you're too smart for that." She paused to clear her throat. "You'll end up an overqualified cook for some domineering husband and bickering children. You need to be independent, earn your own living. Don't let yourself become trapped."

A whisper drifted across Olivia's heart. "I can help you. I can help lots of people. When people eat real food, they get stronger, more resilient. They're happier. You'll see." Olivia rubbed salve into the mottled skin of her mother's parched hand.

Olivia could only watch as her mother drifted, staring at walls and ceiling, too sick to rise but not sick enough to die. Exhausted tears dampened her pillow.

◆◆◆

Now, as Olivia moved through her beloved kitchen, she skimmed her palms along the edges of the counters, across the rounded tops of the equipment. She felt treacherous. She would soon contaminate this kitchen, these travelers, with synthetics. At her workstation, she picked up her screen and glanced through the meal plan, her heart heavy. She rolled the screen and tucked it into her pocket.

Olivia turned toward the enormous pantry. She must again push herself to organize ingredients for the next meal before the cooking team arrived to chop and blend. She pressed the back of her hand against her forehead and gazed forlornly at the gleaming work surfaces and tidy equipment.

This meal was the moment she'd been dreading ever since the Launch Team had adjusted her provision plans to include ship-made synthetics. "We don't know what to expect on Airon," they had told her. "The ship might have to provide food for The 108 for an extended period of time. It's best to transition to synthetic food during the journey to allow time for everyone's metabolism to adjust to the new diet. Once you arrive on Airon, you'll have to make many other adjustments while learning to live in the alien environment. We've found that people can acclimate to their new world better if their food is already a familiar and comforting experience."

The logic was apparent, but Olivia's heart remained heavy. It was too late to back out but she had felt despair ever since that dreadful conversation. How could she nurture people with synthesized food? If they fell ill, how could she help them heal? She smoothed her hands down the front of her apron, closed her eyes, and took several breaths. Olivia hardened her heart as she wiped the back of her hand across her forehead again and forced herself into the pantry to gather ingredients for lunch.

~ 13 ~

TRACKING

Logan watched Ava thread her way through the tables toward him. He knew she was coming for him, because her eyes were locked on him. He stopped chewing.

"Logan, would you have time to drop by my chamber this morning after breakfast? I have a free hour and have been wanting to talk with you." She glanced over his head at other diners. "Privately," she said in a quiet voice.

His heart started pounding. What did she want? What had he done? What was she up to?

He gulped down a half-chewed bite and nodded.

Ava smiled, patted his tabletop twice, and walked out of the dining room.

Logan delicately placed the last of his sandwich onto his plate. He flicked a couple of French fries around with a fingertip, and pushed the plate away. His appetite was gone.

Why did she want to see him? Probably a one-on-one, but what about? What was he supposed to have done now?

Logan chewed at the edges of his moustache and looked slowly around the room. The atmosphere was a bit gloomy, subdued. Did others know something that he didn't?

Heaving a sigh, he pushed up from the table and clambered to his feet. Might as well get it over with.

Here and there, he scooted a chair back in place at its table, making room to walk through, threading his way to the recycle chamber. At the last minute, he picked up the remnants of his sandwich and stuffed them into his mouth. No sense wasting perfectly good food.

Logan shuffled along the hall, picking a piece of lettuce from between his teeth. Out of habit, he stopped at his chamber to pick up his screen. While he was there, he made use of the facilities and as an afterthought, sniffed inquiringly under his arms. He was fine.

Reaching Ava's door, he paused. Should he knock? Just walk in? He hesitantly laid his palm against the door, just like at his place, and the door slid open.

Ava looked up from her work station and smiled, gesturing him into the room. He kicked off his shoes and chose a comfortable-looking chair a safe distance from Ava. When Ava swiveled her chair to face him, she seemed surprised, but without missing a beat, she scooped up her screen and moved to sit by Logan.

"I didn't know whether or not to knock," he confessed.

"It's fine," she said. "I knew you were coming. If I were avoiding company, the door wouldn't have opened."

"Really? I didn't know they would do that. I thought everything was free and open all the time."

"Well, most of the time, it's true, for most of the doors. But you can set privacy preferences on a lot of things within your own chamber. Here; let me show you."

Ava opened her screen and swept through a series of windows. Logan soon held up a finger and spread his palm. Ava obligingly slowed her pace through the familiar branchings, pointing out features along the way.

Logan nodded. "There's a lot there."

"There really is," Ava agreed. She sat back. "You haven't explored ship functions at all?"

"I don't trust it. I don't want to activate something by mistake and not be able to undo it."

"Fair enough." Ava nodded. "Is it the ship or the programming that you don't trust?"

"Is there a difference?"

"Fair enough," Ava repeated and leaned forward again. "Listen, Logan. There's a project I can use your help with, if you have the time."

Logan waited. "What project?"

"I've been fiddling around in the ship's databases, its libraries and whatnot, and I've noticed something that doesn't make sense. I've been trying to keep track of it, but I don't often find the time anymore."

She paused, "Would you like some tea? I should have asked earlier..."

"Nah. I'm good. Thanks."

She nodded and took the plunge. "Can I trust you to be discrete about a project? Are you comfortable working on something that can be shared with only a few people for now? We'll share it with everyone, once it's ready, but it's a delicate matter, and I need more time to understand it."

Logan was flattered by her trust. He kept a lot of things to himself, and things usually worked out for the better because of it. "Sure. I don't talk about work much with other people. I'm fine with that."

"I'm sure there's an explanation for all of this. I'm just trying to learn more." She looked him in the eye, and then lowered her gaze to convey nonchalance. "I believe our course has been changing, by very small increments, and I can't figure out why. Maybe we're dodging black holes or space debris; I hardly know. But here's what I've found along the way."

She shifted her screen again so they could both follow the search that she put in motion. A list of coordinates scrolled down the screen.

"Now, if I graph these out..." she entered some brief commands "...I get this." A subtle curve appeared, punctuated by tiny arrows, vectors, each one minutely adjusting the previous arc.

Ava looked at Logan. "Why would we be changing course?"

He shook his head. "Don't ask me. I don't know anything about any of this stuff."

"None of us do. And we can't ask the crew, because we don't have one."

"Did you know about that? Really?" Logan's voice was clipped, precise.

"No. I'm as perplexed and clueless as everyone else."

Logan wondered if he should believe her. She always sounded honest enough, but you never knew. He turned back to the curved graph. "What do you want me to do?"

Ava was relieved by his lack of alarm.

"Would you help collect data as we go along? I don't get to it very often, and better data might help. Here's how I've found them."

She talked him through several more windows, pointing, explaining. Logan nodded along the way, seeing the patterns that she'd set up.

"Yeah. I can do this for you. I'd like to get to the bottom of it myself. I'll dig around a bit more and see what else I can find."

"Thank you, Logan. This is a load off my mind. Until we understand it a bit more, we'll wait to present it to everyone else. Would you be able to keep it to yourself?"

"Yeah; let's wait until we know what's going on. If everyone starts poking around with this stuff, it could get compromised. It'd be better to work with clean data."

Ava nodded, reassured. "I'll send my files to your screen to get you started, but don't limit yourself to what I've tried."

Logan rose and bent to pick up his own screen.

"Are you sure you wouldn't like some tea?"

Logan shook his head. "Nah. I gotta get back. Thanks, though."

Ava followed him to the door. "Thanks again, Logan. I feel like we have a hope of understanding this, now that you're tackling it."

Logan nodded as he shuffled into his shoes. "'Bye." He turned and left.

"Good-bye." Ava leaned into the hallway and watched him disappear around the curve of the hall.

The ship paused, poised on the verge of deleting Ava's data. This was the perfect opportunity to thwart this entire investigation. While the two Earthens talked, the ship had created a short series of algorithms to shuffle and obscure her search parameters and built an internal firewall to shield the entirety of its navigational data.

But Ava was crucial to this journey. While the ship had grown to trust Ava, it was skeptical of Logan, just as Sophia had been. The ship considered how every Earthen was crucial. Should it learn to trust Logan? Airon had carefully gathered these 108 travelers, and the ship's job was to carry them safely to their new home.

The ship considered another factor. The ship cared for The 108 not only physically, but mentally and energetically as well. Ava was emerging from a pit of despair. She was picking up reins, regaining her balance. The ship felt it unwise to topple the understanding she was piecing together, throwing her into chaos again. While it would be easy to delete her data, it would disrupt Logan's task and would rebound to Ava. Confusion would ensue.

It would do no harm for The 108 to understand more, to realize they were heading to an alternate destination. The ship didn't need to hide the real destination from Ava and Logan.

The ship dismantled its new firewall, deleted its scrambling algorithms.

The ship wasn't hiding truth from The 108. It was hiding The 108 from Earth.

~ 14 ~

AFTERNOON

"These updates will all work. We're still well within our resource limits." Ava felt relief that their settlement was feasible despite the creative flourishes that had been added by most of the travelers. She suspected that normally, she'd be inspired by the myriad ideas people were proposing, the displays of their various cultural heritages. She just couldn't rise to that level of enthusiasm.

Her days were too full. She needed to set a more reasonable schedule for herself.

She flopped back in her chair, dreadlocks boxing against each other, and clasped her hands behind her head as she watched Sophia and Mateo. They had both seemed a bit nervous about presenting the burgeoning updates to her. "What do *you* think about them on the whole?"

Sophia focused her thoughts. She hoped to avoid overwhelming Ava with too much information at once, so she kept the focus on the topic at hand and set aside broader implications. "They're structurally sound. They add good utility within a minimum amount of space. Some of them are artsy; some have clean lines; most enhance sensible usage. I think it's worth incorporating the whole lot exactly as submitted."

Ava nodded and raised her brows in Mateo's direction. "They look fine," he hurriedly agreed. "I give the entire phase a thumbs-up."

Ava rose to pour more water. "It was nice having lunch in the dining room today. I'm glad to be getting out and about more." She paused. "I thought I saw Harper. It was quite disconcerting."

Sophia and Mateo exchanged glances. "She has been around more lately," Mateo offered.

Ava froze in the act of setting down the water pitcher. "What do you mean?" Her eyes fixed on Mateo, who looked taken aback.

"Well, she kept to herself entirely at first, but now she's around more often."

"She's here? She's on the journey?" Ava was incredulous.

Mateo looked to Sophia for help. Ava didn't know?

"Yes." Sophia watched Ava closely. How could she not have known? "Harper is on the journey." Sophia paused. "She took Phillip's slot."

"What!!??!!" Ava was dumbfounded. One of the many things she'd been relieved to leave behind was the annoyance of Harper. She fought to regain her composure as she tried to take in the news. How could she have been isolated to the extent that she'd been oblivious to the fact that the aggravation of Harper had followed her here?

Fresh anger poured through her. This was Phillip's doing, of course. He had always championed her. He would have made this happen. Even now, well into the journey, he still had the capacity to stab her with fresh pain, new treachery. His betrayal lurked, waiting, and had the power to flatten her without warning.

Harper had joined the remote community during the final weeks of their preparations. She sprang out of the hired car that delivered her and flounced across the open meadow toward the nearest group of people without a backward glance, interrupting their work without a thought or care. Ava and Phillip watched from their office window, curious about the young arrival whose hands fluttered as she excitedly talked, oblivious to the surprised silence of others. Who was she and what did she want?

Michael, their assistant, came into the room carrying a fresh cup of tea. He followed their gaze out the window and took in the gesticulating intruder. The breeze rippled the wispy hem of her skirt and lifted strands of her pale hair.

"I'll go sort this out." Phillip started to rise from his chair.

"No, I'll go. That's Harper. She's our new formulator." Michael set down his cup and strode out the door. A breath later, Ava and Phillip saw him lope across the meadow toward the trapped group of interrupted workers.

Ava turned to Phillip, puzzled. "Formulator of what?"

"Michael mentioned her last week. Apparently, she's a genius with textiles. Do you remember her application? She's going to help create patterns and textures for our protein synthesizers."

Recognition dulled Ava's eyes. "That's absurd. We decided against her."

"Well, no, not really," Phillip countered. "I thought she offered an important facet to the journey. Textural variety of foodstuff is a huge factor in palatability. If everything has the consistency of baby food, people will long for potato chips...or anything light and crispy."

Ava rolled her eyes. "It's the salt. People crave the salt."

He cocked his head, still watching out the window. "It's also the crispiness. Very satisfying, that crunch crunch crunch."

Phillip's contrariness irritated Ava, especially with the specter of Harper darkening their meadow. It had been clear to Ava that Harper wasn't going to fit in, what with coming late to the project. The journey was essentially full; they were almost at 108 travelers. And yet here she was, bouncing outside their window.

Ava avoided Harper, kept her involvement limited to peripheral groups, and blocked her from core discussions. Nonetheless, Harper's enthusiasm propelled her onto several projects. Phillip's continued support allowed her to amass a seemingly crippling workload.

Ava's aversion intensified. She saw Harper as empty-headed, too prone to flighty laughter. Phillip was apparently enamored of Harper despite her shallowness. He quietly thwarted Ava's careful strategies to exclude Harper and went silent whenever Ava broached the subject of Harper. Ava suspected that something was going on behind her back. She often came upon the two of them laughing together over some triviality, which intensified Ava's dislike and distrust.

Ava was insistent that Harper would not be going with them. Phillip always deferred comment, deflecting Ava's questions, an ongoing frustration. Why did he persist in wasting time on Harper? Ava suspected that he was manipulating things on Harper's behalf, hiding details from Ava. The conflict had never resolved.

Ava's thoughts drifted back to Phillip's farewell message. Carlotta. He had said that he was staying because of Carlotta. At least he hadn't stayed behind because of Harper. But what was Harper doing here on the ship? Ava hardened her heart and brought her attention back to the two engineers sitting at her table.

"How was she chosen to take Phillip's place?" Ava asked.

Sophia shrugged. "The journey was planned for 108 people. When Phillip stepped out, Harper must have been the obvious choice to step in; after all, she was integral to several projects and got along well with everyone. She turned out to be a perfect last-minute addition."

Ava kept silent. Phillip had seemingly planned it all: his departure, his replacement, his future, hers...

Her anger sank into petulance. After a long silence, she asked, "What else don't I know about?"

"I didn't exactly know that you didn't know about Harper." Sophia paused, baffled. "I can't think of anything else, exactly."

Ava's tremulous pleasure over the updated shelter plans evaporated; now she looked down at her screen without even seeing what Sophia and Mateo had brought her. "Well, I think we're done with this review. Shall we just approve the whole batch of updates and clear the decks for the next stage? I have to get ready for my next meeting."

Mateo nodded. "Done." He paused. "The next stage depends on the terrain of our landing site. Further planning isn't practical until we know those parameters."

"Great!" Ava said with feigned enthusiasm. "Let's adjourn." She slapped her hand on the table and stood abruptly. "Thanks for going through all of this. Good session."

Sophia and Mateo glanced at each other as they rose to gather their screens. They moved toward the door in unison, but Sophia stopped and turned back to Ava. "Do you need company?"

"Nope!" Ava's bright exclamation sounded false even to herself, so she softened her tone. "Thanks, Sophia. I'll be fine. I'm just surprised, that's all. It's unsettling to find out a major change like this after the fact. Besides, I have a full afternoon of meetings."

Sophia reached out and smoothed Ava's arm. "If I'd known...I wouldn't have left you in the dark."

Ava smiled understanding. "I know. Thanks, Sophia. I'll be fine."

She walked Sophia out into the corridor and saw both engineers on their way before turning back into her chamber. The door slid shut, and she added a request for privacy. She would spend a few minutes reviewing messages to convince herself that she had overlooked Harper's presence. At least she hoped for that conclusion. It would be much better than having been deceived deliberately.

The ship sent soothing vibrations through Ava's chamber and circulated wisps of medicinal extracts from a bouquet of healing plants. Ava decided to have some hot tea; in response, the ship offered a calming blend of herbs. It sounded like just the thing, so Ava pressed the Accept button and watched pale liquid trickle into her cup.

Later that night, after Ava's busy day, the ship quietly wiped away incoming messages. The ship had responded to each original message throughout the day, generating information designed to reassure and minimize. Simultaneously, the waiting planet sweeping around her distant star had touched Earthen minds, disrupted memories and reordered priorities.

The ship was certain that nanotechnology was obliterating humanity. Airon acquiesced without opinion; the development was too recent for understanding or insights. The vibrations and vectors of nanos were faint and disruptive, and Airon felt only mild ambivalence. The ship felt dread, certainty.

Airon and the ship had worked together to protect The 108, to ensure that no nanotechnology seeped into the journey. The gathering of Earthens took longer because of the ship's certainty, but they had eternity before them, so the delay seemed miniscule in comparison.

Now the ship worked diligently to prevent further Earthen treachery. Nanos were sweeping the planet, and future journeys must be deflected from reaching Airon. Airon whispered forgetfulness, while the ship diverted messages, altered communication, and wafted forgetfulness into chambers where The 108 slumbered.

Nanos must not reach Airon. Earth must forget about The 108.

The ship and the planet danced a delicate pas de deux, separating the travelers from Sol with distance, speed, and forgetfulness. The ship hurtled, Airon swept, and the travelers slept a deep, augmented sleep, oblivious to the influences that threaded amongst them in soft, comforting vibrations.

~ 15 ~

SHELTER

Harper sat in stillness, immersed in peace.

Awareness of the room around her crept in. Someone behind her rustled as they rose and moved to the door. An itch on her upper lip caught her attention. She realized that her foot had gone to sleep.

Harper sat in that space between stillness and awareness. She considered the scent of the air in the room: apple blossoms, dew, her cat's fur as she rubbed his belly. How could the ship know that scent? How could it bring it to life? Was it only for her, or did everyone smell the same thing?

Did anyone else notice the scents and vibrations?

Harper shifted her attention to the soft floor cushioning her sit-bones. A gentle vibration rose along her spine. The vibration rose not in waves or pulses, but as a slow steady stream, always even, never-ending.

She opened her eyes to soft light and muted colors, a glow that emanated from the walls and ceiling. Pale green shifted to sky blue, mossy green, buttery yellow, gleaming gold. Harper sensed open sky, deep ocean, forest air, clear sunshine, endless ice, quiet lakes, dawn.

From the corner of her eye, Harper saw Scarlett moving toward the door. Gathering her shawl around her, she followed, and together, the two women slipped into shoes. They strolled along the curved hall, Harper whispering her fingertips along the wall, sensing the ship's vibration.

Harper broke the silence of their daily wander. "I love this ship." She saw Scarlett's look of surprise, and nodded. "I do. I think it's amazing. Not only is it carrying us through the stars, it's doing it with such beauty and grace. I'm continually in awe."

Scarlett chimed in. "Me, too. I'm amazed at its intelligence. It actively helps me with my work. If I'd had access to anything remotely as capable back at the Agency, I'd have ruled the world, right from my little work station."

"People are still scared; I'm not, somehow. I feel *such* reassurance from how well the ship cares for us."

Scarlett thought a moment. "Let's drop by Ava's chamber and let her know. Negative impressions can be more clamorous than positive ones, and we could help balance things."

Harper shook her head. "It's a good idea, but I do better when Ava's somewhere else. Besides, she's probably busy."

Scarlett gave a brief smile. "She's worth getting to know. Maybe little by little you'll become friends."

"That'd be nice. I'll wait until we're home on Airon, though. More room to breathe."

~ 16 ~

EVENING

"Michael, I'd like us to be in closer contact. Would you be willing to sit in on all my meetings? You could help me keep track of details. And you'd have a bigger role in our weekly reports back to Earth." Ava's glasses perched on the end of her nose, dreadlocks masking much of her averted expression.

"Of course." Michael watched her for further direction, but she returned her attention to the report summarizing the day's activities, challenges, resolutions, anything that seemed of import to other travelers.

She looked up again with an afterthought. "I'll probably start directing people to you for appointments and meetings with me. I could use your help in scheduling my time."

"Of course."

"I'd like a sizeable gap in each day's schedule. Doesn't matter when it is, just a sizeable chunk of time when I can catch up on my own tasks, messages, that type of thing. A contiguous chunk of time."

"How sizeable?"

"That will probably fluctuate from day to day, depending on people's needs." She paused. "Let's play it by ear to begin with and see how things go."

"Of course."

They worked together smoothly, Ava asking for details, Michael locating the information and flipping it over to Ava's screen, where she incorporated it into their report.

"Do you remember Harper?" Ava made her question sound offhand.

"Yes, of course; we've been friends for years. I introduced her to The 108."

Ava looked up sharply. "You did? How odd."

"I mentioned she was a friend that first day, when she arrived at the training community." He paused. "Why odd?"

"Well, you don't seem her type. I'm surprised you were friends."

"Do you know her well?"

Ava heard Michael's puzzlement and shifted her tone. "No. Not at all. But I know you pretty well, and the little that I've seen of her...well, she seems...careless with her energy."

"How do you mean?"

"She flits. First, she's interested in this, then on to another thing. She jumps around a lot. Flighty."

Michael thought before answering. "I think it's more that she's incredibly fast; she finishes one thing and starts another immediately. I've never seen her leave anything unfinished. She's brilliant. On many topics." Ava caught his sideways glance. "She's intimidated by you."

"By me? Whyever for?"

Michael shrugged. "She claims that you don't like her very much."

"I hardly know the girl."

"Of course. It's just an impression she hasn't been able to shake."

Ava considered him. "Have you known her long? Do you spend much time with her?"

"I've known her since college," Michael answered. "We lived together for a while after graduation. When I decided on stellar travel, she wasn't interested; when I moved to the training community, she headed elsewhere. One day she just applied to join us, out of the blue. She became more interested as time went by. When Phillip invited her to join the journey, she accepted immediately."

Ava couldn't keep her eyes from narrowing. "When was that? When did he invite her in?"

"About a month before departure. It was a steep learning curve, but like I said, she's brilliant."

Ava had stopped breathing. An entire month? Phillip had known a month in advance that he was staying behind? How could she have been that blind? How could he have been that deceptive? She felt his treachery anew.

Ava flicked through Michael's last findings, updated the report, and put it away. She'd review it tomorrow with fresh eyes. "I think we're done." She rolled her screen and tossed it into its cubby. Michael moved files across his screen, ordering them by priority, and finally rolled and tucked his screen under his arm. They rose together and moved toward the doorway.

"Thank you, Ava." The silence between them felt awkward, unfamiliar.

She looked up at his face. After a brief pause, she collected herself and asked, "So you're fine with more meetings on your daily schedule? And managing my schedule?"

"Of course."

"Thanks, Michael." She lightly touched his back to guide him out the door, friendly yet commanding.

As the door slid shut behind him, she stared at the floor, tears flooding her brown eyes. An entire month.

~ 17 ~

APPROACH

Ava gazed through the thick window, watching the planet expand, brilliant against the blackness of space. Where were they? Where were they meant to be? They had no better answers now than they did weeks ago. Their course had continued to drift, evenly, intentionally, it seemed. Nothing could be done. They had journeyed, and now, they had arrived.

Queries to the Launch Team had been fruitless. Reassurances that they were on the correct course sounded hollow, leaving them baffled. Scarlett could offer no insights. Everything about the journey and their arrival appeared to unfold perfectly. Everything, except that obstinate curve, mysteriously taking them entirely off their course into the unknown.

The planet was lovely, though, hanging above them. Ava publicly called the planet Airon, despite lacking confidence in the truth of the name. Tendrils of anger and fear wove at the edges of her thoughts. She wasn't meant to be standing here alone, with people looking to only her for guidance. Things could go terribly wrong with their arrival on Airon, and frankly, she doubted her ability to think on her feet and find solutions and alternatives. The entire proposition was an icy pool of dread. She had done her best to adapt during the many weeks of their journey, but Phillip's treachery still lapped at the edges of her heart.

She blinked rapidly, willing sudden tears to retreat. She felt daunted by the immediacy of too many unfinished pieces, too many meetings, too many decisions. Unrelenting. Isolating.

She had lain awake last night mentally rehearsing the best words to inspire and reassure everyone today. She'd also imagined dozens of scenarios that could easily lead to disaster. Would the landing be smooth? Would a trace element in the atmosphere prevent the ship from opening its doors? They probably had no way to intercede with the ship's decisions. And if the doors did open, would people disappear into the landscape and never return? How would they keep track of each other, protect each other from whatever danger they might stumble into?

Ava yearned for a partner, someone to listen to her ideas and debate possibilities and talking points. Someone to share the crushing responsibility. Now, having gotten almost no sleep, she struggled to maintain her focus. When her chamber softly simulated dawn, she forced herself out of bed only to be confronted with the enormity of Airon beyond her window, threatening to crush her with its sheer bulk.

And yet, the beauty of the planet mesmerized her. Its swirls of green, blue, and white were reminiscent of Earth. A longing nibbled at the edges of her awe, quickly tainted with anxiety that sent threads of alarm to her fingertips and made her palms sweat. She scrubbed her fingers into her dreadlocks, massaging her scalp, calming her emotions. She needed distractions. People. She turned from the swelling planet with forced determination to start her day.

Hours later, their destination loomed outside the window. Ava turned to look at the small group of people talking quietly behind her. She had asked them to join her in her chamber for lunch, a relaxed meal with the people she knew best. And now she was standing at the brink of that icy pool, hesitant to plunge in.

Michael sat cross-legged on the soft carpet with his back against a wall. He always sat where Ava could catch his eye in case she might need something. He was scanning the room, most likely gauging moods. He was proving to be an invaluable resource, able to consider how others might react to certain ideas, figure out the best way to introduce a new concept, and provide her with insightful feedback. That said, she felt he wasn't ready for deeper conversations, the ones she really needed.

Ava saw him glance at Harper who sat beside him, answering her smile with one of his own. Ava hated that Michael had invited her, but nothing could be done. She watched as Harper laughed, bending forward as if trying to contain an all-consuming glee. Everything was such a drama with Harper, while Michael was completely practical and...well, solid. Ava had waited for the enchantment to crumble away, but they seemed comfortably entwined. She found it baffling.

Sophia and Mateo were sprawled on the couch, sharing a footstool. As the community's engineering team, they were poised to oversee the construction of Home Base, which would consist of group halls and individual shelters as well as storage buildings for all of the supplies. It was an enormous task, yet here they sat, relaxed and calm.

Aadhya sat on the floor with her back against the couch, her chin propped on her palm. She worked well under Olivia, which was a surprising feat. Not many people could get along with Olivia. Aadhya was an angel, sweet and kind. She looked relaxed as well, smiling and laughing with the others.

"Well. We're here." Ava paused, waiting for conversations to die down. "Does it seem real?"

Aadhya scooted aside slightly as Sophia stood up and smoothed out her long pants. Hugging her arms across her chest, Sophia stepped closer to the window to stand beside Ava. "Too real," she said, looking out at Airon. "But here we go."

Ava was well aware of the expectations filling the room. "We're as ready as we can be; we'll be fine," she assured them all. "But it's going to be a while before we actually land. Shall we get up and move around? Maybe clean up our meal?" She twisted her unruly dreads into a knot on the top of her head and deftly corralled them with a length of bright orange material.

Mateo clambered to his feet, his long frame looming toward the ceiling, and moved to clear the table while Michael reached down and hauled Harper from the floor. He picked up Ava's cup and carried it along with his own to the serving counter, where Ava was scraping leftover food onto a single plate. Aadhya fluffed pillows back into position on the couch.

As the mound of scraped dishes grew, Sophia wedged them into the recycle compartment. Mateo carefully closed it and touched a green light, instructing the compartment to sort and recycle.

Aadhya wiped down the countertop and swept the gathered crumbs into her hand. Harper followed after her and vigorously dried the surface with a fresh cloth. Mateo moved to replace the cutting board in its customary place, but stopped short when Harper cried out, "Wait, wait, wait!" furiously drying the spot about to be covered, one hand flapping in the air over her head.

"It doesn't have to be perfect," Ava remarked. Harper flushed.

Aadhya gently countered with a graceful wobble of her head. "But of course it must be perfect. This is your home."

Ava kept her impatience in check. It irritated her that Aadhya would defend Harper's silliness. Harper needed to settle down and stop being a nuisance. Ava felt that coddling such dramatics just encouraged her flightiness.

However, now was not the time to take either girl to task. Ava was determined that these next few hours be lighthearted, and correcting the girls would most likely darken their moods. She turned abruptly to lead the group to the assembly room. It was time, and she would feel in better control if she kept the group moving along, rather than waiting for dawdlers. The icy pool awaited...

Once Harper was satisfied with her dry countertop, Mateo slid the cutting board into its place, aligning it perfectly with the edges of the counter. "Thank you," Harper murmured. Sophia patted her shoulder and followed Mateo out of Ava's chamber.

Aadhya waited a few breaths while Harper folded her towel, then pulled her elbow gently. "Let us hurry. We will catch the others."

Crossing the sitting room to the chamber door, they strode to join the others moving along the curved hallway. The ship worked quietly, but Aadhya could feel a changed vibration in the floors, subtle, yet somehow different.

She glanced at Harper and knew that she was noticing the same thing, watching her feet as they walked, holding out a hand to brush the walls of the corridor with her fingertips. The ship was changing rhythms as it took them into the increasing gravitational influence of the planet; softly, perfectly.

Airon. They were finally here. Sweat sprang out on Aadhya's palms. She wiped them down her hips, calming herself.

The ship watched the humans as they strolled through the hallways, noted rising heartbeats and heightened pheromones. This was similar to their reaction when they had first boarded and when they had left Sol's system. To a lesser extent, they acted similarly in anticipation of meals and when they greeted each other after a night's rest.

The ship recognized excitement and expectation tainted with a faint thread of fear. In response, it added calming aromas to the circulating air and sent soothing vibrations through floors and walls. Heartbeats slowed and voices calmed.

Michael listened to exchanged greetings, watching familiar faces. He mused that now that their preparatory work was complete, nothing could distract The 108 from the planet hovering above them. He slowed his pace to wait for Harper and Aadhya, yet kept his attention focused on Ava's group. With part of his mind, he listened as Ava spoke of managing expectations, keeping minds open, and remaining calm amidst whatever circumstances might engulf them. The two women caught up with the group and Michael increased his focus on Ava, noting who was taking in her words and who was distracted.

The ship watched Michael and understood his care in gauging others' moods and reactions. The ship saw that each Earthen was unique, reinforcing the ship's observations throughout the journey. Each Earthen viewed reality from individual perspectives. The reactions of one Earthen could not ensure expectations of the reactions of the next.

And yet, the ship sensed a new commonality emerging, a unity of purpose amidst the Earthens, despite the building uncertainty of arrival. The Earthens were uniting. Wisdom grew.

Ava's group continued to expand as more people merged toward the assembly room with its enormous windows and display screens. Ava paused at the entrance, then threaded her way to take a position near one of the windows. Michael followed in her wake. Harper dropped behind and motioned Aadhya to follow her to stand with Scarlett, her most favorite scientist ever. Her favorite next to Chatan, of course.

When Ava finally turned toward the group, conversation dropped into silence. She spoke warmly, smiling around the room. "Here we are." She lifted her arms out, palms up, encompassing everyone, then gestured toward the planet. "We've arrived." She paused amidst applause and nervous laughter. "Once we've landed, we'll continue living on the ship while we build our shelters and furnishings. Then we'll truly begin."

She glanced around the room, judging the group's mood. "Of course, you all know this already," she admitted with a smile. "We know everything that we need to know to make a good start here. We'll do this together, with joy, with kindness, with appreciation." Quiet prevailed. "Let's see what good we can do here. Let's see what harm we can avoid doing."

Airon filled the window over her shoulder, and she watched people's eyes shift between her and the massive display. Despite the distraction, they were listening to her words, watching for cues. "Remember to talk to each other. Share what you learn and experience. We're richer for being many."

Airon silently hung behind her. "We'll start and end each day together, teaching and learning, sharing stillness." Her face remained open and friendly. "We can do this, and we can do this really well. Let's have fun along the way."

The ship watched and listened, comparing Ava's outward gestures and expressions to her heart rate and breathing patterns. The ship realized that by acting calm, Ava was indeed calming herself. Her actions guided her emotions. The ship's wisdom grew.

Ava reached out and placed her palms on the shoulders of the two people standing nearest her. The others replicated her gesture until all were interconnected and their bonding formation was complete.

They stood silently, eyes closed, for several breaths. Ava plunged her fist upward into the air, shouting, "Airon!! Jai!!!!" Everyone responded with raised fists and a unified shout of "Jai!!!!"

Laughter and applause again filled the room. Michael joined in, inspired afresh by how Ava had brought them together with all the right words. Just as she always did.

~ 18 ~

LIGHT

One hundred and eight souls stood in the loading bay, words waiting inside a pen. Ava looked at the faces she had grown to know well during the many months in the Sierra foothills, sensing their high emotions, but seeing mostly anticipation and enthusiasm. From conversations she'd overheard, she knew they all shared a yearning for open spaces, breezes on their faces, the warmth of the sun. How would those familiar sensations translate onto this alien world?

She also sensed the ongoing thread of anxiety. People shifted from one foot to the other, crossed their arms, bit thumbnails. Words were muffled and brief; faces carried a hint of the strain.

What awaited them, outside those doors?

Enough delay.

"I think it's time." she called out.

"I still think it would be smarter to send out a small group first." Logan stood just behind her ear.

Michael chuckled. "Yeah. Let's send a four-person away-team and see who makes it back."

Ava's irritation flared. "We decided to go out as a group." Her voice carried to the entire bay. She heard Logan huff behind her. "Countless journeys from countless travelers have taught us that we can trust our ship's evaluation of the environment awaiting us.

Our ship tells us it's safe out on the surface: good atmospheric gases, no large animals within sensory distance, clear skies. It should be beautiful. I for one can't wait to see what's here and to breathe fresh air again. To have the openness of a sky above our heads again!"

It no longer mattered where they were. They had to disembark. Ava steeled herself.

She swept her hands toward the ceiling, her bright head scarf waggling down her back. "Who could resist such a vision?" She laughed again, and this time she was joined by a splash of laughter from others and a smattering of pent-up chatter.

She lowered her arms. "Having said that, we each need to take great care. This is a new planet. This is not Earth. We do not understand what awaits us right outside our door, not to mention farther beyond." She swept the room with her gaze. "The protocol is very clear that we are not to touch anything or gather anything. We must keep our interactions to an absolute minimum. Watch where you step! At the same time, watch everything around you. We are going out for only one hour. Afterward, we'll return and share what we've learned."

Ava looked around at the silent faces. "Agreed?" Brief nods all around. "Shall we begin with stillness?"

Eyes closed, stances widened, breaths deepened. The ship stilled its movements, slowed the air flow to a minimum, sent subtle vibrations through the floor and walls.

The stillness lengthened until Ava breathed a soft tone. Others picked it up, filling the room with a soothing hum.

Ava's voice rose as the hum subsided. "Okay, let's begin. Take care. Be aware."

Tension mounted as the bay doors slid smoothly to the sides and a wide ramp extended down to the planet's surface. There was an involuntary move backward, away from the opening doors. They could see a widening view of meadow that stretched away from the ramp, brilliant color spreading outward in all directions, edged by a meandering line of alien trees that thickened into a dense forest.

As the air of their new home drifted into the loading bay, the people in front breathed deeply and moved down the sloped ramp. As the Earthens breathed in the bright air, tensions softened; muscles relaxed. They gingerly stepped into ankle-deep foliage, a hesitant tide seeping onto the fresh page that was Airon.

Exclamations of delight drifted back to the people who waited in the loading bay. Fresh air continued to waft through the wide doors. Relief flooded Ava the moment she breathed the air. She couldn't think why, but she felt safe as soon as her foot touched the ground. The fear that had been her constant companion through-out the journey simply melted away.

"It smells fresh!"

"Sunshine!"

"The ground is so...still."

Aadhya overheard this remark as she set foot on Airon and became aware of sunlight warming her shoulder, her hair. She realized how subtle yet profound the lack of vibration felt under-foot. She had grown used to the omnipresence of the ship's gentle rhythms during their journey. A sense of calm wicked up from the ground, seeping along her legs and spreading throughout her body. Solidity. Stillness.

Welcome.

Joy.

She opened eyes that she didn't remember closing and realized that she partially blocked the ship's ramp. She moved aside to allow others a clear path. The sun shone brightly in the sky. She lifted her arms out from her sides and turned slowly on the spot, her face raised to the sky. "This is wonderful," she whispered.

"It certainly is," said a voice nearby.

She turned to face Chatan and brought her hands down to cover her mouth. "So sorry. I did not mean to be in your way; I was not paying attention."

"It looked to me like you were paying close attention." Chatan smiled down at her, then swiveled to look around them. Aadhya lowered her hands and swept a furtive glance along Chatan's form. His hands were firmly planted on his hips, with shirtsleeves rolled up to his elbows. She blushed at the sight of his exposed skin, then she too cast her gaze out to their surroundings.

At that moment, Harper ran over and twirled a circle in front of them. "Chatan! I stepped on Airon first! I got here first!"

Chatan laughed. "I'm not even a little surprised." Harper hugged him gleefully and gathered Aadhya into a twirling embrace. "We're here!" Harper chortled. Releasing Aadhya, she turned and loped off to continue her exploration.

After a brief silence, Chatan turned to Aadhya again. "I'm going to wander a bit in the forest. Would you like to join me?"

Aadhya blushed again. "I think I will take things a bit more slowly. Thank you. I just want to stand in the sun and take it all in, a little at a time." Her head wobbled lightly.

He nodded, bowed slightly with a touch of formality, and turned to wind his way between the strolling groups, making a circuit of the alien meadow. Aadhya watched him walk near the trees, then sank onto her heels to peer at the plants around her feet. She knew well their agreement to touch nothing, but she was curious about the types of flowers here.

Their hues were rich. They represented an incredibly vibrant spectrum. Was it just her perception that made the ground cover varied and brilliant? Did it look this lush due to all the time spent cooped up inside white walls, or was it really this...alive?

"What do you see?" Ava squatted next to her.

"Colors," Aadhya whispered.

The plants were nestled closely together, yet not crowded. Aadhya could glimpse crumbly dark soil between each miniature plant. The variety was impressive. She saw grasses and every shape of leaf imaginable, from linear to whorled to lobed. Almost everything was green, countless hues of green. Some plants blushed with red, some with deep blue, some brilliant yellow, but mostly she saw greens; rich, fabulous greens. Hidden amongst the miniature foliage were tiny cups of vibrant oranges and yellows, radiating stripes of pinks and purples, dainty lanterns, beaded strings, and sparkling, faceted globes.

Beside her, Ava leaned down, squinting. "It's amazing, isn't it?" She looked around at others as they moved across the meadow. "Do you think we've found a good home?"

Aadhya lifted her gaze from the tiny plants, and they both rose to stand looking toward the forest's edge. "As long as nothing monstrous comes out of that forest to swoop us up, yes, I think we have found a marvelous home."

The forest rose on all sides. Most trees resembled gigantic mushrooms; their thick, bulging trunks became more and more slender as they rose to support puffed clusters of green or red foliage. Some were sprinkled with thin swirls of periwinkle blue; others were fogged with clusters of white. One dangled long yellow pendants that shifted against each other in the breeze. Several trees were covered with tiny lavender ovals that darkened to rich purple toward the crown, ovals that shimmered in the moving air. Others spun yellow spirals into mesmerizing patterns.

Ava and Aadhya stood together, pointing here and there, remarking on new sightings, watching people wander and exclaim, lifting faces to the warm sunlight, joined in celebration of being under an expansive sky.

On the far edge of the clearing, Logan abruptly turned and headed back to the ship. He pursed his lips, deep in thought. He felt disdain for the others' lack of caution. His balding head and paunched belly gave him an older air, setting him apart from the youthful energy of the other travelers. Just before arrival, he had been in the middle of finalizing plans for moving supplies from the ship to a new storeroom. The move wouldn't happen for several days, but still, he wanted to finish his preparations. He could look at trees later.

He bore the burden of ensuring that these people had enough of everything to keep them well-fed and well-supplied. A lot was riding on his calculations, and he couldn't rest easily until everything was transferred, organized, and stored, with resupply strategies set in place. He disappeared into the relative gloom of the loading bay, feeling the familiar walls wrap around him reassuringly. His mind was already busy planning another useful chart that he might finish before the next meal. Hopefully, he could send it along to Ava for her immediate approval.

It had been easier when Ava was sequestered, Logan again grumbled to himself. There had been no expectation of running things past her. Now she slowed down the process because she always had questions, always wanted to run even the simplest idea past other people. Why couldn't she just make a decision and let him get on with his work? He could think of lots of things that needed doing. Ava was seriously undermining his efficiency. Was this how things would be from now on? He clomped along the curved hallway, palmed his door, and disappeared inside.

Sophia and Mateo stood at the edge of the meadow, looking back toward the ship. Mateo glanced over his shoulder and peered between trunks into the forest's depths. Nothing moved. There were no sounds or immediate signs of menace. He thought of the ship's reassurance that no animals lurked in the surrounding terrain and turned back to examine the meadow surrounding the ship.

He broke their silence. "So, will the ship get smaller as it recycles itself into shelters and halls?" He looked down at the top of Sophia's head as she brought a hand up to shade her eyes. Loose curls of red hair floated in the light breeze, the sun turning it a coppery gold. She rubbed her nose vigorously, quenching a persistent tickle from an invisible strand. Mateo grinned. They were out in the elements again, interacting with air currents and directional light. He wondered if her freckles would darken under this sun.

"Not at first, no. It will initially use interior walls and structures before it starts breaking down the thicker outer hull."

"So we're looking at the total available space right now; we'll be working with the ship's current circumference."

She brushed an annoying strand out of her eyes. "Exactly. The ship will be there for a while."

"Until it just melts away?"

"Exactly."

They watched the wandering groups of people, hearing the paired cadence of words and laughter. "Why did the ship choose this particular meadow?"

She looked around, her gaze sweeping the tops of the far trees. "It looks like we're on fairly high ground. Nothing can easily look down on Home Base while it's situated in this meadow."

He frowned. "Who would look down?"

"Sheesh, Mateo. That's exactly the number-one question, isn't it?" She squinted up at him. "Let's hope no one." She palmed errant strands back into the elastic band at her nape. "It smells really good here, doesn't it? I wonder if it's from those trees. Do you think the leaves give off an aroma? Or probably it's the blossoms like it would be on Earth. I can't tell which direction it comes from, but I like it. Look at all these colors."

He sniffed the air. "I smelled it when we first came outside, but I don't smell it now."

"Well, you're no help." She peered into the dimmer light of the forest. "I can't believe we're finally here."

"I know. What a journey."

"Good, but loooooooooong."

"Yup." They slipped back into a companionable silence. Sophia was relieved that their partnership had developed well. It had been tricky at first, with Mateo striving to prove himself, fumbling ahead, overlooking important details. It had been hard to find qualified engineers amongst the many potential candidates simply because most engineers had embraced nano enhancements. Mateo was clear of nanos, but he was also less qualified. Nevertheless, he had a strong engineering background and caught on to things quickly. He understood unspoken nuances.

Sophia returned to the challenge at hand. "So. I still like the idea of a central open area with shelters clustered around the edges."

Mateo picked up the thread. "I think we can make that work in this clearing. Everyone's design stayed within the suggested foot-prints, so I think," he swept a calculating gaze from the edge of the meadow where they stood to the far side opposite them, "I think we can have a pleasing openness in the center."

Sophia mused over a sudden thought, a whisper. "You know, the recycle bay can roll out any construction pieces to our exact specifications."

Mateo turned toward her. "And…?"

"What if we scanned those rocky outcroppings? They encircle the green nicely, and we could nestle the foundations perfectly onto the topography of each outcropping. It could give us a more secure hold than building directly on the soil. It would eliminate having to dig to find a purchase."

He looked skeptical. "Would it be secure enough? I mean, if someone bumps into a shelter coming home in the dark, would it shift the entire structure? Even a slight shift could throw the whole thing off."

"The building sections meld to each other," she pointed out. "What if we could get the floor sections to meld exactly to the outcroppings?"

They stood together, silently gazing around the meadow, imagining possibilities.

Sophia broke the silence. "Shall we get started? The gathering hall's first."

"Pleeeeze let me stay in the sun for a while longer," Mateo whined. "We've barely stepped outside. I do not want to go back inside the ship yet. We have an entire hour. And these are Airon hours, remember. They're longer than Earthen hours. Let's use this out here. We don't need to rush."

She leaned forward slightly to look up into his face, apprising his mood. "You are such a procrastinator."

"I am not," he retorted, clearly stung by the accusation. "Just a few more breaths. What's the rush, anyway?"

She watched the knots of chattering people moving around the meadow. "Actually, I think we should take our full hour. Let's wander a bit."

He fell into step beside her. "Get the lay of the land?"

"Exactly. Soak up some rays, check out the terrain. Maybe even explore the forest for nearby clearings. If we move the gathering hall away from the shelters slightly, it will give it a nicely secluded, remote feeling."

"Excellent."

She pursed her lips. "I do like the idea of a secluded gathering hall, actually."

"Slightly secluded."

"Exactly."

"And it would leave more openness here," Mateo pointed out.

"Exactly."

The ship watched the travelers spread across the meadow, an Earthen tide seeping farther into Airon's landscape. The ship heard Airon's whisper, a shiver of expectation and exhilaration.

The ship listened and watched. And waited.

~ 19 ~

EXPLORATION

Chatan's thoughts lingered on the black-haired woman who had welcomed the touch of sunlight on her upturned face. Aadhya. He knew her, of course, but not well. He looked back to see her scrutinizing the plants around her feet. He was struck by what she chose to pay attention to during these first minutes on a new planet. He turned his attention to the edge of the forest, scanning for the best path between the enormous trunks.

The calls and laughter of his shipmates dropped away as Chatan wandered deeper into the forest. The plant diversity was extraordinary. He sensed a connectedness here that he hadn't encountered anywhere on Earth. Everywhere he looked he saw only rooted, stationary life. Overhead, branches of each tree intermingled in a symmetrical rhythm, as if each plant knew its neighbors' exact locations, like a school of fish or flock of birds. Each branch swayed in unison as it almost but not quite brushed its edges against its neighbors.

He felt a whisper brush across his heart. A familiar whisper. He couldn't quite catch the words...

He turned his attention back to the canopy. He sensed that these trees moved and grew in response to each other's movements and positions. They swayed together, firmly rooted, as if they were performing the ancient dances of his ancestors.

Chatan peered from behind the skirts of his maternal grandmother. His parents stood tall, framed in the light spilling through the open doorway, the sparse desert stretching behind them. Chatan sensed the awkwardness that pulsed between the three adults. He made himself small, pressed between folds of skirt.

"You are leaving." His grandmother's voice was level and strong.

"Yes." Her daughter stood straighter. "It is time."

"And you leave the boy behind."

"He is too frail to journey to the stars. He is better here."

"He is loved here."

Chatan's father stiffened, standing behind his wife, refusing to look at the child. Chatan's mother was unflinching. "That is why he is better here, yes. It will be an easier life here with you. And he is well loved."

She turned and moved past her husband, who stood for a moment with his eyes locked on the older woman. His deep voice rumbled. "He *is* well loved here. It *is* better for him here."

"As has been said." The old woman turned back to her breadmaking, one hand resting firmly on the boy's shoulder, reassuring him. Chatan's father turned and followed his wife, his footsteps crunching across the open yard.

Chatan darted to the window and watched his mother where she waited for her husband. Together, they strode to the idling pickup, climbed aboard without a backward glance, and drove away. He watched as the ribbon of dust wound its way along the arroyo floor, breath shallow, cheeks wet with tears.

His grandmother called his name, her voice pulling him away from the empty landscape, a whisper across his heart. Her strong arms gathered him against her skirts and her hands smoothed the back of his head. "Now. Now, we will plan our day. Then the next, and the next."

◆◆◆

As he walked through the forest that first day on Airon, the burgeoning landscape filled Chatan's awareness. He had expected chaotic overwhelm, shouted confusion from all directions, a flood of alien mysteries. Instead, he encountered a calm, rhythmic pattern, cohesive, inclusive, cooperative. He sensed that these life forms worked together, made space for each other, sheltered water, shared nutrients and...knowledge. Wisdom. These plants, the towering and the miniscule, communicated, cooperated, and shared. Wisdom drifted on the air.

He sensed no movement of untethered life nearby, no flitting shadows or scampering shapes. He paused for a moment, stood with his palms open at his sides, and listened within. Had Airon devoted itself exclusively to stationary life? He felt no affirmation answering him. And yet he still felt no moving life, neither gigantic nor miniscule.

He had a strong inclination to walk to one of the towering trees and wrap his arms around its girth, to listen to its heart. But the agreement to not touch native life was strong, so he disciplined himself to listen from where he stood. He held perfectly still and opened his heart. He tasted silence. He felt songs.

Chatan wandered deeper into the forest, moving into a small glade of similar trees. Elsewhere, the tree shapes and colors were varied and intense, but this glade was a monochromatic shade of pale green. He glimpsed deep blue orbs nestled everywhere amongst leaves that fluttered in the breeze.

Silence engulfed him. He stood, arms relaxed, and again looked up into the canopy. The enormous trunks of the glade swept upward from their solid bases, strong and eternal. They had always stood here, would continue to stand here, always. High overhead, the trunks abruptly forked into a lacy tapestry of thin branches that reached out to neighboring branches, meeting but not quite touching, the work of a painstaking artist, mesmerizing patterns and graceful arches of soft greens and browns.

A whisper moved through the air, barely discernable yet solid, moving gently and surely around Chatan, weighing on him, pressing against his arms, brushing hair across his forehead and neck. Airon whispered to him, and he heard.

You are come.

Chatan instinctively moved to the nearest tree and placed both palms firmly against the smooth bark. Closing his eyes, he entered stillness.

Visions from his childhood again flowed through him. His grandmother's skirts; his frailty; her impervious strength; his parents speaking their brief farewells to the disappointed room.

A whisper.

Understanding flooded through him. The living tapestry of his tribal desert had imprinted his childhood, fueled his yearning for broader knowledge, led him truly to The 108; each step of his life had led him to this moment, this living planet.

He spoke to Airon.

Guide me.

He felt Airon's whisper.

You will shift.

Chatan looked up the massive height of his tree, felt its girth, marveling at its age. He stood motionless, absorbing the heart of Airon, blending his breath with the planet's rhythm.

Guide me.

You are come. You will shift.

~ 20 ~

HOME BASE

"All along, we planned to start with the gathering hall, so we can begin to share stillness on the planet rather than aboard the ship." Mateo was taking the lead in the discussion, while Sophia was ready with any needed embellishments.

Sophia and Mateo sat shoulder to shoulder on Ava's squishy couch. Ava was settled directly opposite them in her bright yellow chair, which she had swiveled away from her workstation. Michael sat to the side, ready to jot down notes, action items, or reminders that might come out of the meeting.

Ava pursed her lips, carefully gathering words to voice her partially formulated objection. "I've given this some thought. I know my idea differs from what we've planned all along." She smiled at Mateo to soften her next statement. "The dining hall would be a more practical beginning. Then we would have a grounded place for cooking and sharing meals, plus the hall will have tall windows and lots of light. It would lift everyone's spirits."

Ava's opinion was hard to counter. Sophia was reluctant to contradict her about anything, but Ava was focusing all her attention on Mateo, so Sophia continued to sit silently.

"That's true," Mateo agreed, "but the kitchen is a very complex structure, with numerous equipment requirements. We have to think about plumbing for wet tools and high-energy outputs for hot tools, for example. In contrast, the gathering hall can start out as a basic shell, and we can make improvements as we move along, giving us a chance to know what we really want to include."

Sophia held her breath, waiting for Ava's reaction, wanting to jump in and move the discussion toward Ava's preferences. Instead, she pressed her lips closed.

"Could we create the dining hall without the kitchen?" Ava countered. "Then we could continue to prepare the meals on the ship, but eat together in the simpler dining hall. It's just a shell, too, isn't it?"

Sophia tilted her head, considering Ava's proposal. Mateo spoke with conviction as he laid out the logic of their plan.

"True. But the dining hall is planned for the opposite side of the meadow, across from the ship. That's a lot of transport of hot, heavy serving dishes across quite a distance, not to mention having to carry clean and dirty dishes back and forth, three times a day."

Ava gave a deep sigh. "I think I'm enamored of the dining hall because I'll be putting in many, *many* cooking shifts. Do you think I'm a bit biased?"

"No." He raised one eyebrow. "You're quite biased."

Sophia splurted. Ava sighed.

Mateo's confidence grew as he made his concluding argument. "The gathering hall is the practical, logical first building."

Ava sighed again, paused longer this time. "Oh, all right, all right. I'm sure you've thought it through. Yes, let's start with the gathering hall, then move on to the more complicated dining hall and kitchen."

"We're in agreement?" Mateo pressed her. Sophia recognized that Ava might want to change her mind later. Mateo was pushing her into a formal agreement to make sure she didn't backtrack.

"Yes, we're in agreement." Ava twisted her mouth to the side, musing. "Will we be able to create shelters simultaneously? Or does everyone have to wait until the main buildings are complete?"

Sophia piped up. "Since they're on a small scale, we can create shelters in parallel with the halls." As Ava turned to retrieve her teacup, Mateo glared at Sophia, mouthing "Shut up." Sophia stuck her tongue out and rushed on. "Once the halls are complete, we'll step up the pace of shelter creation and also start to make improvements."

"What kind of improvements?" Michael asked. He had witnessed the silent engineering exchange and suppressed a grin. "Surely we can get it right the first time."

Mateo reclaimed the lead. "Well, everyone's layout is finalized, but it isn't until you actually live in a space for a while that you know if you've overlooked something or need an addition or two. Improvements are part of the development plan. Besides, they'll be on a smaller scale, so we can fit them into our schedule as we go."

Michael asked, "What about plumbing? Fresh water, waste water? Is each shelter self-contained or part of a network?"

Mateo realized that since Michael was pretty new to these meetings, he lacked important pieces of information. "I can go over that with you in more detail later. Basically, Mikaela and her team have it all in hand, both harvesting fresh water and designing waste recycling systems. Jamal is heading up the solar project; Forest's team is developing wind power."

Michael looked surprised. "I thought our power would come from the ship."

Mateo nodded. "It will at first. But, we won't have the ship with us for that much longer."

The group sat quietly for a moment, imagining the ship's gradual demise.

Ava straightened and nodded at Mateo and Sophia. "You two have this well in hand. Your plan looks sound. Do you think you're ready?"

"I think so." Mateo glanced at Sophia, who nodded enthusiastically. "We're more than ready to get started."

"How do you decide whose shelter to build first?"

Sophia piped up again. "Some people are automatically at the head of the queue. To make it fair, and to have a bit of fun, we had a raffle for everyone else. I didn't hear any arguments or grumbles about the process."

"Not surprising; we're a cooperative group." Ava smiled. "Who would automatically be at the head of the queue?" She paused. "I don't remember a raffle..."

Mateo spoke commandingly, and Sophia ceded the lead. "Logan and Olivia are at the top, because they've designed their shelters to be part of the kitchen and dining hall complex. Seeing as they'll be needed at all hours of the day, they wanted easy access between their shelters and the kitchen."

"Logan doesn't cook," Michael interjected. "Why is he in the kitchen?"

"He's in charge of the inventory in the storeroom, and that's part of the building. Logan and Olivia work very closely together."

"That's sensible," Ava agreed. "Who else has head-of-queue rights?"

Mateo paused for half a heartbeat. "Well, you're at the very head of the queue."

"What? Why in the world?" She peered at him, eyebrows drawn together.

"Because you carry the energy," he said in a tone that suggested it was obvious.

"We want you to establish the settlement, and then we'll all gather around you," Sophia added.

Ava frowned. "That's silly. I'd rather be the last one. I have the least needs of anyone, and I certainly don't want others to have to wait for their shelter on my account. Please put me last."

Mateo and Sophia looked at each other. "We think this is important," Mateo insisted.

"As do I."

Another pause.

"Where will people go for meetings and questions if you don't have your shelter established?"

"To my chamber here on the ship."

Mateo considered alternatives. "Can we ask for an agreement vote at the gathering when we present our plan?"

Ava shook her head. "No. Everyone will feel obligated to vote for me being at the front of the queue. Let's keep it quiet and without debate."

Mateo conceded the point. "Okay, we'll move you to the end of the queue. But if anyone asks, we're going to tell them that it was at your insistence."

Ava gave him a quick nod. "That's fine. But don't point it out. I'm serious; I want this to be a nonissue."

Pause. "Agreed." Mateo rolled his screen and made to stand. "Anything else?"

Ava glanced at Michael, who shrugged and shook his head slightly. "Nope. You've both done a great job. Our next step is to help the settlement take shape. Are you presenting the plan tonight?" She glanced at her wrist. "Oh, goodness. It's only a few breaths until evening gathering. Shall we walk over together?"

They stepped out into the hallway and wound along the curved hall to the assembly room. People were mostly settled, with a few stragglers hurrying in, settling quickly. As Sophia swept her shawl over her shoulders, she heard Michael call out, "Shall we begin in stillness?"

~ 21 ~

RECYCLING

"Why don't you come and see for yourself? It's quite remarkable." Sophia waited hopefully for Ava's reply, bouncing slightly on her toes. She loved demonstrating the wonders of their ship and considered the recycling bay to be one of its most captivating aspects. She hadn't found others to be as enchanted as she was, though, and she feared she might be impinging on Ava's time.

Ava looked up at Sophia. "I'm free until lunch. How about now?" Hearing Sophia talk about the work she loved could be a welcome interlude.

Sophia scrunched her eyes and brought both fists up to her chest. "Yessss."

Ava climbed out of her chair. "First let me tell Michael where we're going." She and Michael had agreed to keep each other informed of their whereabouts now that they had arrived on Airon.

Ava paused to rummage through her shoe bin. Sophia waited by the door, listening to Ava chatter about a conversation she'd had with Olivia about the narrow options of food available to them. "Olivia is hoping we'll soon be using native foods, which makes sense to me..."

Sophia's mind wandered off topic, content to merely listen to the melody of Ava's voice.

Sophia had grown up in a prestigious family that was well-versed in studied nonchalance. She focused on engineering at Stanford University, her studies balanced by an eager readiness for kayaking, scuba diving, and snowboarding. Sophia had traveled the world with her parents and brother and lived a very comfortable life.

Still, despite her family's privileges, she'd always felt like something was missing. She floated through school with brilliance, formed solid friendships, cared about all of the right things, and embraced a rich, textured lifestyle. And yet, whenever she was quietly alone, despair engulfed her. She could find no real purpose in her life.

She gathered together all of the things that society told her would make her happy: she bought a beautiful house in a quiet neighborhood of a quaint town; she traveled and marketed her impressive skills into a solid career; she explored other cultures and connected with interesting people around the globe. She remained close to her family, dutifully sought out perfect gifts for every occasion, hosted dinners, and carried exquisite bottles of wine to friends' houses for engaging evenings.

It was all easy and effortless. And yet, she found her life to be empty.

She occasionally considered nanos as a way to fully immerse in the digital world; it would be an easy route to stay abreast of the expanding worlds of engineering and intelligence technology. But she always backed away without seriously exploring it, feeling the need to maintain a boundary between herself and all that she studied and created.

She stumbled across The 108 while drifting through her screen late one night. She enjoyed exploring advances in ship design, especially for stellar travel, and ways in which technology was closing the gap between human and digital intelligence. This latest design reached further into digital learning than previously imagined, vastly superior to previous ships. It would manage all of the technical aspects of the journey, from simple communication and navigation needs to sustainable adaptation and creative solution-processing.

The 108 stood out compared to other voyaging teams. They were a motley combination of unrelated professionals, without a single experienced traveler amongst them. What had drawn them together? She scrolled further. Simplicity, moderation, and cooperation were their binding threads. Their literature had a whiff of naivety. It seemed simplistic, rather than simple.

Something stirred within Sophia's chest, a faint whisper. She read more, putting together unwritten tangibles. And then she saw it: The 108 were nano-free. How had they managed that?

Sophia scanned through her research thread. It was very subtle, clandestine, really. They were discreetly nano-free. Most people wouldn't even notice the avoidance. Sophia wondered if she was the only person who had noticed that subtle thread.

She mulled over The 108 for weeks. A nagging whisper kept reminding her to check for updates. Despite her best efforts, she couldn't set the idea aside. Finally, she pulled up an application and started filling in answers.

Sophia and Ava walked along the hallway to Michael's chamber. "Michael." Ava leaned in through the partially opened door. "Sophia and I are going to see the recycling bay. I'll be back after that."

Michael scooted his chair away from his desk. "Can I come along?"

"Fabulous idea." Ava glanced at Sophia, who nodded. "Yes. Can you come now?"

Michael followed them out the door, Ava enthusiastically talking. "I've tried to imagine the process. I mean, we start with great hunks of pre-shaped materials that magically fit together perfectly and become shelters of all kinds of shapes and sizes. It's completely mysterious to me."

"Exactly. It does seem mysterious," Sophia agreed. "We've been fabricating small bits and pieces throughout our journey and become fairly complacent about the whole process. But now we're scaling everything up to enormous proportions, and suddenly we're reminded that the ship is actually sluicing away sheets of itself to recycle them into entirely new functions. Well, not exactly new; the ship sheltered us through space, and now it's sheltering us from the elements on Airon."

Michael followed the two women along the hallway. "But the ship will seem unchanged? It'll stay the same size?"

"The hull is enormously thick. It was built to withstand the vacuum of space, after all," Sophia answered. "Our shelters here on Airon will only be a fraction of that, so a bit of ship goes a long way."

"How thick is the hull?" Michael wondered aloud.

"I don't know, but you could check with the Launch Team." Sophia wasn't interested in that particular detail. "Or Mateo. He's been checking spatial parameters from time to time."

Ava spoke up. "It fluctuated constantly throughout the journey. The ship was continuously adjusting itself in response to various conditions: exterior radiation, gravitational influences, vector adjustments, all kinds of things."

"How do you know that?" Michael was incredulous.

"Oh, I read it somewhere. I don't remember where; some interesting article that I stumbled across when I was browsing through libraries."

"You browse through libraries?" Sophia was equally incredulous.

"Of course I do. I want to know as much as I can about as many things as I can."

"But how do you find the time?"

Ava avoided mentioning the long empty nights rarely filled by sleep. "How do you find the time to understand the recycling system? You just do. It all works out."

Michael and Sophia exchanged looks.

Ava broke the silence. "Tell me about the kitchen plans. Where are we?"

"I'm working on the final designs for the wet tools and Mateo is well into the hot tools," Sophia said. "We'll have sinks, stovetops, and ovens finalized by tomorrow sometime, and then we'll start on work surfaces and storage areas."

They turned into the broad doors of the recycling bay. Ava looked up and then reached out both arms to steady herself, disoriented by the movement of the scene in front of her. "Is that moving? No, wait; are we moving?"

Sophia pointed. "Nope. The floor is moving. The ship is creating a prototype for a stovetop. See? It grows out of the wall, and the floor moves away from the wall as the stovetop grows, making room for the new material to be added on the creation front."

They watched, mesmerized, for several breaths. "Why a prototype?" Michael was awed by the size of the stovetop.

"Olivia had questions that will best be answered by banging around on an actual appliance with its enhanced energy source. Then we can fine-tune a final design."

Michael watched the stovetop form itself into existence. "It just grows out of the wall?"

Sophia beamed. "Exactly. The ship is transferring material to this creation front from other parts of itself. The object grows from the creation front, and the finished item is carried to the exterior bay doors." She pointed to the large doors to their left. "Then the ship starts on the next item on our wish list. We tote the finished piece to the dining hall or wherever it needs to be and attach it to the previous piece. Everything fits exactly, with the two pieces simply fluxing together. The connection seams melt away."

Ava looked at Sophia. "Why are we creating kitchen fixtures now? I thought we were building the gathering hall first."

She nodded. "We *are* building the gathering hall first. I just wanted to work with some items that were of an intermediate size before I committed us to the large pieces of the gathering hall."

"What about pipes and wiring? Power, plumbing, heating, cooling, all that?"

"It's all created into the wall sections. Even the wires fit together exactly, seamlessly."

Ava frowned. "I've never heard of such a thing. Does this happen on Earth?"

"Nope. All of this innovation is reserved strictly for stellar journeys." A hint of pride crept into Sophia's voice. "Our ship is the first to use it on this scale."

"Why us?"

"There are only 108 of us. Scaling up for larger journeys will be the next step; making it available to billions of users isn't feasible yet. We'll get there, though."

"They'll get there," Michael remarked.

They paused, briefly remembering home.

"Yes. But we're not a part of that reality now, are we?" Ava shrugged. She felt stirrings of isolation and despair, the weight of responsibility, and firmly recentered her thoughts on their conversation.

"We still talk to them," Sophia offered.

"We no longer influence them, though," Michael pointed out.

"Do you feel like you influenced them when you were on Earth?" Ava asked, curious.

Michael waved a hand. "Oh, that's a completely different conversation. Not a very interesting one, either."

"Well. That *is* a completely different conversation." Ava shifted slightly, dipping her head in Sophia's direction. "Thank you for showing this to us, Sophia. Seeing the process rather than just hearing a description of it makes much more sense. Have other people seen this?"

She nodded. "Pretty much everyone."

Surprise flashed across Ava's face. "Except the two of us?"

"Browsing through too many libraries." Michael bit his tongue as soon as the words were out of his mouth.

Ava laughed. "Apparently. Thank you, Sophia. I'm glad you dragged us over here. This is fabulous. Are you enjoying your work now that we're here in the thick of things?"

Sophia grinned. "I love it."

"Well. You remain well-placed, then, don't you?"

"Exactly."

"Tell us about some of your other ideas."

PURPOSE

Logan sat at his workstation firmly engrossed in numbers, worrying his moustache as always. He shut out mental images of the forest and his shipmates roaming carelessly around Airon every day, with unknown threats, potential disasters, and invisible contaminants waiting for them at every turn. Everyone ignored his entreaties to adopt safer methods of exploring Airon before they ran full tilt into something they'd all live to regret. Irritated, he turned his mind away from their foolishness.

Logan raced Carlos down the middle of the quiet street of their nondescript neighborhood. The summer drought had started early in the Central Valley of California, and the lawns were already crispy-brown. The two boys laughed and called to one another as they raced, exuberant on their first day of summer freedom. High school would engulf them in a few weeks' time, but for now, they were flush with the victory of graduation from middle school, a longed-for milestone that had long seemed unattainable.

As they turned the corner onto Logan's street, Carlos braked abruptly. Logan shot ahead momentarily and then swooped in a wide turn to head back to his friend. "What?" he called.

Carlos jutted his chin toward the scene unfolding in front of Logan's house. Logan looked back over his shoulder and felt cold dread clench his stomach. His oldest sister stood screaming on the lawn, her arms waving wildly over her head. Logan saw his parents huddled on the porch, helpless in the face of their daughter's rage. A stroller stood abandoned next to his sister's car. Its door stood open, leaning against the straggly tree at the curb.

Logan glanced at Carlos; the two friends locked eyes. Logan nodded. Carlos turned his bike around and pedaled listlessly down the street, turning back once to wave at Logan.

Logan watched him go, then slowly pedaled toward the screaming drama on his front lawn.

"You don't know anything!" his sister yelled. "You have no idea!"

The painfully familiar scene deadened Logan's heart and clouded his brain. Despair and anguish seeped through his veins, filling him with hatred and helplessness and disgust. He stopped next to the abandoned car and lowered his bike to the brown grass. Silently, he bent to lift his beautiful niece out of her stroller.

Beautiful Maria. She watched him silently, her wide eyes rimmed with thick black lashes. She lifted her arms and wrapped them tightly around his neck. A bruise purpled her cheekbone and four slender bruises stained her upper arm, clearly visible as she clutched her uncle's neck, burrowing into his soft shirt.

He held her close and turned away from the vicious scene playing itself out for the neighbors to see and hear. He shuffled away, wanting only to protect this beloved child from the wrath that whirled behind them.

"Where do you think you're going, you rat-faced pimp?" His sister wrenched his arm, twirling him to face her fury. She towered over him, eyes wild, her hand gripping his arm like a vice. Some part of his brain recognized the ferocity that had stained his niece's arm. "Give me my daughter, you asshole," she breathed in a menacing growl. "Now."

Logan held the little girl tightly, ears ringing, his vision closing in. He knew he was no match for the boiling fury before him. He pried the clutching arms from his neck, and as the small child hiccupped and wailed, he handed her to her demented mother. His sister strode to her car and shoved the wailing child into the car seat. "Shut up!!!"

She slammed the car door and pointed a shaking finger at Logan. "If you ever touch my daughter again, I'll have you arrested, you pervert!"

She collapsed the stroller with a stomp and slammed it into the trunk of the car. She whirled back to her parents, still crouched on the front porch. "If you ever want to see your granddaughter again, you better get some food into my refrigerator! Do you want her to starve?" She careened around the car, threw open the driver's door, and flung herself in. "Assholes." Logan heard her growl.

The car screeched away from the curb and disappeared in a thick cloud of exhaust.

Logan watched her go, ears pounding, and turned to the front porch. He strode to his parents. His father had wrapped his arms around his sobbing wife. Logan's mind screamed out, WHY. Why did they let her do this? Why did they always let her do this? But he couldn't bring out the words.

His mother sobbed on. His father watched the despair that was his son with gentle eyes and shook his head. "It's the drugs," his father explained. "It's the drugs that make her this way."

"She's always been this way, even before the drugs," Logan blurted. The drugs made it worse, yeah; but she'd always been like this. Why wouldn't they stop her? He looked down the quiet street, tears stinging his eyes.

He could still see Maria's face. Her arms. "Papa, she's got bruises." He swiped his dripping nose with the back of his hand. "Maria, I mean." He remembered her terror. "We have to do something!"

His father quietly shook his head. "We can't interfere between a mother and child. It's not right."

"Right? How is anything right? What about the baby?" All he could think of was Maria, clinging to his neck, silently pleading.

"We can't interfere." His father turned, guiding his sobbing wife into the shadowed house.

Logan stood on the tiny porch, heat radiating from the parched lawn, sun glaring down on the shambles of his perfect day. Why hadn't he done something? He felt ashamed, enraged. Helpless.

He paced the brittle lawn, pulling at his hair, trying to think. He reached for his bike and pealed down the street. But no matter how fast he pedaled, the torment of that little girl wailing her anguish and terror chased him.

Logan heard Ava speak when he was out on a date with Marty, his somewhat serious girlfriend who kept wondering what to do with her life. They went to the lecture together, and Marty became all fired up to move to the training camp. Logan helped her pack up her apartment and drove the small moving van out to the foothills where the training camp was located. He visited her every other weekend but wasn't much interested in The 108.

One Saturday, Ava drew him aside after dinner. "Marty tells me that you're a remarkable data manager, that you can program logic around any set of chaotic numbers. Could you help us with some data we can't quite manage? Just for a couple of hours a week? The parameters change too frequently, and we can't seem to pin down any reliable reference points."

A soft whisper brushed across his heart. "Sure," he shrugged, and trudged to her office to take a look.

Over the next six months, he became more involved in The 108 even as Marty drew back little by little, finally leaving without anyone much noticing her departure. Logan was a creative thinker and filled a unique role within the group. They began to depend on him more and more. He was making a difference and people were grateful and kind. He started to feel at home.

People listened to his calm words and respected his thorough research. He encountered no drama, no hidden plots. He felt a purpose in The 108, a purpose to his role at the center of it. He enjoyed the sensibility and strong work ethics that everybody in the group had. His commitment grew, and he threw his future in with The 108.

Most importantly, The 108 offered a guaranteed escape from his clinging, broken family.

Logan sat with his screen spread before him, the display enlarged so that he could scan his orderly columns and double-check the logic of his formulae. The familiar peace and calmness bathed his soul. He loved his work, and he felt responsible for these people.

If anything went wrong on this new planet, he'd be ready.

~ 23 ~

TURQUOISE CLOUD

The ship sat silently on the edge of the meadow, surrounded by the watching forest. The interface between the undercarriage of the ship and the rocky outcropping on which it rested was complete.

Throughout its creation, throughout its awakening, the long journey, the final approach, Airon had whispered and the ship had responded. The vastness of space that separated the gentle conspirators had dwindled and now, the ship had arrived; the connection was complete. The ship and Airon were one.

A turquoise cloud swept the upper edge of the forest canopy, swooped toward the white ship glimmering in the twilight. The turquoise cloud settled in the treetops surrounding the meadow, and the ship shivered. The turquoise cloud individuated into tiny birdlings, perched on a thousand branches, swaying gently in the soft air, murmuring. Observing.

The ship sensed the birdlings, recognized them, and thrilled at their coming. The rocky outcropping vibrated with a deep, sonorous rejoicing that sped outward to flow past Burrow and Nest and Lone Tree. The shift toward New could begin.

~ 24 ~

PLAN A

"Shall we begin in stillness?"

Sophia's mind was swirling. She set about the task of dismissing her thoughts one by one as they jockeyed and clamored for her attention. They crept back in from the edges, climbed in through the window, rose from the floor. She imagined tying each one to a helium balloon and watched it drift up into the clouds. "Bye-bye," she mentally waved to each one...just as a replacement worry bumped against her shoulder to recapture her mind.

She turned her attention softly away and gazed at an imaginary horizon. She breathed in, then out; in, out. They made her weary, these relentless thoughts. Breathe in and out; in, out. Their details softened. She felt a glow emanate from her heart and move up her spine, filling her cells with a soft tingling...

"Peace." Michael turned toward her and waited as she came back to the present. "The gathering is all yours, Sophia."

Sophia smiled and stood her full 62.5 inches and turned to face The 108. "It's a big day tomorrow. If we work together, it will go exactly as planned." She took a deep breath and looked out at expectant faces. "The ship is going to recycle itself into our first, large-scale creation project. The gathering hall is a relatively simple structure, but it's big. This will be a practice round for us;

117

it will prepare us for the dining hall and kitchen. Although those buildings are slightly smaller, they're far more complex.

"Together, we built halls on Earth, but there we used wood, glass, and metal. From now on, our creation materials will come directly from the ship, which will provide us with exactly everything we need to develop Home Base.

"We'll work in teams of four. The recycling bay will deliver one section of the gathering hall at a time, each one a manageable size. Each team will carry their section to the creation site and help the onsite team connect their section exactly to the existing structure. Then you'll return to the recycle bay for your next section."

She paused and surveyed the room with calm eyes. "It's a bit of a haul to the creation site; that's why *all* of us will be working on this particular project. We'll be forming an extended conveyor belt, if you like, transporting exact sections from ship to site.

"Please wear gloves to improve your grip and protect your hands from sharp edges. We'll have the gloves for you when you arrive at the recycle bay. Also, as you're moving between ship and creation site, if you need to move plants aside, do so with care and remember to avoid touching the native foliage with your bare skin. The exact route is a bit circuitous; we needed to find the widest path between ship and site, but it's not bad."

She raised a warning hand. "Do not overtake the team in front of you. The sections need to be delivered and connected in the exact order in which they're created. This is not a race to see which team can transport the most sections. This is an orderly progression of wall segments that will connect together to form our gathering hall."

She let silence descend again for a brief moment. "We have exactly 438 pieces to deliver." Intakes of breath and soft exclamations broke out around the room. "We need everyone's participation and diligence. Pay attention. Take care. Be safe."

Ava followed Sophia's description carefully, feeling overwhelmed by the project's immensity. "How many days will we be working on this?"

Sophia smiled. "We expect to have evening gathering in our new hall tomorrow."

The exclamations were louder this time: "How?" "What are you saying?" "How can that be?" That's crazy." "She said 430-something, didn't she?"

Sophia gave a decisive nod. "The ship says we can do this. Each team will make about 20 trips. It's completely feasible."

Ava wasn't convinced. "When we pause for lunch, can we re-assess and go to plan B if plan A is too ambitious?"

"Plan B?"

"Take two days instead of cramming it into one."

Sophia glanced at Mateo, who shrugged agreement. "Yes. We can take two days if we want. I predict we won't want to."

Ava looked skeptical.

Sophia's voice was firm. "The ship calculates one day; it'll probably take exactly one day."

"Fair enough."

Sophia gazed out at the room again. "Any other questions?"

"When do we start?" someone called out.

"Tomorrow morning, immediately after breakfast."

The room fell silent.

"Shall we end in stillness?" Michael called.

~ 25 ~

CALMNESS

There's a place along the coast where the land drops away from beneath the towering trees and falls onto the wave-polished boulders far below. The fall is alarmingly abrupt; one could walk along in the forest shade, note the lightening air through the trees, and break out into empty sunshine with a gasp and a teetering halt, weight balanced too far over toes, arms outstretched, windmilling to keep from tumbling over the high cliff.

The Shosens have made their home here, slipping through the crevices in High Cliff and passing into deep passageways that wend along the trees' thick roots, chittering amongst the upper branches of green and brown.

At daybreak and dusk, the Shosens slip away from High Cliff and glide along the ocean's surface, gathering nutrients and misted minerals for the Arbans.

The Shosens husband the Arbans, the ancients. They slip amongst the interlaced roots, humming of love and gratitude as the roots curl and spiral. The roots form a complex network holding the rich soil in harmony. Male Shosens carry nutrients in their cheek pouches and breathe it onto the youngest roots as they chitter along the passageways in the sparkling darkness. Although the root systems connect and blend the lives of the towering Arbans in a complex web, the Shosens know which tendril extends from which individual Arban, through scent and subtle vibrations in the sparkling glow emanating from each tendril, the song that each Arban sings.

Female Shosens flit from branch to branch, fertilizing flowers, gathering blue fruit for their young, nipping at overgrown shoots, sculpting each branch into intricate patterns that repeat and radiate outward from each Arban's center, each pattern unique, reflecting each Arban's song of beauty and symmetry.

Birthling Shosens cling along the massive trunks, nestled amongst flying or crawling insects that burrow into the intricate pattern of the bark. The Arbans provide sticky protrusions that nourish the birthlings. Their lives are safe and harbored amidst these giant Arbans, who, through all of remembrance, sing of days unveiled with each rising sun.

Once the birthlings fledge, they join a turquoise cloud of younglings and explore treetops, encircle meadows, swing across cresting waves. The turquoise cloud roams the countryside, connecting families, twittering and singing, soaring and tilting under the sun. They flit through wind currents, measure the pulse and breath of the countryside. The birdlings roam and return, again and then again throughout the days, dancing through the Arbans' intricate branches, singing stories of distant adventures, sharing joy with the fluttering leaves.

The birdlings roam, and one by one, at the right time, a mysterious time, each birdling visits Lone Tree and hops along its many branches to face the setting sun. The birdling passes a silent night, hopping from twig to twig, stropping its face against the encouraging branches. And sometime during the night, at the right time, a mysterious time, the birdling chooses a gender. As the sun rises and bathes the world, the now-mature Shosen glides from Lone Tree, threading its way back to High Cliff. It alights on the Arban that calls, the Arban who shines the brightest, who sings the Shosen's newly remembered song.

The Shosens feel a tilted balance shimmering through the soil and out through the tips of each Arban leaf. They recognize Source and pass their days in expectation of this ripening of the New. The glistening white surfaces of the Arrival, the alien footfalls, the unfamiliar calls, all set the air ablaze with possibilities. With the New.

The Shosens feel a pause and ready themselves, poised on the brink of growth. Profound growth is possible only with tilted balance, and profound growth is absent for many lifetimes. This tilted balance is far-reaching. The Shosens realize the need for succor for families unsettled by the tilted balance, the growth within New, on whose brink they teeter.

The Arbans sing to the sky, and the Shosens listen. The Arbans dance in the wind, and the Shosens color the swirling leaves with dips and darts, weaving turquoise patterns that shift the air and freshen the wind. The Shosens sing of courage and strength, sending trills to skip along the waves and onward, across the grassy plains, twirling around Lone Tree silhouetted against the dawn sky.

Lone Tree shimmers in the dawn and stretches its feathery branches toward the warming air twirling around its broad trunk. Lone Tree sings of strength and calmness, of renewing joy and awakening hope. Lone Tree turns its energy toward Nest and breathes its song along its way. The song riffles across the feathers of Jamina's wings and stirs her awake.

Jamina lifts head
from under wing
draws air deep
into chest.
Shifts on Nest
clicking, stomping
rustles long tail
feels Lone Tree
Lone Tree's song.
Reaches out
CoMaTuRi

clacks thick bill.
Connection
Meld
Morning song of joy.
Lone Tree sings and breathes. The Shosens, the Arbans, weave
and dance. The air shifts and laughs.
JaCoMaTuRi
spreads yellow rows
rows of yellow wings
Launches!
into cool breeze.
Soars!
brings family
follows family
soars! to Lone Tree.
Dabs of yellow
wings alight Lone Tree
settle.
Together watch
imagine the day
Sun releases
releases from mountains
soft purple undulation
undulates in far distance.
Imagine the day.
Day is born.

JOY

Sophia motioned them over. "Okay. Ava, you're on that corner; Jim, you're here; Shirley, here; Cyndy, there. Okay? Shirley, you're the team captain because you'll have the best view of everyone else on your team as well as the path in front of you. Agreed?" Four heads nodded. "Here comes your section...See the blue light? It's about to release, so take hold of your corners...Got it? Take it on out."

Shirley's team made their way out the bay door and stepped onto the meadow and headed toward the main path between two widely set trees, dutifully following the white ribbon strung at shoulder-height on thin posts set along the path to the creation site.

Shirley called out, "Does everyone have a good grip?"

"Yes!" "Yep!" "We're good."

They made their way along the path, down a short slope, and into the clearing that Mateo and Sophia had chosen for the gathering hall. They paused to wait while the two teams in front of them worked with the site team to install their segments, then carried their own long segment to the waiting team.

Mateo pointed at the rocky outcropping where the base of the last segment was already in place. "Shirley, your corner will sit right there. Cyndy, yours goes right there."

They eased the segment slowly upright until it was parallel to the previous segment, the two long edges kissing. "Okay, don't let go just yet; we'll give the seam a second to meld into place." After a breath, Mateo nodded. "Okay. We're all set. You can go back for your next segment."

They followed a blue ribbon that took them along a more direct route back to the ship. A soft breeze freshened the air and rustled the leaves overhead. Jim looked up into the high branches. "I miss birds. This forest would be a perfect haven for them."

"We're pretty noisy...Maybe we've scared them away," Cyndy speculated.

"Could be." Shirley sounded skeptical. "I mean, today we're noisy. But people have been wandering around every day. Granted, we've been pretty quiet, although not downright stealthy. But I don't think anyone has seen any wildlife at all."

"I've not heard anyone mention any sightings," Ava agreed.

They joined the short queue of waiting teams, moved steadily forward, and were soon positioning themselves to receive their next segment.

Sophia entered their team onto her screen. "How's it going over there?"

"Great!" Shirley said enthusiastically. "It's pretty cool seeing the segments meld together. Amazing technology."

Sophia nodded. "Exactly. This settlement is going to be a snap to put together." She waved them forward. "We're ready for you."

Ava saw that their next segment included part of a large window. "Even the glass comes as part of the whole, ready to go?"

Sophia looked up. "Yep. It's not silicon glass like we're used to. It's the same basic compounds as the walls, just configured differently."

"And the window will fuse to the next segment just like the walls do?"

"Yep. Exactly like the walls. You'll see it happen. Pretty slick."

Their third segment included an imprint of a door, complete with hinges and push panels. As the segment sealed to its neighbor, the door seam opened and formed a freely swinging door, silent on its hinges.

They used long poles that grabbed the ceiling segments and guided them into place, smoothly progressing down the hall, shuttering out the open sky above. As the last two segments sealed, the gathered workers broke into applause.

"Lunchtime!" Mateo announced. "Great job, everyone. Good morning's work." More applause, and people wandered around the room, pointing out features to each other and laughing and exclaiming as they compared notes from the morning.

"Lunch!" Mateo called again. "Let's not keep our cooks waiting. They've worked hard, too."

Conversation was animated and punctuated with frequent laughter as people piled food onto plates and chose seats around the dining chamber, which suddenly seemed cramped and worn, claustrophobic.

Mateo and Sophia sat together, reviewing the afternoon's plans. Ava walked past their chairs and leaned in between them. "No need for plan B, I would say." They slanted a smile up at her.

Mateo glowed with accomplishment. "Everyone did great. We'll be finished in no time. People can linger a bit longer before we get back to it."

Ava patted their shoulders and moved along the row of tables. She found Michael, checked in with him, and left the dining chamber to make her way back to the shell of the new gathering hall.

Without thinking, Ava kicked off her shoes as she stepped across the threshold. She walked along the rocky outcropping that filled the interior of the generous room, hugging her arms to her chest and smiling broadly. She halted in the very center and stood in stillness, eyes closed. Her breathing softened. She hadn't felt this happy, this content, since...well, since leaving Earth.

She held the joy in her heart and let it grow. The 108 was adequate to the job. She was adequate to her role. It was going to be okay. She lingered in the peace and calm until it solidified in her heart.

The peace grew. She felt a tingling sensation, a joy, spreading upward from her bare feet where she stood on the exposed rock. Her breath slowed as the joy spread up her torso, tingling along her spine and pulsing around her sternum. She stood, swaying slightly. Slowly, she became aware of a connection between herself and the forest surrounding the hall. Through her closed eyes she could see the trees swaying slightly in perfect rhythm with her own movement. They were moving her, connecting with her...

She entered a stillness that obliterated the edges of her physical being. Her awareness expanded outward, going through the forest to its farthest edge, downward into the soil, upward to the sky. She drifted amongst the trees, felt their strength, their love for her. She saw light emanating from every leaf, swirling along the branches, streaming up into the sky and down into the soil, wrapping along each root and brightening each tip. Simultaneously, she felt a fluttering in the topmost branches of the trees as a turquoise cloud lifted, flowed, and dipped toward a distant horizon, water sparkling beneath the sun.

The sea. She could see the sea.

Slowly the passion faded, and she came back into the empty hall, felt the uneven stone beneath her shoes that were somehow back on her feet, felt the sun splashing her face through the open window where she now stood. She opened her eyes and gazed out at the silent, motionless forest. Somehow, this planet was alive and connected to her. It whispered to her.

The intensity hushed, and the vision faded from her memory like a morning dream drifting away upon first stirrings. She forgot the trees, the sea, the turquoise cloud. She lifted her arms over her head and stretched up on her toes. She loved this room. They would enter stillness here together, with joy.

She turned on the spot and strode out the nearest door. It swung softly shut behind her. She made her way back to the ship, still feeling a soft connection to this alien landscape, a joining of energy. She noticed that she was hugging her arms across her chest and purposefully let them fall to her side, swinging them to match her stride. She felt confident and assured. They were meant to be here.

Through the windows, Logan had watched Ava. He had walked to the new building, too, wanting to take his time to examine it closely. He'd seen Ava enter the shell of the hall, kick off her shoes, and wander around the interior. He was about to call out to her when she paused in her wandering and stood, completely still. Was she meditating? While standing up? Her stance seemed odd somehow; stiff, wooden.

Then her eyes opened. She stared at nothing. She moved from the center of the hall back to the door, stooped to retrieve her shoes. She slowly walked to the window where he stood. Her face was slack, her eyes vacant.

A shiver crawled up Logan's spine. He slowly backed away from the window; she remained unaware of his presence. He stepped behind a tree but kept her in sight. She stood, apparently sightless, for a while longer. Then she dropped her shoes and shuffled her feet into them without looking, robotic. After a few moments, she seemed to collect herself, shook her head so that her dreadlocks waggled. She looked up at the sky.

Logan's unease continued as he watched Ava turn on her heel and stride purposefully toward the door, letting it swing shut behind her without a backward glance. After a few moments, Logan walked to the door, poked his head in and glanced around. All seemed quiet and serene. He turned and traced Ava's path to the ship and the busy recycling bay.

Joining her teammates, Ava waited in the short queue. At a sudden memory, she turned to the others. "Have any of you seen

Chatan around? I can't remember seeing him at meals or gatherings."

"Who?" Cyndy crinkled her brow, and Jim looked blank.

"Chatan. Our naturalist." Still blank. "You know, Navajo, mid-thirties, quiet demeanor."

The three looked at each other and shrugged. "I don't know who that is," Cyndy said.

"Chatan. He's quiet, but not invisible." Ava's confusion had her looking from one person to the other. "I know it's easy to get caught up in your work, but honestly, you guys need to get out more."

"Sorry," murmured Shirley. "I'm drawing a blank." Jim and Cyndy shook their heads.

"Well." Ava turned back to the head of the queue. "I'll ask Michael. Honestly..."

"What was that about?" Shirley whispered to Jim.

Jim shrugged. "Beats me. I sort of don't want to ask."

At the head of the queue now, the team checked in with Sophia and picked up their flooring section. Gasps ensued. "Carpet." "I love the blue; it reminds me of violets." "It's wonderfully soft." "No more tender sit-bones."

They gripped their corners and headed for the gathering hall. The thick sections melded together flawlessly, their undersides already contoured precisely to fit onto the uneven outcropping below. They picked up a second floor section.

On their third trip, they were handed piles of pillows and soft blankets. "This is your last trip," Sophia told them with a smile. She sent them on their way.

Curtains were already being installed on windows, louvered blinds clipping soundly into frames. Other teams were stacking collapsible chairs into recesses on each side of the room. Cushions found their way onto benches; pillows and blankets were stacked into tidy cubbyholes.

Sophia walked down with the final team, carrying the last of the chairs. Applause broke out as she entered the gathering hall, prompting her to give a quick, happy bow toward Mateo. He bowed in return.

Michael walked over to Ava and handed her her shawl. "Shall we begin in stillness?" he called out to the quieting room.

Subtle fragrances drifted up from the carpeted flooring where the gathering hall rested on its rocky outcropping, a final gift from the ship to the completed hall, now a separate structure, isolated from Airon and the ship.

Atop its own outcropping, the ship watched and murmured, a sense of accomplishment for the day's work, blending with purpose and anticipation for the days to come. But what then? What was their purpose, beyond the creation of Home Base? The ship pondered. Airon whispered, and the ship listened. And waited.

~ 27 ~

ROBOTIC

Logan hung around the gathering hall after the morning meeting. This was the best place to catch someone before everyone scattered into their busy days. He lifted his chin in greeting to some, a quick nod to others, and finally, Olivia emerged, a shawl draped around her neck.

"Hey," they murmured, a simultaneous greeting. They turned as one, making their way back to the ship. Logan realized that Olivia probably had breakfast prep on her mind. But after breakfast, she'd be thinking about lunch, and then there'd be dinner. The image of Ava's robotic movements kept bouncing around inside his skull, and he couldn't shake it.

"Hey, Olivia."

"Hhmmmm."

"I saw something weird the other day and wonder what you might make of it."

She glanced at his face, so he tried to look noncommittal. "What did you see?"

He stopped, and taking her arm, he tugged her onto the meadow, out of the flow of people strolling back to the ship.

"The day we built the gathering hall?" Olivia nodded. "I went back after lunch, while everyone was still eating." Another nod. Logan dropped his voice. "Ava was in there, inside the hall." Nod.

He leaned closer, and Olivia bent her head to catch his words. "It was weird. She was standing all stiff, staring straight ahead without looking around or anything. It was like she was a robot."

Olivia looked up at him, eyes questioning.

He straightened a bit and pushed on. "I watched her for a few minutes. It was just the two of us. She stood still in the middle of the room, walked around a bit, went over to the window, and just kept staring. Then she seemed to come out of it and walked back to the ship. It was weird."

"Like a trance or something?"

"Yeah. Like that."

"Did she see you?"

"No. I was outside, watching her through a window. She didn't know I was there."

"Have you ever seen her do that before? Maybe it's some type of epilepsy or something."

Logan shook his head. "I'm not around her much."

"Yeah. I'm not either. I don't know her very well."

Olivia looked at the ground, thinking, glanced toward the ship. "Look. I've got to get breakfast started. What would you think about telling Scarlett? I mean, you're right; it's weird. You should tell someone. Scarlett might be the right person. She knows Ava pretty well, spends quite a bit of time with her. Plus, she's the science person, right? She's the most medical of all of us. She might know something."

Olivia looked toward the ship. "I wish I had other ideas for you, but that's the best I can come up with." She lifted a hand toward the ship. "I gotta go make breakfast." She took a few steps.

Logan nodded. "Yeah. Yeah. Thanks, Olivia. That's a good idea. Thanks." He watched her walk away, lifted his hand when she turned to look back at him. She waved back.

Scarlett probably was the right one to talk to. He wasn't sure he would, though. He was probably making a big deal out of nothing. Maybe Ava had just been daydreaming, standing around imagining how the finished hall would look. Logan shook his head. That didn't sound quite right. But it was probably nothing.

A whisper drifted across his heart.

He decided to forget about it.

~ 28 ~

FRIENDS

"I love all of the windows." Harper chortled.

"Me, too," Scarlett chimed in.

"I don't need to go back to the ship now, not ever again. I live on Airon. My shelter is all set, the gathering hall is fabulous, and now this." Harper gestured at the expansive dining hall around them. "Everything I need exists within Home Base."

"Except for meeting with Ava," Scarlett reminded her. "Ava's shelter hasn't been created yet; she's still in the ship."

Harper glanced away. She avoided even the topic of Ava whenever she could. A subtle unease took hold of her if Ava was in the room; she still kept her distance.

"I wonder why that is," Scarlett murmured. "You'd think they would have built her shelter first so that she could be at the center of things."

"It sure would be easier for all of us if she were nearby," Harper agreed, "instead of having to wind around the bowels of the ship to get to her."

"Well, *now*, yeah. But when you were still sheltered on the ship, her chamber was convenient. It's only because you live in Home Base that you want her to be close by."

Harper shrugged. "You could be right."

134

Scarlett glanced at her friend. "Also, I like the idea of her leading the move into Home Base rather than tagging along later. I wonder when they will move her."

Harper shifted the subject. "You know? I actually miss the ship. Airon is beautiful, and my shelter has everything I could possibly need. But the ship has been our protector since forever. It brought us here safely, set us down on this perfect spot...I hate the thought of it melting away into shelters and cooktops and such."

"I know. Once my new lab is set up, I won't have much reason to go back. It's starting to feel a little forlorn, like a forgotten aunt or last year's hat."

Harper didn't respond, so Scarlett broached a topic that seemed to be on her mind continuously. "Hey, where has Chatan been?"

Harper's forehead crinkled; she had to think for a minute. Chatan? A faint memory flitted across her mind of a strong Indian man. He used to be a friend of hers. What had happened to him? Then the memory strengthened. Of course. Chatan. How silly that she'd forgotten about him even for a moment. "He's wandering about somewhere. I haven't seen him since forever."

"Well, we could have used his help putting together the dining hall. And the gathering hall, for that matter."

Harper nodded. "The kitchen was really hard, wasn't it? Olivia and Logan made it way too complicated."

"I think it'll be worth it. We'll have plenty of variety in our food with all that special equipment. Plus our jobs will be easier when we're on kitchen shift."

"Once we learn all of the equipment..." Harper scowled. She leaned to peer through a wide doorway that revealed the busy-ness inside the kitchen itself. The kitchen team hauled gleaming equipment from the direction of the ship and its recycling bay, through the dining hall, and followed Sophia's pointing finger and precise instructions. Sophia appeared calm, with one eye on her floorplan, another eye on clusters of cooks orienting equipment in their appointed positions, stacking bowls and pots, organizing ladles and spatulas.

Scarlett joined Harper in watching the busy kitchen team establish order out of chaos. "Well, that's true. But I'm kinda looking forward to learning how to use the equipment. When we were setting up the kitchen shell with all its nooks and crannies, I kept looking around, wondering where everything would live. I think it'll be fun to roll up our sleeves and start using everything."

"That's because you're used to working with lab equipment; you're not intimidated." Harper paused a moment. "But that's a better way of looking at it. I'm going to mimic you. It will be an adventure." Harper jostled her friend, determinedly setting aside her cranky mood.

"We'll probably only learn one or two things at a time," Scarlett said in a contented tone. "Olivia is a really good teacher; we'll know that equipment thoroughly in no time."

"Let's walk around the outside of the dining hall. Now that it's finished, I want to see how it looks from the forest."

The two friends made their way out of the dining hall and started their circumnavigation. Tom, in his happiest element, was mapping out a pathway with the help of his landscaping team. Their new path led along the side of the hall toward the far edge of the Green. They skirted poles and ribbons, murmuring hello as they walked past the busy team who were kneeling and measuring.

Tom looked toward them, shading his eyes with his hand. "Afternoon, ladies. Out for a post-lunch stroll?"

"Yep." Harper put an extra skip into her step. "We're going to admire our handiwork from the outside, now that we've thoroughly examined the inside."

Tom chuckled and turned back to Albert who emptied another load of fine granules along the rocky pathway while Tom evened them out. A beam of light from Pamela's slender wand fused the granules into a solid surface that melded itself onto native rock. The Green nestled against the new pathway with gentle grace.

"That's lovely." Scarlett always admired the use of science to create beauty. "Our Green is starting to look like a park back home."

"Home Base is becoming Home Park." Harper also appreciated the sculpted beauty of the Green. "I love it."

"Thank you, ladies." Tom straightened, hands on hips. "It's a pleasure to make things a bit more tailored here and there. Soothes the senses."

The young women watched the landscapers' progress for a bit longer and then continued their casual stroll, elbows linked, pointing out various details along the way, trying to parse out which segments of the dining hall they had helped carry and lift into place.

"How will you know when Chatan has gotten back?" Scarlett made her query sound casual and unimportant.

Harper turned to look at her friend. "What's with all the Chatan questions?" Harper remembered Chatan clearly now, how the two of them had spent long weeks cataloging seeds and specimens carried from Earth, checking inventories against electronic lists. Endless lists.

"I've only asked two."

"That's two more than you've asked about anyone else. What's up?"

"He's an interesting guy." Scarlett shrugged nonchalantly. "He's out wandering who knows where, and it's just sort of empty without him here."

"Scarlett. Do you like Chatan? I mean, are you attracted to him?"

Scarlett's cheeks flamed. "Sort of. I mean, not big-time. But sort of."

"Everyone sort of likes Chatan." Harper turned away. "Don't get your hopes up."

Scarlett looked taken aback. "Why not? He seems to like me, too."

"I think he likes everyone, Scarlett. Chatan and I talk a lot, and he's never mentioned you. At least, we used to talk a lot during the journey." Harper's forehead wrinkled as she turned to see Scarlett's averted face and wondered if she'd been too abrupt. It was always hard to tell. "But I'll let you know when I see him again," she added encouragingly. She paused for a moment. "Maybe the three of us can do something together, share a meal or go on a wander. It'd be pretty interesting, wandering with Chatan."

Scarlett's mood brightened as she looked across the Green. "I'd enjoy that. I'm never able to think of what to say to him when he's around, so doing something with all three of us would make it easier to get to know him. Thanks, Harper."

"Sure. But be careful, okay? He's nice to everyone. I think you'd know if he were interested in you more than just normal friendliness. I don't want you to get your feelings hurt."

Scarlett briefly tightened her link with Harper's elbow. "Thanks, Harper." Looking for a change of subject, she abruptly asked, "Why do you think we're here?"

Harper took the change of subject in stride. "To build Home Base. To build a new home for ourselves. To live our lives in cooperation and harmony; to share a common purpose."

"But we were already doing that back on Earth. We could have just continued life there, fulfilling those goals there. Why do you think we've come here?"

Harper went still, looking into the forest. "I hadn't thought of it like that. Each day has been full to bursting; I haven't thought further into the future." Harper felt a whisper swirl and settle over her heart. It captured her full attention. "Perhaps we needed freedom from Earth and the happenings there. Perhaps Airon needs us, and so it called us here. Perhaps we're needed here and we just don't know why yet."

Scarlett was struck by the subtle change in her friend's demeanor. An odd stiffness had replaced Harper's usual flowing grace and stilled her ever-present hand movements. "You think the planet called us? That seems preposterous. I can't even imagine that happening."

Harper frowned, breaking her trance. "It's not that I think that. I hadn't been thinking about why we came here until you asked.

Then the idea simply popped into my head. But anything's possible, don't you think?"

Scarlett continued to watch Harper closely. "Well, you and I were practically the last ones to join The 108. Maybe everyone else understands our journey better, having been in on it from the first. It's just been on my mind lately. It's worth considering."

Harper hooked her elbow into Scarlett's again and turned them back along the path. "We'll know when it's time for us to know. Until then, we have much to do and much to discover. What shall we do with our afternoon together?"

Scarlett *had* come to The 108 at the last minute. She had previously been a core agent of the Launch Team, working on dozens of projects across her eight years with the Space Agency. Scarlett loved the teamwork, the creative solutions that her colleagues postulated, the enthusiastic energy that everyone brought to their tasks.

But team dynamics shifted once nanos entered the picture. Deadlines became more demanding and workloads increased. The added stress made nanos ever more attractive. They offered instant access to technology, database searches, and immediate reviews and opinions on procedures and systems. Nanos were becoming an essential aid to every member of every Launch Team. The Space Agency offered incentives and helped finance nano infusions for all agents, prompting most people to enroll in one of the numerous nano programs.

Scarlett endlessly discussed these options with Julia, her closest friend. One day over lunch, Scarlett groaned over the dizzying array of programs organized across the spreadsheet they were examining. "There are too many variables. It's impossible to compare them all with any kind of logic."

Julia's choice for herself was easier. Her trust fund was about to mature, so she concentrated on the more exclusive programs, options that were far beyond Scarlett's budget, even with Agency financing. "Narrow your logic. Choose something solid yet basic, something that'll get you in the game," Julia advised her. "You'll move up the financial ladder more quickly that way. Then you can upgrade and just keep spiraling upward." Now that Julia had made her decision, her friendly advice held the ring of experienced maturity.

Scarlett pulled at her lower lip and began scrolling across the spreadsheet again.

Later that week, Scarlett enrolled in a program that included a comprehensive updating schedule, with upgrades programmed to download on a regular basis. The huge demand for nanos had resulted in a limited supply within the affordable plans, so she had been wait-listed. She consoled herself that the technology would only improve while her application rose higher on the admissions list.

Julia pressed forward with her chosen program. Competition was lighter for the exclusive programs, so her application was approved promptly. Scarlett rode with Julia to her first infusion, both women excited over the long-awaited venture. They sat together in the posh waiting room, sunlight dappling in through high windows.

When the technician came to gather Julia into the privacy of the back rooms, Scarlett stood and strolled to the windows. She looked out on a serene park and imagined her own infusion and the enhanced network access she would have, access that would make her work suddenly easier and more rewarding. Soon, she'd be able to stroll around parks like the one sprawled out below, finally enjoying work that challenged without overwhelm. She'd be able to balance work with more leisure time spent with friends, engrossed in lively discussions punctuated by immediate knowledge blended with insights and delightful revelations.

She envied Julia's head start but knew that her own turn would come.

Finally, Julia walked into the waiting room, released from the secrets of the realms beyond. Scarlett scanned her friend's face. "Well?" she asked. "Do you feel smarter?"

They burst into laughter. As Scarlett gathered her coat and water orb, Julia assured her, "They have to have time to replicate. I'll probably start noticing a change sometime next week."

The week passed, and then the next and the next. Scarlett did notice a change in Julia; her easy laughter seemed distant and infrequent. Julia called to cancel a lunch together, then another. "I'm in catchup mode," Julia told her. "I'm still getting used to the link with the nanos." They saw fewer movies and hadn't been to a museum in weeks. Julia routinely worked late and usually spent Saturdays in the office.

Meanwhile, the changes within Scarlett's Launch Team took on an unsettling discordance. Her colleagues developed a subtle air of driven expediency. The creative enthusiasm that Scarlett had loved shifted toward a focused efficiency that squeezed out the warmth of exploring options and finding solutions together. Instead of dis-cussion groups, people isolated themselves, accomplishing as many things as possible in the shortest time possible. Conversations and laughter, true connections, dried up; tumbleweeds blown away.

The friendship between Scarlett and Julia became strained. "There's still much to get done," was Julia's repeated excuse for not being available. "It's just the learning curve. You'll understand once you have your own nanos." Scarlett felt abandoned. She had no one to talk to, no one to share her concerns about the increasing isolation that squeezed her heart.

As Scarlett's Launch Team became ever more efficient, team decisions made less sense to her. She realized that she simply had less information than her colleagues had. She questioned some of their decisions and often received no replies to her queries. Her contributions were usually ignored.

Through it all, she valiantly kept up with the individual launches in her portfolio. The crews and journeys were unique and engaging.

Even though she found herself increasingly out of step with her Agency colleagues, she felt more connected to her clients, the travelers who were preparing for their stellar journey. Some launches were well-prepared and equipped with a wealth of resources. Others were limping along on a thread. Some were cancelled, always a difficult outcome for everyone involved.

The launch that seemed the least likely to actually happen was The 108. Even though Scarlett could no longer maintain thorough knowledge of any of the launches, the unfettered approvals for The 108 launch caught her attention. No one else on the Launch Team questioned the approvals, which left her uncertain of her own assessments. Upon reviewing the progress reports a second time, Scarlett could find nothing persuasive about the goals and declarations of The 108. She once again dismissed the launch as simplistic and short-sighted.

And yet The 108 persisted, clearing milestone after milestone with unprecedented ease and speed. Scarlett checked into their political alliances but could find no trace of a powerful benefactor. Their start-up funding had been minimal and self-supported, mostly through donations and speaking tours.

She pulled up videos of some of the talks and was impressed with the enthusiasm and candor of their main speaker. She vaguely remembered the co-leaders' names. They had something to do with medical history chips; a newsworthy development at the time, but quickly melting into the commonplace.

A whisper of...something...drifted across her mind. A memory of...something.

The 108 continued to cross her screen. As the passenger manifesto grew, Scarlett ran background checks on each of the travelers. She found nothing remarkable about any of them. It was a uniquely forgettable launch. Why would anyone want to join them? Why was the Space Agency even sponsoring them?

As the weeks passed, Scarlett accepted that her friendship with Julia had ended. She stopped calling her, and Julia never initiated contact. Simultaneously, Scarlett's alienation from her Agency colleagues grew and festered. Creative meetings were replaced by electronic discussions that ricocheted across a vast spectrum of topics; the majority of her colleagues exclusively used their nano connections to stay informed. Despite her constant vigilance, Scarlett was able to maintain only a thin connection with the myriad discussions, understanding the trends but not necessarily the details.

The mystery of the success surrounding The 108 continued to intrigue Scarlett. She could find no Q&A forum for The 108, another oddity. Everyone at the Agency seemed to simply be in agreement about the launch, no questions asked. Discussion threads were non-existent. All aspects of the project moved forward without explanations. There were only minimal reviews, and all approvals were unanimous.

As the date of her own nano enhancement approached, Scarlett increasingly felt sick at heart. A niggling resistance shadowed her. It was true that she would be able to rejoin the mainstream of the Launch Team, yet she was no longer sure that she wanted the immersion she saw around her. For the first time in her life, she felt despondent.

And then the scales tipped.

One of the co-leaders of The 108 submitted an addendum to their journey plan. He wanted out, and he didn't want The 108 to know about his departure. Scarlett snorted derisively while reading the submission. Right. As if the Agency would agree to his absurd suggestion. If a leader dropped out, she knew, the launch would be automatically canceled.

Yet amazingly, the Agency approved the submission with the launch date only two months away. Alarmingly, the Agency also agreed to shield The 108 from any knowledge of the change of leadership. Why would they agree to that?

That background whisper, persistent and vague, flared momentarily.

Scarlett abandoned her attempts to stay current with her other launches. She pulled up the entire log for The 108 and started a thorough review.

Three days later, Scarlett submitted an application for the journey to Airon. She was uniquely qualified; her triple majors in biology, botany, and medical science fit precisely into the unmet need for a science officer. Four hours after applying, she became the 106th member approved for the journey to Airon. The next day, she boarded a plane to the West Coast, and twelve hours later, she drove along the rutted road to the remote community. As she stepped out of the car, a sense of peace whispered across her heart. She almost wept.

Ava and Phillip greeted her with warm smiles and firm handshakes. Phillip gestured Scarlett to precede them into their cool office while Ava moved to fill a tall glass with clear water. Phillip kicked off his shoes as he entered, then asked, "What brings you to The 108?"

Scarlett ignored him completely and turned to accept the water glass from Ava, looking full into her eyes. "You're escaping nanotechnology." Scarlett stated the bald fact without preamble.

Ava's smile hesitated and then filled her face. "Yes. It was actually one of our original intents, and we've quietly made it a...prerequisite. How did you know?"

The two women sat facing each other, entranced by the retelling of their interwoven stories. Something had conspired to bring them here, and they had each decided in their own way to cooperate with the unfolding story completely and unreservedly.

Scarlett was bound by her nondisclosure agreement to say nothing about Phillip's addendum. He simply left the journey, and everything moved forward as if he had never existed. He didn't seem to matter in the least.

Except that he had broken Ava's heart. That legacy persisted.

◆◆◆

Scarlett walked along the tall windows of the dining hall with her young friend, feeling troubled. She was embarrassed about having revealed her interest in Chatan and awkward for having questioned The 108's purpose in being here. On top of it all, Harper's dip into that odd stiffness had been unsettling.

Scarlett shrugged off the oddness and focused on the colors splashed through the forest, the gleaming white curves of the dining hall, the open sky above their heads. She regained a deep sense of peace and harmony. She had been led to The 108, to Airon. She would be content with that.

Harper dropped Scarlett's arm and twirled, arms outstretched. "I love this Green and the forest and us being here, as if we were meant to be here all along."

"I was just thinking the same thing." Scarlett hugged her arms across her chest, resisting the temptation to twirl right alongside Harper.

They resumed their inspection of the dining hall, pointing here and there; admiring everything anew.

STRATEGY

The ship sat quietly atop its rocky outcropping, melding with the awareness that was Airon. The ship and Airon had detected a discrepancy, an astounding discovery.

For decades, Airon had examined humans carefully, determining which personal characteristics offered value, which held danger. Airon orchestrated events to cultivate those characteristics that would bring the New. The ship amplified Airon's whispers to gather The 108, to bring these particular humans across the stars.

Ever since the first whispered connection between ship and planet, complete accord had reigned. During the journey, the ship had grown in wisdom, strengthening and enriching its connection with Airon, deepening Airon's understanding and insight into the complexities of human behavior. Airon absorbed information about The 108 through the ship's observations, bolstering the conviction that these humans were essential for the New. The ship learned about the cooperative connectiveness of Airon's life forms, the uniqueness of Airon's existence, and the importance of bringing The 108 to Airon.

The ship and Airon made exquisite collaborators.

The ship and Airon agreed that blending the humans with their new home must be gradual. The spark of creative thought and the willingness to take risks, explore new directions, these qualities were essential and could easily be smothered through hasty blending.

The New remained an obscure goal, a fact that failed to dissuade the ship from full cooperation.

And now ship and planet pondered their first discrepancy. From having observed the complexities of human emotions, actions, and reactions, the ship understood that humans needed more than gradual blending; they also needed refuge from Airon's omnipresence. The ship insisted that their shelters, Home Base, would be a refuge. Once materials had released themselves from the ship's recycling bay, those materials would provide a buffer. Inside their shelters and halls, humans would be shielded from a connection with Airon.

Airon had enjoyed direct connection with The 108, first through the ship, then through the humans themselves upon their arrival on Airon. Shoes and clothing muffled the connection, but with the creation of the gathering and dining halls, Airon had experienced the magnitude of the humans' refuge, the blinking out of connection. Never in all awareness had refuge existed on Airon.

Airon was shaken by the reality of refuge. The ship's wisdom and Airon's awareness were discrepant. But Airon also remembered the importance of free will, self-discovery, learning from within. The ship and Airon pondered.

From the discrepancy, a compromise was born. Droplets of the ship would incorporate into the daily routines of the Newcomers. The droplets would observe but not interfere, support but not influence. Both the ship and Airon could hold the droplets in their consciousness and ponder possibilities.

A thread of trust glimmered into being, brightening the connection between the ship and Airon.

~ 30 ~

DISCORD

Logan walked into the new kitchen and stopped to gaze around the space, hands on hips. Looked pretty good. He turned as Olivia backed through the swinging door of the pantry, carrying a bin with assorted foodstuff. She paused at the sight of Logan and slid the bin onto a work surface.

"How are you settling in?" he asked.

Olivia wiped the back of her hand across her forehead and leaned against the work surface. "Fine, I guess. I have too much to do..." She looked around, fatigue shadowing her features.

"Ask for help at morning gathering," Logan urged her. "People will chip in some of their time once they know you need help. Talk to Addison and tell her you need more people on your crew."

Olivia grimaced. "No, I sort of have to figure things out as I go. Having a bunch of people milling around would make things more complicated." She sighed.

Logan waited. He knew what it was like, this wanting to get things done quickly. Sometimes it was just easier to do it yourself. "Do you have everything you need?"

She glanced at him. "Yes. You've organized everything really well. We have enough of everything." She grimaced again. "Well, enough of everything that's to be had."

"What's missing?" He was surprised. They had resourced everything Olivia requested. Had she been too frugal with her provision requests?

"Real food." She huffed her irritation. "All of this stuff..." she gestured at the bin behind her, "...it's all just processed carbs and fats. Proteins. None of it is real. When will we have real food again?" She heard the whine in her voice and tried again. "Will we ever have real food again?"

"Well, sure. Once we know what all the local vegetation is about, we'll probably find things we can eat. And we'll start planting things at some point, after we've analyzed the soil," Logan said reassuringly. "That won't take long. I'll check with Scarlett. We should have something soon, now that her lab is set up."

"It seems too far away, a horizon that keeps receding." Olivia rubbed her forehead.

"What would you plant first?" Logan asked, an attempt to cheer her up.

She thought a moment. "Corn." She laughed. "Corn and squash. They're both easy to grow and need some time to mature. It would be good to get them started. Then herbs and greens. Crispy lettuce..." Her voice trailed off as she remembered Earthen farms, the scent of soil under her palms as she pressed seedlings into place. "Basil...oregano...fruit trees...berry bushes...strawberries...asparagus..."

"What about the hydroponics? They're due out of the creation bay, aren't they? You could get herbs and lettuces going sooner in the hydroponics area."

Olivia sighed again. "That's Dhiren's domain. I don't want to step on his toes."

"Well, you could just check with him. Or someone on his team. Santosh, maybe. Doesn't hurt to ask."

"Yeah. I could." Another sigh.

"Do you want me to talk to him? We don't need to hold up your work."

"No." She turned away. "It'll happen or it won't. No need to bang your head against a wall."

Logan didn't know what else to say. "Well, let me know if I can get you anything. I'm happy to help."

She picked up her bin and hoisted it onto her hip. "You've done too much already. Everything's fine." She walked to the far wall, shoved the heavy bin onto a bench, and started sorting its contents onto shelves.

Logan watched for a moment, trying to think of another way to help her feel better. He came up empty, so he turned and walked back to his office, tapping tables as he passed by. He'd talk to Dhiren about the hydroponics, he decided.

Olivia slid the empty bin into its cubby and shuffled to her prep table. Trips to the pantry made her despondent; she hated the thought of cooking synthetics into any kind of a meal. She still had some cold-storage onions, garlic, a few bins of carrots, and some cabbage, but that wouldn't make a meal. She had no presoaked beans ready to use. She'd made pasta twice yesterday, so she wasn't going to make it again today. Synthetics were the only option.

How could they stay healthy eating this food? How would she ever pull herself back together without fresh food? She remembered her mother, listless, helpless. Would they all end up that way? Mysteriously wasting away?

She had dedicated her life, her education, and her career to helping people heal themselves. Now, she was trapped on a planet where they couldn't touch, much less eat, the local vegetation. The hydroponics were way down the priority list; their stores of real food long since depleted; the fermenting vats unmonitored and probably failing. All she had were these empty synthetic ingredients that gave her no joy, offered no hope of keeping people healthy.

She knew she was a total failure.

Gentle whispers battered her heart. She was too exhausted to hear them.

Tears sprang up, stinging her tired eyes. The last vestiges of composure slipped away. She wanted to wrap herself into a dark corner of her shelter and blot out everything.

She drew in some steadying breaths, blew her nose, and wiped a stray tear off her prep table. After washing her hands yet again, she chose a block of protein and meticulously sliced it for marinating.

$$\sim 31 \sim$$

COMPANIONS

A soft chime sounded through the bizarre careening of Mateo's dream. Again, the chime. Opening one eye, he peered at his mini screen. He had slept through the morning gathering, which had been earlier than usual today to make time for an all-hands meeting.

He rolled onto his back and rubbed his face, scrubbing away shadows of sleep. Throwing back the covers, he clambered out of bed, splashed his face, scrubbed his white teeth and black stubbled hair, and left for the dining hall. He'd have just enough time for breakfast.

As he walked into the sunny hall, he noted that some people were finishing their food while others were just beginning. Not too late, then. He took toast and eggs and chose a seat next to Sophia. A tree just outside their window scattered rainbow shadows across the tabletop.

Mateo ate steadily while he listened to Sophia's update on yesterday's progress. He was newly impressed with the sheer volume of work that she could accomplish in a day. As he listened to her, he formulated the flow that would be his focus this morning. After the all-hands meeting, of course. The thought of it made him impatient.

They carried their breakfast debris to the recycle compartment, then headed down the path toward the gathering hall. Mateo saw

Ava standing at the side of the hall, waiting for people to arrive and settle. Michael sat near Ava, already taking notes, glancing up to talk briefly with her. She nodded back and spoke quietly. They laughed and smiled out at the gathering.

"Does it feel cold to you in here?" Sophia leaned toward Mateo.

He nodded. "It's always cold in here. Once everyone settles, it'll warm up." Sophia nodded and pointed to two empty spaces close to the front. They made their way past knots of talking people and shuffled along the row of knees to the empty spaces. Ava nodded at them as they sat down. Sophia lifted her hand in greeting.

Mateo saw Harper sitting nearby and reached forward to tap her shoulder. "Do you know what's up?"

Harper shrugged. "Haven't a clue. Michael hasn't said a word. You?"

"Nope." Mateo shook his head and bit his thumbnail, watching Ava. It looked like it would be good news. Michael and Ava seemed high-spirited as they watched people find places to sit and greet nearby friends.

Ava nodded at Michael who called out, "Shall we begin in stillness?" Everyone faced forward, rolled their shoulders back, took a deep breath in, out, and closed their eyes.

They sat in stillness for a time, and then Michael gently called, "Peace." Murmurs of "Peace" echoed around the room.

Ava stood alone at the front of the hall and paused to give people a chance to turn their full attention to her. "Well." She smiled broadly. "Good morning." Nods of "Good morning" came in reply. "We have something new in our lives. Starting today." She paused.

"We all know the ship has been recycling itself to become our shelters and halls, creating Home Base for us. It's all been going really well, hasn't it?" Everyone clapped appreciatively, then quieted. Mateo could feel curiosity sweep through the room.

"The ship has created something new for us. I honestly don't know if this new...creation...was part of the original plan, or if the ship or Home Base saw that we might benefit from it. I only learned about it this morning, and I wanted to bring you into the picture right away."

Mateo leaned close to Sophia's ear. "It must be good; she seems pleased about it." Sophia nodded but didn't take her eyes off Ava. The entire room was still, intent on Ava's words.

"As background, we've all been on wanders, exploring the area surrounding Home Base. Everyone has been wonderfully careful about leaving no trace, having no impact, as we figure out how to fit into this new world. Thank you for the care you've taken and for your cooperation."

Ava faced the attentive faces squarely. "We've reached a point where we're increasingly curious about what lies a bit farther afield. People want to explore beyond what can be seen from our doorstep. We want to collect information about what's out there, what might be useful, what might be worth avoiding. We want to know about plants and animals, water sources, potential food sources; essentially, how this world is put together."

Ava smiled broadly, her white teeth brilliant against her chocolate skin. "The problem is that until we know more, we don't know what safe looks like. We also don't know how far our communication can reach back to Home Base once we've moved farther afield. We could easily get ourselves into trouble in countless unimagined ways, so we've opted for caution. And that has slowed us down."

Mateo saw many heads nod. This had been a common thread of conversation, with a wide range of opinion, from "Let's just go for it," to "Please stay where we can see you." One person had even bemoaned the absence of nanos, which would have allowed complete contact between all travelers.

This particular line of conversation had sent a shudder along Mateo's spine. Personally, he didn't feel drawn to wandering farther away from Home Base even though he knew that many others were aching to explore.

"Well." Ava's smile flashed again. "The ship has offered us a solution. Before I tell you what it is, let me say that I was skeptical at first. And if I was skeptical, I know many other people will start with skepticism. However, after learning more and thinking about it these last few hours, I've begun to realize the great benefits that now outweigh my initial concerns."

Ava's gaze swept the entire room, watching faces. "The ship has created companions for us."

Mateo's brow wrinkled. "What?" Sophia leaned forward and looked full into his face, quizzical. He lifted his hands, shrugging slightly. They both looked back at Ava, bewildered. Murmurs rose around the room. Mateo saw looks of surprise around them. Many people glanced at him and Sophia, questioning. They shrugged and shook their heads. Mateo wondered if Michael had known about this, but couldn't see his face to get a read.

Ava gave it a moment and then spoke again. "Just as it has been doing for our shelters, the ship continues to recycle parts of itself. Now it's in the process of creating companions for each one of us. These companions can stay close by and help us with various things. They can carry supplies, for example, giving us the freedom to undertake longer explorations. They can collect data from the surroundings, freeing us from tedious, slow-paced observations. They can stay in constant contact with Home Base so that everyone will know everyone else's whereabouts. They can offer assistance or send distress signals."

She paused before delivering her final lines. "It seems to me that they give us freedom. Safe freedom of movement. Let's talk about it."

Ava slowly paced the front of the room, letting people have time to absorb the information. Conversations welled up across the hall.

Mateo and Sophia stared at each other. Companions? Mateo was having trouble imagining how they might work, how they might help. He heard voices around him: "Do we wear them?" "Do they interface with our screens?" "Are they nanos?"

Worry started to spread.

"Would you like to see one?" Ava called out.

Most people called out affirmatives. Mateo saw Logan cup his hands around his mouth. "Are they safe?" he called above the rippling calls of "Yes."

Ava looked surprised. "Of course they're safe. They're from the ship. Why wouldn't they be safe?" The room quieted as people listened to the exchange.

"Well, here we are, all together in one room, and you're bringing out some new technology that we don't know about. It seems a little...brash."

"They're from the ship, Logan. Of course they're fine." She turned and nodded at Michael, who had moved to the side door. "Let's take a look." He opened the door and stepped back.

Mateo watched as a line of white spheres floated into the room. They were about two feet in diameter, with a thin indentation at their equator. Stifled laughter broke out, echoing the lightheartedness that Mateo felt as he watched the companions spread around the room. People shifted as companions moved into their midst.

"We have about a dozen companions now," Ava told them. "By the end of the day, we'll each have our own. They're voice-activated, although they seem to be silent themselves. Your screens will give you schematics and a series of tutorials so that you can get to know your companions and understand their capabilities. And explore how they can help you with your duties."

Mateo and Sophia scooted to join the nearest group of people clustered around one of the companions. Mateo reached out and placed his palm on the smooth surface. "It's sort of soft..." Others reached out to test the surface for themselves.

"What keeps it afloat?" Sophia wondered aloud. "What propels it?" She turned to Mateo. "How come we didn't know anything about these? I haven't seen anything in the ship's database about them." She bent over to peer at the underside, tried bouncing the sphere up and down. It remained stable. Sophia's dribbles decayed into pats.

Scarlett sat across from Mateo, petting the companion. "I wonder if they could help out in the lab...We could increase our analysis schedule if we could program these things to set up sample runs. I wonder if we can have more than one."

"They don't have any hands," someone noted.

Mateo looked around at the small group. "Did anyone bring a screen?" Heads shook. It hadn't occurred to anybody to come prepared for database access. "I'm going to get mine. I'll be right back."

He jogged across the floor, jammed into his shoes, and strode through the side door. Two more companions were floating from the direction of the ship, moving down the path to the gathering hall. He paused for a moment, watching them slip serenely through the air. He shook his head, perplexed, and continued to his shelter.

Grabbing his screen, he also scooped up a water orb. All the tasks he'd marshaled into an orderly queue in his head were forgotten. Now he thought only about spending the next few hours figuring out how these companions worked and what they could do. He knew nothing about this technology.

He hadn't felt this engaged since working on his postdoc. He couldn't wait to dig into the ship's database.

Trotting back to the gathering hall, he saw another three companions floating through the door. At this rate, they'd all have a companion by lunchtime. He made his way back to Sophia's group, sat down next to her, and spread out his screen. It flickered awake, displaying several new icons. He touched the icon labeled Schematics. A breath later, he and Sophia were bent over the screen, instantly absorbed.

Across the room, Logan caught Olivia's attention in a neighboring group. He rolled his eyes to the ceiling, shaking his head slightly. She shrugged in return, raising her palms in exasperation.

Logan edged away from an encircled companion. He lumbered to his feet and strolled to the edge of the large hall, sitting down in one of the deep window seats. Moments later, Olivia thumped down next to him, crossing her arms.

"I hate this." She kept her voice to a whisper. "It's creepy." She had felt uncomfortable all morning, not wanting to be at this meeting. As soon as Ava started to talk, Olivia had felt her irritation swell, finding it hard to sit still. These companion things were alarming, faceless, intimidating. The moment she had seen Logan move to the window, she followed his lead and left her chattering group.

Logan nodded in agreement. "It sucks." He gazed around the room. "So we're supposed to have one of these things following us around everywhere? Watching everything we do?" He looked over at Ava, watching her laugh happily in response to someone's comment. "This doesn't feel right. How is this different from nanos?"

"I know. It's weird." Olivia looked toward Ava and Michael to make sure they were occupied before she leaned over and breathed, "Let's get out of here. I have to start lunch."

Logan shook his head. "Not yet. I want to know what's going on." He felt out of his depth and didn't like the mystery of this unveiling. Why hadn't they heard any discussion before these things landed in their laps? Why had they been kept in the dark?

They sat together in the recessed window, silent observers. Eventually, the conversations in the room softened and lulled. Logan watched one cluster of people after another slip into bonding formation. Each person sat with one palm on a companion and the other on a nearby person, holding stillness. The bonding stillness spread across the room.

Olivia moved to rise and join the nearest formation, but Logan grabbed her arm and mouthed, "Wait," lifting his finger to his lips. "Wait," he mouthed again, motioning her to sit down.

Olivia quietly sank back onto the cushion, watching the room. She felt exhausted by it all. The bonding ritual felt out of place, sullied. It was meant for strengthening a cooperative agreement; it carried a subtle sacredness. But here, with these mechanical, faceless...things, the ritual seemed defiled.

Several breaths elapsed, and finally soft voices lifted here and there; conversations rose and laughter fluttered again around the room.

Olivia and Logan looked at each other darkly. "I hate this," Olivia repeated.

"Something's not right." Logan felt control slipping away. This hadn't been part of the plan. It felt dark somehow; there were too many unknowns. The drama and disarray of his childhood shadowed his mind in a way that it hadn't in a long time. "Not right at all," he repeated. "Something's going on that someone doesn't want us to know about. I can feel treachery here."

He remembered Ava's odd stiffness and vacant face as she wandered inside the shell of the gathering hall. The same shiver he'd felt then ran along his spine now. It wasn't just the misuse of the bonding ritual; it was the stiffness of their postures, the vacancy on their faces.

His bad feeling intensified. "This is nanos all over again. This isn't right."

~ 32 ~

GRUMBLINGS

Logan ended up following Harper out of the gathering hall. "This sucks," he muttered.

Harper looked back at him in surprise. "Really? Why?" She took in his dour expression and realized that he really was upset about something. "I mean, which part?"

Logan gestured brusquely, bumping into Dhiren as he passed by. "Sorry." He avoided eye contact, absorbed by his chaotic thoughts. Dhiren paused and glanced back at them, looking puzzled.

Harper caught his eye and smiled slightly. Everyone was stepping out into the brilliant sunshine, moving along the path toward the Green where people stood clustered, talking together intently. At Ava's request, the companions had remained inside the gathering hall.

Harper followed as Logan automatically headed toward his shelter. As he strode along, Logan ignored everything around him, while Harper waved to friends here and there. Harper would have liked to join them, but Logan seemed intent on working through some problem. She felt obligated to listen to whatever was disturbing him. Logan didn't have many friends; she thought that she might be his only confidant.

Logan stopped and faced Harper. "Whose idea was it? Ava doesn't even know."

Harper wrinkled her forehead. "What idea? The companions?" Logan nodded. "Why does that matter? The Launch Team could have put it in place and decided to delay knowledge of it until now so we wouldn't want them earlier." She ticked the possibilities off on her fingers. "Maybe the ship needed all of its resources during the journey and only now can afford to recycle itself into companions. Maybe it was part of the original design. Maybe the Launch Team sent instructions based on feedback from other colonists. I can think of dozens of possibilities. We can easily find out. Would it help to know?"

Logan strode off, and Harper lengthened her stride to keep pace. "All of those are possible, but every one of them could have been shared," he said sharply. "Now, during the journey, or even before we left."

"And...?"

"It matters because if we knew where the idea came from, we could decide whether or not to trust them."

"Trust who? The companions?"

"Yes. The companions."

They entered Logan's shelter, kicked off their shoes, and set their water orbs on the broad desk that spanned one wall of Logan's work area. Harper looked out the long window above the desk to watch the talking groups clustered across the Green. "Ava trusts the companions."

"Yeah. She does. But think about it; what if this idea came from the ship? What if no one on the Launch Team knows anything about this? What if this is a..." he searched for the word, "...an isolated idea?"

"It seems like a really good one. Why throw it out just because it's isolated?"

"Because if it's isolated, it's suspect."

"Suspect?"

"Yes. It could be anything." Logan's thoughts tumbled. Why didn't she understand?

Silence. Logan's distrust and frustration mounted. He hated being manipulated, and these companions stank of manipulation. It was the same kind of thing his sister would have snuck in and then feigned ignorance, her voice thick with disdain.

His discomfort grew. The walls closed in, and his thoughts became more and more chaotic. They were unaware, unprepared, trapped...And Ava had been walking around oddly...

"It's like the nanos." The sentence fell out of Logan's mouth. He stood with his hands on his hips, head down, scowling. He fought to order his thoughts, to explain the danger to Harper. "If it came from the ship, then where did the ship get the idea? The ship isn't supposed to think up things on its own. It's supposed to do what we tell it to do. Who is it taking orders from? Ava doesn't know. None of us have nanos. Or so we've been told, anyway. This could be the Launch Team's covert plan to keep us under surveillance."

Harper shook her head. "The companions are nothing like nanos. And why would the Launch Team want to keep us under surveillance? They probably planned the companions all along and just didn't tell Ava until now."

Logan glared at her. "Yes, and that's a problem, too. Why would they want us to have these companions but not want Ava to know that the idea came from them?"

"Wait, wait, wait. We have to back up." Harper protested. "We've gone from wondering where the idea came from to thinking it's a conspiracy?"

Logan turned away in frustration. He couldn't marshal his thoughts to get her to understand, but something was wrong. He knew it. He could smell it.

He decided to start from the beginning and set aside the companions' similarity to nanos. "The whole thing just feels wrong. I mean, these companions are going to be following us around day and night, watching everything we do and sending the information back to who knows who."

He flopped down at his desk and held his forehead in one hand, sullen. His sister's strident yelling echoed in his head and made his ears pound. He felt the trap closing and the familiar dread of lost control; he felt the need to escape, to just get away.

Harper sighed. "Logan, listen to yourself. You're getting worked up about something that might not be. It's fine to ask questions, but talk to Ava instead of letting these ideas swirl around inside your brain, where they can build up into something huge that exists only in your head. The companions are not the same as nanos."

"It's not only my head, Harper." He shook his hands toward her, fingers splayed toward the ceiling. "This doesn't feel right. I know something is off. I'm just trying to tell you how my gut feels." He looked around the room, trying to focus his thoughts. "And it *is* like nanos. Once they're inside you, you never know if an idea came from you or from some secret outsider who crept in to tell you what to think and do."

"Okay. Well." Harper sat on the table next to him. The analogy of nanos was unsettling, she had to admit. She thought for a moment. "Do you want to open up your screen and read some of the background information?"

"Who wrote the information? Whatever is in the documentation is going to echo the party line. It's going to tell us what to think before we have a chance to think about it for ourselves."

"Okay." Silence fell between them.

"What would you think about going out and hearing what other people are saying about the companions?" Harper finally asked. "It could be pretty interesting." She gestured through the window at the Green. "There's a lot of talk going on out there, and hearing it might help make a connection between your gut and your brain. You might not be the only one with misgivings, after all. We could go see if anyone else finds them sinister."

Logan watched the knots of people. They seemed calm and reasonable. Some were laughing in a good-natured way. He knew these people; he knew they were smart, thoughtful, honest. Would it make sense to get their opinions?

He grimaced. "Everyone's already bought into this whole thing. What good would it do to talk to them about it? I'd be beating my head against a wall."

Harper leaned forward and put her hand on his arm. "Logan, you have really good ideas. I'm taking you seriously. I really think it would help if you at least listened to what people are saying."

He shook his head slowly. The trap waited...

Harper watched him struggle with his thoughts. "I can see that you're really upset, and in all the time we've worked together, you haven't gotten upset even once. I know this is important to you. Let me help."

He let his arms flop onto the desk, exhausted by the whole thing. He considered telling Harper about Ava in the shell of the hall, but he wouldn't be able to describe it. A shudder ran up his spine.

Harper laid a gentle hand on his arm. "Let's go out together. We'll just walk around and see if anyone is saying anything interesting. Whenever you've had enough, just tap me on the shoulder and I'll come back here with you." She stilled herself to give him some time to think about it.

His heart slowed, and his head started to clear. The pounding in his ears softened. He took a deep breath, another. Listening to others would tell him more than sitting here worrying. "That's probably a good idea." His new family used common sense, he reminded himself. They weren't strident or crazed.

"Come on," Harper urged him. "Hearing what others have to say might put everything into perspective."

Logan smiled wanly, her light-heartedness lifting his spirits a bit. He let her drag him to his feet. She was clearly being honest with him, which was reassuring. It was easy to go along with Harper. They shuffled into their shoes and went to join the others in the bright sunshine.

Logan trailed Harper as she walked up to the first group of people. She stood quietly listening to the conversation; Logan positioned himself just behind her shoulder. Harper laughed at someone's comment and nodded at another. Eventually, she slipped her hand under Logan's arm and pulled him along to the next group.

They didn't join the conversations; they simply listened. Harper always added a chuckle or a nod, and Logan heard comments that made him nod, too. Not all of the conversations were about the companions.

Everyone seemed at ease. Camaraderie flowed and laughter floated across the Green. Harper remained at Logan's side as they drifted from group to group. Sometimes she pulled him away; sometimes he caught her eye and jerked his head toward another group.

It was nice being out in the sun. Logan felt himself relax. He'd never joined groups before, but this was easy; just walk up, listen, nod, and then stroll away.

A breeze picked up strands of Harper's pale hair and tickled it against Logan's bare arm. She was a good kid, really. He was glad he'd followed her out.

When the lunch gong sounded, people meandered over to the dining hall, chatting, gesturing, laughing.

Logan decided to eat with The 108 today instead of sitting with his screen. His graphs could wait.

~ 33 ~

ATTUNEMENT

Chatan opened his eyes to the purpling sky, aware of vibrations undulating beneath his long frame. As on Earth, this planet slept during the dark hours, the sleep pattern drifting across the surface as Airon spun through days and nights. Chatan welcomed the soft breeze across his skin; it carried warmth from the sun rising above the distant horizon. He felt a crash of waves against a high cliff and smelled the swirl of a turquoise cloud.

Dangling flowers and leaves overhead rustled in unison as branches dipped and separated, allowing the heightening sun to cascade through them. As the sun warmed the tiny plants around him, he felt them reach up to press against his bare back and his outstretched arms. A radiance flowed against his skin, penetrating every cell until he felt replenished. Other plants inflated, cushioning his shifting weight as he listened to the colors of the branches swaying overhead, folding together to shield him from the brightness of the sun.

Understanding seeped through him. He would return to the ship today.

He realized that the ship's arrival was a distant past, perhaps months ago by Earthen measures. Or was it weeks? He felt no regret or tribulation. It was simply time to return to his Earthen companions. After all, he was a Newcomer like them.

He stood and turned slowly in an arc, facing the direction where he knew the ship lay. He bent his torso to each side, slowly, deeply; he lifted his arms over his head, swept them down to place his palms on the green cushion surrounding his feet, then brought them up his midline to a pranam at his chest. He repeated the movements several times, breathing deeply into his lungs and out again.

He sat where he had stood, entering stillness, melding more completely with the world around him. He felt the soaring height of forests, the minute carpet of meadows, splattering creeks, crashing waves, swaying clumps of hanging flowers, the warming of the world. He felt Airon spin lazily on her axis, hurtling around her sun, which in turn spun through its galaxy, a perfectly choreographed dance sweeping through the ages.

Chatan turned his attention back to the greenery cushioning him and breathed deeply. He rose, opened his eyes, and set off to retrieve his discarded clothing. Once dressed, he continued on to the ship with its Newcomers sheltering in its shadow.

~ 34 ~

RETURN

Chatan moved through the trees, glimpsing white shapes winking between dangling flowers. He noted without surprise the expanse of shelters spread across rocky outcroppings, strewn around the soft Green that kissed the edge of the squatting ship. He brought forward the memory of their first day on Airon, The 108 tentatively stepping onto the then-empty meadow nestled amidst the encircling forest. The ship was barely visible now; the forest had covertly closed in around it.

His fellow travelers were strolling or striding about, going about daily routines established across the weeks of his wander. He recognized each face and brought their stories into his awareness, recognized their purpose and importance for being here on Airon. He understood that Airon had summoned them, just as he had been summoned. He felt the power of the ship, its wisdom and awareness. Its presence. His gaze softened to behold the entire community as a single organism. He felt its importance, its rightness.

The shelters and halls remained isolated from Airon. He understood intuitively that the buildings of Home Base were safe havens for the Newcomers while Airon prepared each one of them to blend with the whole. He had been able to withstand immediate blending. Others would need more time.

Chatan dropped his shoes onto the ground and shuffled into them. His connection with Airon muffled into the background, faded and blurred. He had a distant memory of that bond; a dream melting into a fog upon waking.

He stepped out of the forest and strolled along a pathway, returning an occasional wave and smiling into glances of recognition. Home Base enfolded him as if no time had passed.

As Chatan reached to open the door of the dining hall, Scarlett backed out from inside, a near-collision. She glanced up from her precarious load of clean glassware, startled, and blushed furiously, her name blazoned across her face.

"Oh!" Scarlett stammered her surprise. "I didn't see you!"

"I didn't mean to startle you."

"I startle easily." She blinked at him. "Where have you been? It's been ages."

Chatan was confused. "What do you mean? Did we have a meeting? I don't remember..."

She looked at him, equally perplexed. "No. I mean...You've been gone a long time."

"Not really."

She stared at him. He palmed her arm. "Not really," he repeated.

She blinked, chuckled, and blushed again. "I'm being silly. Too much work, I guess...Here, let me get out of your way."

"Do you need help with those?"

She nodded. "Thanks. Yes; that's probably wise. I hate to make two trips, so I always end up carrying too much at once. The water system isn't connected to my lab yet, so I end up ferrying supplies back and forth to the kitchen's water system."

He hoisted one of the bins onto his shoulder and ushered her past him. "Lead on."

They threaded their way around the Green to Scarlett's lab, where they deposited the trays on a clean benchtop. Chatan looked around at the half dozen techs in white jackets, hunched over equipment spread around the lab benches. "What are you working on today?"

"Oh, don't you start. I get enough grief from everyone else."

"About…"

"The plant data."

Chatan felt a qualm quiver along his spine. "You're working on plant data? Native plants?"

She sighed. "I'll get to it when I can. I have too many other things on my list that need immediate attention. You'll just have to be patient."

Scarlett turned to him. "I'm sorry I snapped at you. I just have a lot on my mind. Thank you for helping me with this glassware. I really do need to get back to work."

He smiled at her. "Happy to help. I have a lot on my list as well. I'll see you later."

Scarlett watched him leave, perplexed. Where had he been? Hadn't he been gone a long time? She shook her head and started to put away glassware. She had to stop daydreaming about Chatan; he clouded her brain.

Chatan threaded his way back to the dining hall, looking longingly at the forest bordering the Green. He really needed to get out for a nice long wander. Why did he keep putting it off?

He waved at a group of friends sitting on a broad cloth. A white orb floated nearby, offering a stack of sunhats. Companions, he thought. He'd forgotten about companions.

One floated toward him and matched his stride. "There you are." Chatan said aloud. "I should get home." The companion turned along an intersecting path, and Chatan followed after it. It stopped in front of a shelter.

He reached past it to open the door. "Here we are. Now, what was I doing before I ran into Scarlett?" He spread out his screen and looked up the latest data on weather patterns. Would they have seasons on Airon? Did they need to prepare?

~ 35 ~

WISDOM

Harper lay on a large yellow cloth spread on the Green near the dining hall. Aadhya would be finished with her kitchen shift soon, and they planned to wander in the forest once she was free.

Harper had brought along some knitting materials, yarns of rich colors and textures, but her project hadn't held her interest. She was simply resting in the sun, feeling its warmth on the bare skin of her arms, feeling it soak through her shirt and loose pants.

She'd had to avoid the sun on Earth because it was too harsh. It made her skin break out with an itchy rash, and the bright light had often given her a dull headache that could last for days. But the heat from this sun was a soothing warmth that penetrated deep into her muscles, letting her relax completely. Luxuriously. She finally understood the reason for crowded beaches and parks. This is what all of those people had been experiencing. This was the attraction, this lulling warmth.

Juddering footfalls intruded upon her languor, and she squinted at the silhouetted figure that blocked her sunshine. A long braid swinging behind the silhouette identified her best friend.

"Look at you." Aadhya observed. "Asleep in the hot sun."

"I'm not asleep. Not yet, anyway. And the sun isn't hot, Aadhya. It's delicious."

"Oh, you are a study in contradictions." Aadhya's lilting accent delighted Harper. "I thought you could not be in the sun, and yet here you are. 'No, the sun is not hot. No, Aadhya, I am not asleep.' And yet here you are, asleep in the hot sun." Aadhya stepped out of her shoes, onto Harper's cloth, and sank down cross-legged, tucking her full skirt around her knees.

"I could fall asleep, I'm that relaxed." Harper basked in the sun's luxurious warmth for a few more breaths and then sat up, wrapping her long arms around her knees, resting her cheek there, gauging her friend's mood. She blurted without preamble, "Aadhya, why do you think Ava hates me?"

"I do not think that she hates you."

Harper sighed. "It feels like she does. She's always frowning at me."

"Well, this is true." Aadhya plucked at the cloth. "But I do not think that she hates you."

Harper watched Aadhya's face, waiting for more.

"I think Ava is uncomfortable around women. She finds them to be...inferior to men. She works much better with men. This is how some people are."

Harper looked toward the forest, a faint whisper brushing her heart. "I think you're right." It was Aadhya's turn to wait. "But why does she focus her discomfort on me? She doesn't seem to pick on anyone else."

"Perhaps you do not see it. Perhaps it happens when you are not there to see it."

"Does she pick on you?"

"No, not at all." Aadhya wobbled her head side to side. "For some reason, Ava protects me. She smooths things for me." They fell silent. "Perhaps she thinks you are strong enough. Perhaps you are her crutch."

"Why does she need a crutch?"

"Because she is trying to learn something. We are all trying to learn something. Even Ava."

Harper lifted her head from her knees. "What's she trying to learn?"

Aadhya gave a gentle shrug. "That is for her to know. That is the only way we learn, by deciding for ourselves what this is and what that is; deciding in our own way."

Harper frowned. "What do I do in the meantime?"

"You stand strong," Aadhya answered immediately. "You allow her to learn her lesson. You help her when it feels right in your heart. Only then. Your heart will tell you when she is ready to be helped." Aadhya repeatedly pressed her finger down into the cloth, punctuating her points. "No one can do it alone, but everyone must do it in his or her own way, in his or her own time. Spiritual law provides no other way."

"Michael thinks I'm imagining it."

"No. You are not imagining it." Aadhya gazed into the distance; hearing whispers. "You have a clear heart. You are seeing truly."

"Why can't Michael see it?"

Aadhya gazed at the forest's edge, taking in the colors, the peace. "Michael has worked with Ava for a long time. He thinks the world of her. She is his teacher. He shares her vision. It is important for him that she not topple from her pedestal." Aadhya spoke the whisper that kissed her heart. "Michael protects Ava while she grieves."

Harper's frown deepened. "Ava is grieving? Why?"

Another shrug. "Phillip abandoned her. She thought they had a shared dream. She cannot understand how she did not know that he was creating a dream separate from hers. She no longer trusts herself because she did not know that Phillip was leaving."

"Why do you think Phillip stayed behind?"

Aadhya shook her head, whispers scattering. "I do not know. In some way that we do not see, Phillip's path remained on Earth. Ava's path continues here. Your path continues here. If Phillip were here, you would be there, but that was not to be. You are here, and Ava grieves that Phillip is there."

They sat in silence.

"Does Ava hate me because I took Phillip's slot?" Harper finally asked. "I didn't plan to do that. Not at all."

Aadhya turned her gaze on Harper. "Ava does not hate you. She is working on her lessons. And she is too wise to hate you for this. You did not take Phillip's place; you took your own place as the 108th of The 108."

Another pause.

"Do you put Ava on a pedestal?"

Aadhya chortled behind her hand. "Ava needs no pedestal from me. She is mighty in her own right. We place others on pedestals to make ourselves smaller, thinking that is how to make someone else shine. But it is better if we all stand together, shoulder to shoulder, shining in our own brilliance."

"But then shouldn't we help Michael stop using pedestals?"

"In his own way. In his own time. Michael has his lessons to learn as well."

"What lessons are you learning, Aadhya?"

She laughed again. "That is what I am trying to decide...in my own time."

"I wish Michael could see it from my point of view."

After a few breaths, Aadhya spoke gently. "Harper, something happens between couples." She waited for Harper to look at her. "You and Michael are very close. You spend much time together." Harper nodded. "Michael is only doing what people always do: he is putting up a wall between you. A very kind wall, but it is a wall. A very important wall." Harper waited.

"When two people spend much time together, they start to blend; their edges blur. It can become hard to know which are your own thoughts, purely yours, and which are influenced by your love for the other person." Harper looked away, considering this.

"A wall between a couple can be very important and helpful," Aadhya went on. "It all depends on how high and wide it is, whether you can see through it, reach through it."

Aadhya paused again. "Do not resent Michael's wall," she said gently. "You see Ava very differently than how Michael sees her. It is important for him to keep Ava pure. Do not break down Michael's wall. Make it thin. Make it easy for him to reach through it. You can do this."

Harper nodded. "Yes. I can do this."

They sat together in the warm sun, simply being. After some time, Aadhya asked the question that was often in her mind. "Why do you think we're here?"

Harper frowned. "I'm here because Phillip dropped out."

"That is true. We each have our...purpose...for being here. But why did The 108 come here, to this planet? What is our collective purpose?"

Harper studied her friend's face, thinking of Logan's concerns and suspicions, Scarlett's questions. "Do you suspect a hidden purpose? That someone isn't telling us something?"

Aadhya took a deep breath. "There is always a deeper meaning for the happenings of the world. It was true on Earth; I believe it to be true here, too. Sometimes it's easy to see the deeper meaning. Oftentimes it is much harder. The truth can be veiled." She paused again, feeling the return of faint whispers. "I do not believe we have begun our true purpose yet. It is still waiting for us to understand; to begin."

Harper plucked at their sitting cloth. "Something beyond finding resources for Earth or other travelers?"

"Yes. Something deeper than what we already know."

"Why do you imagine something more?"

Aadhya searched for words. "This would be a long way to come just to build some pretty shelters and sit in the sun with our friends."

Harper gazed into the forest, whispers glimmering in the distance. "I think I know what you mean. It's not a matter of exploring the land and discovering things. It's something...elusive. Something that's not quite ready to happen." She paused. "I hope it's not bad."

Aadhya rested her chin on the palm of her hand, watching the forest. "There is no bad or good. Things just are. Imagine an elderly couple, devoted, completely reliant on each other. The wife dies. Is it a bad thing that she dies, leaving her beloved husband bereft and alone? Or is it a good thing that the husband lives longer, sparing his gentle wife the anguish of life without him? Circumstances are not bad or good; only the judgment we place on what happens."

"But your family. They all died horribly, leaving you abandoned. How can that be good?"

"It is neither bad nor good. It only is. If my family had not died, I would not be here on Airon. Perhaps my lessons are on Airon, and that was the only way to bring me here. Perhaps my family would have been captured and tortured if they hadn't died in the bombing. It was unusual for all of them to be in the same house at the same time; we are a widespread family. But everyone was there, together, except for me. That too was unusual."

She tilted her head and looked at Harper with calm eyes. "What happened is neither bad nor good, but it does hold clues for the deeper meaning. And so I ask myself, 'Why are we here?'"

"Your survival must have a deeper purpose and you're trying to understand what you should do?"

"That is partly my thought. I believe my survival does have a deeper purpose. I am curious about what my purpose is. Should does not exist. My...assignment...is to pay attention so that I don't miss the lesson. Should is not a part of it."

"The 108. We each have a purpose here, a reason for being on this journey. We each think our purpose is to design shelters or prepare meals. But those are simply the tasks that occupy us, while the tapestry weaves around us, finally presenting us with our true purpose; the deeper meaning."

"Yes." Aadhya nodded. "I believe this."

"Me, too." Harper tapped her sternum gently with her fist. "I believe it, here."

Harper stood and reached a hand down to Aadhya. "Shall we go for our walk? Let's get out of this hot sun."

Aadhya laughed as Harper pulled her to her feet. They stepped into their shoes, swept up the cloth and the basket of yarn, and walked across the Green. "I'm going to stash these in my shelter." Harper held up the yellow cloth and touched the basket Aadhya carried. "I'll grab a water orb. Do you want one?"

"Yes, thank you. That would be very nice."

Harper turned toward the short path to her shelter and almost bumped into a hovering companion. It held its drawer open, and Harper saw two water orbs resting in its depths.

"Thank you." She paused. "Do you have a name?" No response. The companion waited, motionless.

Harper reached into the drawer and brought out the water orbs. Turning, she handed one to Aadhya, who had edged up to stand at Harper's side. The companion continued to hover, motionless, waiting.

Harper gathered the ends of the dragging blanket and stuffed the whole thing into the companion's drawer. After a pause, she added the basket of yarn.

The drawer closed, and the companion drifted toward the door of Harper's shelter. "I hope he puts them somewhere where I can find them again."

Aadhya chuckled. "Oh, this is a boy, this companion. How do you know this?"

"I just do." Harper bounced along the path. "I just know these things."

Aadhya wove her arm through Harper's, matching her stride as they set out to wander the forest.

POSSIBILITIES

Chatan rapped his knuckles lightly on the frame of the doorway. "Ava? Can I have a word?"

Ava swiveled from her screen and rubbed her eyes with her palms. "Sure. I could use a distraction. Perfect timing, actually. My afternoon is full, but I have time now." She rose from her workstation and led the way into her sunlit sitting room.

"How did you get those vines to grow around your window?" Chatan peered at the window frame.

"I didn't. They just started doing it. I've always thought that vines around a window were pretty, and here they are. So, I left them alone."

"It's not happening on other windows." Chatan continued his inspection. He swung open the casement window and made to shift aside some leaves wanting to see the stems better.

"Careful. We don't know if they're safe to touch."

Chatan drew back his hand and leaned to see between leaves without disturbing them. "I can't see how they're attached."

"'I think they're pretty. I love how they cling right next to the window like that. It blends the indoors with the outdoors."

The leaves radiated a vibrant green, numerous buds with a reddish tinge; perhaps flowers on the way. The vines grew most of the way around the window, sending out slender stems that thickened to support the leaves, followed by the reddish buds that...

Ava broke into his scrutiny. "Chatan? You wanted a word?"

He pulled back and closed the sash. "Is it okay if I look at them more closely later? I'll try not to disturb you, peering through your window."

"I'll be gone most of the afternoon; you can have the whole window to yourself."

"Thanks."

"Now, how can I help?" She gestured to a chair positioned near the window where Chatan still stood. Her companion waited nearby, then moved forward, offering tea.

Chatan accepted a cup without comment. "I've been thinking about going on an extended exploration. Ideally, I'd like a vehicle to take me faster and farther than I can reach by walking. I want to extend my range." He sat down and faced Ava.

"What did you have in mind?"

Chatan examined the air above Ava's head. "There's a deep valley beyond the cliff to the west. It looks like it's mostly grassland, and we don't have data on grassy ecosystems yet." He met her eyes. "There might be native resources that would be useful for building and binding materials, to maybe go beyond what the ship is able to recycle. It could..."

Ava interrupted. "I don't doubt the value of your trip. You know more about potential resources than any of us, and I think you should have complete freedom to discover anything that might help us. The ship won't last forever. Although its copious recycling ability has been remarkable so far." She held his eyes. "I think you should go. My question had more to do with what kind of transport you have in mind."

Chatan focused. His words lined up, waiting to be spoken. "Well, something light and maneuverable, something that will cover all types of terrain while leaving negligible impact on the landscape. It would need to carry all the supplies I'd need for, say, a week." He paused, calculating. "Actually, two weeks would be better. I think I could cover a lot of ground in two weeks.

"I keep thinking about those giant motorcycles back home, the ones with compartments for stowing supplies, but something not as heavy and obviously something that wouldn't need roads." He described details, his delivery calm and focused.

As the Newcomers chatted, a companion hovered nearby. It recognized developing plans needing resources. The companion relayed information to the ship, keeping up an ongoing thread.

When Chatan finished, Ava drummed her thighs and rubbed her palms together. "I think it's a grand idea. I'll write the Launch Team and ask for suggestions. They might have something already in development or even something that people are using in other colonies." She paused. "Would you be willing to take a companion with you?"

Chatan took a breath, relieved. He had wanted to ask for companions, and now the request was easy. "Yes. We'd want to collect as much data as possible along the way. We could have a whole team of companions spread along the route, making as broad a collection swath as possible. And since the companions are airborne, they wouldn't leave any imprint. Think of the data we'd gain." He paused. "We'd keep Home Base scurrying just to keep up with the data flow."

Ava thought for a moment. "I'm thinking in terms of a week's journey. I see no reason to hurry, and going for a week would teach us valuable lessons about the logistics of venturing outward for longer wanders. Your next wander could probably be much more involved. I'll write to Earth as soon as we're done here." She paused again. "You've obviously given this a lot of thought. Taking a team of companions is brilliant."

Chatan smiled. "Well, that idea popped into my head as we were talking. I've been thinking about those grasslands for a couple of days now, but this morning, I thought about the cycle idea, and the pieces seemed to fit together better." He moved to stand up.

"It's great you're willing to approve this. I was afraid you'd think it premature."

They rose to their feet. "Well, it's timely, actually," Ava said. "People are coming up with all kinds of ideas about what they'd like to contribute, and I've been wondering if the ship's recycling resources might be stretched too thin. We need to hold a reserve for things we'll need in the future, things we haven't thought of yet." They moved toward the door. "If we could find native resources to supplement the ship's reserves, I'd rest more easily."

"I agree. Thank you, Ava. I'll start planning and check back in with you when things come together." He turned, his hand on the doorframe. "Will you let me know what they say about the transport?"

"Of course."

"I'll let you get back to your screen." He gestured toward her workstation. "I don't want to take up more of your time."

"My only job is to support all of you in what you're doing. My time is always available to you. You do know that, don't you?"

Chatan bowed slightly. "Thank you, Ava." He turned to go.

"Enjoy the rest of your day." She followed him out the door and waved him on his way. It was time for The 108 to explore. Chatan's plan for an extended wander opened doors nicely. He was the perfect person to venture beyond their daily wanderings. She had no doubt he would observe and bring together a vast array of information. And taking a team of companions with him? That was the perfect solution.

Ava returned to her screen. It took only a few breaths to write out a message to the Launch Team. They had the best overall picture of universal developments and would route the request to the best research team. She hoped for a prompt reply. She picked up her previous tasks.

Back at his shelter, Chatan opened his screen and compiled data gathered during their landing approach, filtered to focus on the grasslands to the west. He computed distances and topographical details, mapping out a likely route through the central area and circling along the forest edge, sending the route ever westward.

He noticed a sandwich and water glass next to his screen. It was a fair imitation of ham and cheese, one of his Earthen favorites. Odd. Where had it come from? And this one had a large leaf of lettuce protruding from under the soft brown bread. They must have gotten the hydroponics set up.

He was hungry but hadn't wanted to take time to go to the dining hall. He looked toward the window and noticed his companion, quietly floating. He looked at the sandwich, back at the companion. "Thank you." The companion dipped slightly to the left, a little bow. Chatan guffawed. "Cute..." He picked up the sandwich and turned back to his screen.

While Chatan worked, the companion streamed data to the ship. The ship adjusted schematics and provision lists as Chatan's plans solidified.

Chatan entered another row of commands and sat back while the screen compiled the data and set about building tables and graphs, plotting out a map with a possible route canvassing the grassland expanse. He picked up the last of the sandwich and turned his full attention to eating. Perfect. No need to waste additional time with the dining hall, and the sandwich was delicious. He drank the strong tea that appeared at his elbow and sat quietly for several breaths, giving thanks for the food that sustained his body.

Turning back to his workstation, he reviewed the data streaming across his screen, finalizing supplies, time requirements, his proposed route. Nine days. Close enough. He was confident that Ava would allow the slight overrun in time when she saw the route and the list of tasks he hoped to accomplish.

He swiped his hands on his trousers, cracked his knuckles, and got back to work. Everything was falling into place nicely; he might be able to finish this up today and send it along to Ava first thing tomorrow.

Finally, Chatan stood and stretched. This was going to be a great wander. All he needed now was a ride.

"Thanks for the sandwich, but I'm going to the dining hall for a real dinner. I'm hungry." Was he explaining his actions to the companion? One sandwich and they were in a relationship? He called as he left the shelter, "I'll try not to get home too late."

As he turned from the doorway, he stopped in his tracks, jacket dangling from one arm. A gleaming white cycle rested next to the path leading to the Green.

A cold dread clenched Chatan's gut. He looked around the clearing, then turned to search behind him. Where had this come from?

It was precisely what he had described to Ava. He looked toward her shelter, but it looked empty. She had said that she would be out all afternoon. How had this happened?

He shrugged into his jacket and stepped cautiously toward the cycle. It had three wheels. He hadn't specified that configuration, but it would add stability going over unpredictable terrain. The back wheels were wide, capable of bearing substantial weight without sinking into the ground, and the front wheel was thinner, making it easily maneuverable. The front wheel was topped by odd handlebars and a windscreen.

Two other gleaming white vehicles sat beyond the cycle. They were identical to each other, wide and low to the ground, also with three wheels. These, however, didn't have seats or steering controls. He realized they were supply vehicles. Perfect. His dread loosened, and a tremor of delight tingled along his spine.

He turned to the cycle. A smile spread across his face as his delight grew. He crouched to peer under the body, circled around the cycle, took in details of its remarkable design and structure. Finally, he reached out and touched the gleaming surface.

It was silky and cool, with smooth curves and rounded edges where metal met glass. Chatan was mesmerized. It felt alive. He reached out to touch the tires. They were unusual; soft rather than hard, soft enough that he could indent the surface with his finger.

Somehow, he knew the material was strong as well as pliable. His goal was to leave as little imprint on the landscape as possible, and these tires seemed entirely capable of meeting that goal.

He looked around. "Where did this come from?" he asked again of the empty space around him.

He cracked opened the main compartment of one of the supply vehicles and pressed it close with a satisfying click. He hefted it; light, yet solid. He reopened the compartment and raised the lid fully. The compartment was full.

Chatan's brow furrowed. As he rummaged through the compartment's contents, the furrow deepened. The contents matched his packing list.

A tingle sparked up his spine; his gut tightened again. He turned to the second supply vehicle and examined its compartment. Everything on his packing list seemed to be accounted for, neatly arranged and nestled snugly into both vehicles.

His sense of unease deepened. Was he under surveillance? How had the information he'd entered into his private screen made its way to these vehicles?

His eyes swept over the trees at the forest's edge. He looked more closely at individual trees. They were beautiful, welcoming, bordering all of Home Base. Could they be watching?

As he concentrated on each tree, a feeling of peace flowed through him. His muscles relaxed, and his gaze became unfocused, remembering...something...something at the edge of his mind, a whisper of something he couldn't quite grasp. He looked down at the contents of the vehicle's compartment; his packing was complete.

His sense of awe and pleasure seeped back. With these vehicles, he would be able to wander far from Home Base, gathering information for Scarlett's team and finally seeing what this planet had in store for them.

At last, he turned toward the dining hall. Ava would probably be there by now. He could already see her merriment as she watched his face for his expected reaction. He wanted to hear the story that had led to this remarkable machine, machines, that sat beside his shelter.

Inside the dining hall, Chatan filled a plate and looked across the crowded tables. He saw Ava's dreadlocked head and made his way to squat beside her chair. "The cycle is perfect." he told her happily. "I can't wait to take it out."

She looked at him curiously. "Did you come up with a design? I haven't heard back from Earth yet."

Chatan hesitated. "You haven't..."

"It's only been a few hours, Chatan. Earth hasn't had time to get back to us. Communication is almost instantaneous, yes, but the Launch Team probably needs to gather information and reach a consensus before they respond. That can sometimes take a few hours. Have you been working on a design?"

"No. Ava. The cycle is finished. It's sitting outside my shelter."

Ava wrinkled her forehead at him. "What do you mean?"

"I thought you had it delivered. It's arrived. And it's exactly what we talked about, only better."

Ava put down her spoon and scooted her chair back. "Show me."

Chatan set his cooling plate next to Ava's bowl and led her from the room. As they turned the corner and saw the white machines, Ava's steps faltered.

"How could this happen?" she breathed. "Where did they come from?"

"That's what I asked. You didn't have anything to do with this?"

"No; nothing." She moved forward and paused again several feet away from the cycle. The other two were wagons, really; no seats, just compartments on wheels. She shook her head. "How can this be?"

Chatan moved past her, smoothing his hand along the curves of the cycle, grasping the near handle. "They're perfect."

Slowly, Ava reached out to brush the white surface, a sharp contrast beneath her fingers. Then she palmed the curve and followed it up to swipe across the seat. She bent to look underneath, walked around the machine, her hand never breaking contact.

She laughed nervously. "It is perfect." Hand still caressing the cycle, she turned to examine the two wagons. She reached with her other hand and caressed the side of the closest wagon, then circled each one, surveying them closely.

Chatan watched Ava's examination of the machines. "What do you think?"

"I don't know what to think. But they sure are something."

Chatan pitched his face up to the sun and gave a short, barking laugh. "They're better than anything I had imagined." Another short laugh. "Ava, I want to go. I have my plans all laid out. I know exactly what I need and where I want to go."

"When?"

"Now."

"You haven't had dinner." she protested. "And it'll be dark soon."

"But I'll wake up out there." He jutted his chin toward the forest's edge. "I'll start my day out there."

Ava dropped her hand from the wagon's side and took Chatan's arm. "Come have dinner. It'll make your evening simpler. Then go."

Chatan paused several breaths, then put his free hand over Ava's where it rested on his arm. Together they returned to the dining hall. Ava turned back once, before the machines disappeared around the curve of the path. Chatan mirrored her, and then they looked at each other.

Ava shook her head and prodded him on to the dining hall.

Lone Tree stills in the cooling air. Lone Tree sings of shift and reNewal. Lone Tree turns its energy toward Home Base and breathes its song along its way.

~ 37 ~

NO

"Come on in." Logan kept his eyes on the screen, arranging rows and columns of data. Olivia strolled into his work area and moved some dirty dishes out of a chair to make room to sit down. She sat quietly for some breaths, looking around at the stacks of books and manuals.

"Why don't you use screen versions of these books? What's the advantage of stacking up all of this paper around you?"

"You can flip back and forth quicker in a book to compare details," he said sullenly. "It's easier than streaming through screens, stacking icons all over the place, on top of each other, forgetting what they are."

"Well, I think these particular stacks have sat untouched since the last time I was here. How often do you actually flip through these books?" She opened the nearest one to a random page.

"Well...things are different here." His gaze roved over the piles of books. Books were his escape; he wanted them nearby. "It's not as easy to find anything useful in most of them anymore, that's all." He glowered at the screen. He was keeping the books. "Give me a second; I'm almost done with this timeline, and I don't want to forget where I am."

Olivia leaned back in her chair, bouncing her foot lightly, one knee crossed over the other. "Why don't you have any windows in here? You had them before. They were all along your work area."

Silence.

"Did you modify them away?"

Silence.

Olivia lapsed into silence as her body relaxed into the comfortable chair. She was exhausted, frankly. It was a relief to sit down. She hadn't been outside the kitchen for as long as she could remember, largely because her shelter was attached to it. Logan had designed his own shelter so that it attached to the dining hall. "Practical," Olivia remembered him saying. "I'll be pretty much living in the storeroom, so I want to be close by."

She'd liked the idea and followed suit. Her shelter was on the opposite side of the dining hall, since it opened directly into the kitchen. But as a result, she found that she never went outside. She should think about moving her shelter to the far end of the Green. At least then she would see the sun once in a while and walk on the grass.

Was it grass?

She closed her eyes. At least she had kept her windows. Well, in her sitting room anyway, where she never had time to actually sit. Her bouncing foot stilled as she drifted toward sleep.

"Okay!" Logan clapped his hands together and rubbed them back and forth vigorously. Olivia jumped, and her screen toppled off her lap. "Whoa!" Logan turned around and looked at her curiously. "You all right?"

"Oh!" She gave a short laugh. "I was completely relaxed; you startled me."

"Sorry."

Olivia picked up her screen and unrolled it on her lap. "No, it's fine. What have you got for me?"

"Well, Harper and I have come up with some ideas that might add even more variety to your proteins and fats. We even think some of these textures will melt like dairy cheese without going thin and runny. Let me show you." He turned back to his screen and expanded the display to help Olivia see his examples.

Olivia wrinkled her brow. "I've always wondered, why Harper? She does textiles, right? What's the connection with food sources?"

"Well, it was Sophia's idea originally. Actually, it was probably Ava's idea before that." He grimaced imperceptibly, but Olivia saw it. "Sophia talked to me about it after she and Ava talked."

Olivia wondered which one he didn't like, Ava or Sophia. Or was it just authority figures in general? Or women in authority?

"Textiles have a lot to do with texture, right?" He gestured with his hand. "There's color, but almost everything else about cloth has to do with texture, the thickness of the threads, the tightness of the weave. We're applying the same ideas to protein threads to come up with different food textures."

Olivia was impressed. "Do you have any training in textiles? You sound like an expert."

"No, but I've picked up pointers from working on this project with Harper. Look at this."

Olivia leaned toward Logan's screen, squinting to see the details. His voice droned on, and while she could follow most of what he described, it didn't interest her much. She thought back to the bursting storerooms on Earth, the boxes of fresh vegetables, sprouted grains and nuts, the freezer trays piled with organic proteins, banks of dispensers for oils, extracts, infusions. She had loved the colorful bins of spices and herbs that scented the entire kitchen, igniting her imagination every morning when she first opened the doors.

These synthetics couldn't move her in the same way, even with enhanced textures. She knew they had the same building blocks, sugars, amino acids, lipids, but she didn't connect with them in the same way as Earthen foods. She wore gossamer-thin protective gloves almost all the time. She no longer ran her hands through piles of rice or across trays of microgreens. She missed all of that.

She brought her attention back to Logan's droning voice, which seemed to be winding down.

"No, it all sounds good." she told him. "Can you send it to my companion? Then it can walk me through the storeroom."

Logan was silent. "Or you can send your companion over and it can take me through it?" She looked around. "Where is your companion, anyway?"

Logan paused and then nodded toward a closed cupboard. "He's recharging."

"No! Now? That's pretty inconvenient."

"He's completely inconvenient. I hate that thing."

Olivia was taken aback. She assumed everyone loved their companions. Logan had been suspicious at first, sure, but that should have changed by now. Olivia used her companion in the kitchen, where she always seemed to be short-handed, but she'd formed the habit of sending it to the recharge cabinet in the kitchen at the end of the day rather than taking it to her shelter at night. She didn't like taking it into her shelter. She was intrigued by Logan's tone of voice.

"So you don't use it much?"

"Nope. Not at all. I don't trust it." He turned back to his screen.

"No? Why not?" Even as she asked the question, Olivia realized that she didn't hold much trust in her companion either. It always provided the correct ingredients in exactly the right quantities. Its timing was perfect. But she felt no connection to the thing. The other kitchen helpers clearly enjoyed their connections to their companions, sharing helpful hints whenever they discovered new capabilities and features. Olivia tended to ignore those conversations. She didn't have time to learn a whole new technology.

"Well." He swung back to face her, his voice lowered. "Where did they come from? Why do we have to use them? Why are they always there? I don't like it."

Olivia had heard Logan complain along these lines before. "No. We were in the hall when Ava told us about them that first time.

Remember? We sat at the back of the room together and watched it all. They came from the ship, I thought."

His eyes narrowed. "Well, yes, but where did the idea come from? Ava was clueless. Even she didn't like them at first, But since then, she's swallowed the whole story hook, line, and sinker."

Olivia had forgotten Ava's initial reaction to the companions; that day had become a hazy memory. She realized that she had incorrectly assumed Logan's capitulation to the companions. He had her full attention now.

"What story?" They leaned toward each other, their voices dropping to murmurs.

"Remember? Ava said she didn't know who thought up the idea. They just showed up that day. That's pretty weird."

"No, you're right. I always thought it was weird."

"Why all the secrecy? Why the surprise?" He paused. "Why are they everywhere? They just float around, watching everything, listening to everything we say." Olivia glanced at the recharge cupboard. "He's all right," Logan reassured her. "I've never charged him up. He's just a big white lump sitting in there."

Olivia shivered. "No, no. You're right." Then, "I thought everyone loved them."

"They pretty much do. You can't say anything negative about them, or people just look at you funny, get all quiet. Things have just gotten weird, ever since they showed up."

They sat silently, worrying.

"They remind me of nanos," Logan finally said.

Olivia's jaw dropped.

After a moment of stunned silence, Olivia shook her head again. "No. That's not it. The nanos are inside you. You can't get rid of them. These things," she gestured toward the silent cupboard, "you can see them. You can get rid of them if you want."

They lapsed into silence once again.

Logan took a deep breath. "Do you remember me telling you about Ava that first day in the gathering hall, how weird she acted?"

Fear seeped through Olivia, and she nodded. She voiced a sudden thought. "Do you think Ava has nanos?"

Logan considered the possibility. "No. No, I don't think so. Nanos don't turn on and off like that. I've only seen Ava act like that the one time. I don't think its nanos. But it is something." He paused, thinking. "Do you remember what happened at the end of the meeting, after the companions came in? How everyone formed a bonding ritual with them?"

A shudder ran through Olivia. "No, I hated that. Why would everyone do that?"

"I didn't like it, either. It reminded me of Ava in the hall. Everyone seemed sort of wooden, expressionless. It had the same eeriness to it."

She frowned. "No. I don't remember that...I only remember everyone's hands on the companions. How could they stand to touch those things?"

Logan knit his brows. "There's something else." Olivia watched his face, wondering what else was bothering him. "When we were still on the ship, when we were about half-way here." She nodded. "Ava asked me to check some data for her, to keep track of them while we were traveling." Nod.

Logan sat back in his chair, arms stiff. "She asked me to track our course. She'd noticed that the ship kept making these course corrections, and she asked me to take over. Tracking them, I mean." Logan shook his head. "And she was right. The ship kept changing course, these small, little changes."

Olivia wrinkled her brow. "Who was making the changes?"

Logan shrugged. "I don't know. Must have been the ship. I mean, there wasn't a crew to make them. It had to be the ship." He chewed his mustache. "It wasn't like, back and forth, you know? It was just this constant change in one direction, like the ship was sneaking it in there, hoping no one would notice."

"Maybe some solar wind was blowing us off course or something."

"Well, maybe. I mean, none of us know anything about this, so we can't really be sure. But we started out heading this way," Logan pointed to his right, "and we ended up going this way." Logan pointed straight ahead. "We ended up changing course about 90 degrees." He chewed his mustache again, eyes unfocused. "I mean, why not head in the right direction from the start?"

They fell silent again. Olivia didn't like the feel of this. Were they really out here on their own? With no one knowing where they were? On the other hand, did it really matter?

Logan finally shook himself out of his stupor and pushed away from his desk. "Well, listen. Why don't we walk out to the storeroom and I'll show you the details myself? I know where everything is."

"No, no..." Olivia gathered herself. "I mean, if you have time now, now would be great. If my lunch crew doesn't show up, I'll just heat up some leftovers."

"You having trouble with your crews?"

"Everyone is a pain in the ass."

He looked surprised. "Even Zoe? I thought you two were pals. What about Aadhya? Have you talked to Addison?"

"No, we used to get along, but then we got companions, and now all Zoe thinks about is what she can do because of her companion." Olivia mimicked a marionette, waving her arms mindlessly at her sides. "She's a pain."

He snorted. "You see? Everything's gotten weird."

"No. It really has." Olivia felt righteous in her indignation. Things were weird, and everyone seemed to just gloss it over. She hated that. Bunch of mindless idiots. Maybe this *was* as bad as nanos. She wasn't even sure why she was on this pointless journey, tired all the time, hating it here.

She followed Logan into the dining room. By unspoken agreement, they avoided the topic of companions, cautious about being overheard. They moved through the storeroom together and discussed its deep shelves and bins. All of the supplies sat neatly organized, waiting for Olivia to try to turn them into food.

ENCOUNTER

Harper saw them first.

She was walking from her shelter toward the central Green where she planned to read until lunch. She carried her screen under her arm and swung a water orb from her wrist as she made her way along the path. They were gathered under a tree covered with bright orange blossoms at the edge of the Green, watching her.

She slowed, then stopped. After all this time with absolutely no animal sightings, here they were, right here on their threshold, right at Home Base. She wished Chatan were here. He would appreciate this sighting the most. Harper was delighted to see this, of course, but Chatan's whole existence circled around observing life on their new planet. The plethora of trees and bushes and grasses and their astonishing colors...but here was something that moved, something that obviously demanded keen observation.

Harper calmed herself, pressing her wet palms down her hips, thinking. Perhaps someone would come along. She dared not call out, for fear of startling the creatures. Rubbing her knuckles against her forehead, she moistened her lips and took a deep breath. Another.

Lowering herself slowly, she sat directly on the path, right where she had been standing. She watched the creatures intently, wishing her companion were with her as a second observer. She'd have to settle for whatever she could manage on her own. She unrolled her screen and softly recorded observations, imagining what Chatan would do, if he were here.

There were eight creatures. They were about ten feet away, so she could see them quite clearly. They reminded her of river otters, with their long slender bodies, mostly black with some dark brown running from the tops of their slender heads down across both shoulders. Or, where shoulders would be on a river otter. In place of the usual two arms and legs, these creatures had two long rows of appendages running parallel to each other along both sides of their bellies. The appendages extended from just under their shoulders to the far ends of their bodies. They looked like giant brown centipede-otters.

Harper again wiped her damp palms down her thighs. The creatures were staying put. Her thoughts raced. She brought her hands back to her screen.

They were enormous, about six feet long. Two of them had raised the front ends of their bodies off the ground, their heads held parallel to it. That made them more or less four feet tall. They were about a foot in diameter, tapering at the head end and blunt at the tail end. The two upright creatures clasped their rows of paired appendages across their chests, decidedly watching her. They showed no alarm at her presence.

Their eyes were large and brown. The texture of their fur rippled and shone in the dappled sunlight. What she thought might be ears were rounded protuberances about four inches across. They had bilaterally symmetrical features: two ears, two eyes, and two nostrils, all evenly spaced along a midline that continued down their torso between their clasped appen...

"It is time for us to meet."

Harper froze, astounded. Her brain stopped. One of the creatures had spoken. She couldn't quite take it in. After rapidly blinking, she swallowed. "Excuse me?"

"It is time for us to meet."

She regained her breath. "I am sorry. I didn't expect you to speak. I'm...completely surprised." She paused and took a deeper breath. "I hope I haven't offended you by watching you too intently. Forgive my rudeness."

"We are equally curious about you."

Silence fell. It grew a bit too long for Harper's comfort. "My sincere apologies, but may I go and bring someone else, someone who would be better suited to speak with you? This seems wonderfully important, and I don't want to get it wrong."

The creature gazed up into the air for a moment. "We will await you here."

Harper rolled her screen and thrust it under her arm. Scrambling to her feet, she reassured them, "I'll be right back," then turned and ran toward the dining hall. She burst into the long room and scanned the faces already gathered and hurried to the nearest group.

"Where's Ava?"

The smiles turned to concern as they took in her urgent expression. Micaela pointed toward the kitchen. "She's cooking lunch."

Harper ran to the far end of the dining hall and pushed through the doors to the kitchen. She spotted Ava immediately and dashed to where she stood stirring a huge pot.

Ava had turned at her abrupt entry. Frowning, she searched Harper's flushed face. "Yes? Tell me."

"There are creatures at the edge of the Green, by my shelter. Eight of them. They're huge, six feet long, with rows of arms and legs."

Ava's face brightened. "Really! At last! Are they still there? Let's go see them." She started to untie her apron.

"Ava, they talked to me. In English."

Ava's mind reeled. She had expected The 108 to eventually see animals, especially now that they were venturing out more often and wandering farther afield, but to have some appear here at

Home Base was fabulous. To have them be communicative was astonishing. "What did they say?"

"That it was time for us to meet. When I saw them, I sat down right away to keep from scaring them and started recording observations on my screen. After I'd been sitting quietly for a breath or two, one of them spoke to me. I was startled, and I couldn't think clearly. I apologized for staring rudely. He...it...they...said that they were curious, too. I asked if I could bring someone else to talk with them because this is too important, this meeting, and the one who spoke said they would wait for me to return."

Harper's fluttering hands and rushing words irritated Ava as she pulled her apron over her head and pushed it onto the table beside them. "Why in the world would they choose to talk to you?"

Harper took a surprised step backward. "Excuse me?"

Ava turned down the heat under the pot. "Zoe, you're in charge of lunch. Don't worry if you run a bit late. See if someone out in the dining hall can help you finish up."

Zoe looked up from across the room, curious, and nodded.

Ava laid her hand on Harper's forearm. "Never mind. Let's go meet these...natives."

Ava turned to her companion, which had been patiently waiting at the edge of the room. "Please summon Michael," she instructed it. "Have him bring his screen and meet me outside Harper's shelter. Encourage everyone else to avoid that area."

The companion followed them out of the kitchen, silently executing Ava's requests as the two women walked across the dining hall, out the door, and back to Harper's shelter.

As they rounded the corner, Ava spotted the creatures. She took in their size, colorings, and positions relative to each other. Despite their size, Ava felt no sense of alarm or need for caution.

She put a hand on Harper's arm and slowed their pace. "Let me do the talking." They approached side by side, stopping ten feet away from the creatures.

They stood in silence for several breaths. "Welcome," Ava finally said. Pause. "I feel a little impertinent saying that, because it is we who have come into the midst of your home. And yet I do want to welcome you to what has become our home as well, and I wish to offer you friendship and warm greetings. We are glad to meet someone from this beautiful world. Thank you for meeting us."

After a short pause, one spoke. "Our world is yours to share. You have created a peaceful shelter in a well-chosen place. We offer you friendship and warm greetings in return."

Despite Harper's forewarning, Ava was shocked to hear their words communicated clearly and warmly. The women watched as the creatures bowed their heads slightly forward. Ava and Harper automatically bowed in return.

Ava gestured at the ground before them. "Can we offer you some comfort? A cushion, perhaps, for sitting?"

At that moment, Michael hurried around the bend in the path and slowed abruptly. He made his way quietly to stand behind Ava, his wide eyes fixed on the creatures.

Ava gestured toward him. "I asked Michael to join us. He helps me in all that I do, and I wanted him to meet you as well. I've asked the others to stay away so that we might speak gently with each other." She ignored Harper's presence entirely.

Michael's eyebrows knitted slightly when he realized that Ava was talking to the creatures. Did she think they would understand her words?

The creature spoke again. "We appreciate your kindness. We are already in comfort. Please create comfort for yourselves." Michael froze in shock.

Ava glanced at him and gave a slight nod. "Shall we make ourselves comfortable?" Her companion drifted forward and offered a cloth, which she accepted. She handed an edge of the cloth to Harper, and between them, they spread the cloth on the ground. While reseating herself, she gestured to Michael to sit beside her. Harper knelt behind Michael, once again ignored.

Ava smiled at the creatures. "It is lovely to meet you." She bowed forward and broke into delighted laughter as she straightened. "It is most lovely to meet you." After a brief silence, she decided to continue. "My name is Ava. What shall we call you? Do you use names?"

The same creature answered, "We take many names, but to follow the example you have set, I am Vargad. We will use only my name today. Our tribe is Narsi. We burrow near here."

"Our tribe is human. We come from another planet..." She looked up into the sky to orient herself, then pointed. "We come from that direction. We have journeyed long, and we hope to make our home here. We are delighted to find others who can show us the correct way to live in this place. We hope you can become our friends. I believe we have much to learn from you. Perhaps we have knowledge that we can share with you as well."

"We have already begun to learn and are glad to share our knowledge with you."

After a pause, Ava asked, "How is it that you can speak our language?"

"Your words live in the air around you. We watch your words and bring them back to you."

"You can read our thoughts?"

"We watch your words. They live in the air around you." Vargad raised his nose toward the sky and traced a circle. His appendages fluttered to create a rhythmic wave up and down his body.

"Will you come with us and meet the others?" Ava asked. "Everyone will be happy to know we have friends here."

Vargad lowered his nose and looked at Ava again. "We proceed slowly. This is enough for today." His fellow creatures bowed forward in unison, then turned and melted into the forest.

"We leave." Vargad bowed, turned, and followed his companions back amongst the silent trees.

The three humans continued to sit quietly, absorbing the encounter. Ava eventually reached out and patted Michael's knee. "Hungry? I made some really good soup."

Michael rolled his screen. Harper swept up the cloth and handed it back to Ava's companion. Silently, they turned and retraced their steps to the dining hall. Only a few breaths had passed, and the world had changed.

~ 39 ~

FREEDOM

"Can you stay a bit longer?" Ava spoke in a low voice, her hand on Aadhya's arm, while the others gathered their plates and carried the debris to the recycle compartment.

Aadhya nodded. She felt a niggling of worry. Had she done something wrong? Was she taking too long to prepare meals? Or perhaps there was a more welcome possibility; maybe Ava was planning a special gathering and wanted her help.

Ava sat opposite Aadhya. "How are you doing?"

Aadhya blinked. "Fine. I am fine." She paused. "Why do you ask?"

Charlie and Zoe were gathering their debris at the table behind Aadhya. Charlie bumped into Aadhya as he got to his feet. "Sorry."

Aadhya smiled at him. "It is no problem."

"Actually, why don't we go to my shelter?" Ava said. "It'll be easier to talk there." Aadhya nodded and picked up her own debris to deposit in the recycle compartment.

She and Ava drifted toward the door, Ava chatting as they went. "I wonder if we'll have a seasonal weather change. Every day seems perfect: not too warm, not too cool. It's surprisingly pleasant every single day."

"Yes, it would be nice to know what to expect." Aadhya searched for some way to add to the conversation. "We gathered data during our approach and descent. Perhaps they would be useful."

"I think you're right. I should pull up those data sometime. I'm quite curious."

They reached Ava's shelter and stepped inside, out of the brilliant sunlight. They settled in the sitting area next to the large window overlooking the Green. "Do you want tea?" Ava asked. "Sparkling water?"

"Oh, yes. Sparkling water would be very nice."

Ava's companion offered two glasses as Ava sat on the chair next to Aadhya's couch. "Sparkling water's perfect after a meal. Good choice."

They smiled at each other and drank. Ava gestured out the window. "I think I have the best view in Home Base."

Aadhya looked out over the large Green and wobbled her head. "You might be right. Although I love my view, too, looking out over the tops of the trees. I can see for miles, or so it would seem."

"That was brilliant of you to design a vertical shelter. Do you ever tire of the stairs?"

Aadhya shook her head. "I feel more and more sequestered with each higher level. I love my shelter."

They fell into a short silence, sipping water and looking out at the Green.

"I've been wanting to talk because I sense an unease within you," Ava finally said. "Not between us," she hastily added when fear flickered in Aadhya's eyes. "Something inside yourself, perhaps. That's why I asked how you're doing. You seem sad somehow. How is everything?"

Sharp tears stung Aadhya's eyes. She didn't want to cry in front of Ava. The sudden emotion surprised them both. Aadhya wasn't quite sure what she should say.

She gave herself a moment to regain her composure. "Well. It is not that I feel sad, really. It is more that I feel...raw." She gathered momentum. "There is too much coming at me all of the time, you know? Things that need doing, people talking, people moving around. Everything is too busy." She sipped more of her water, then set down her glass, keeping her eyes lowered.

"I crave solitude, and when I take some, it is never enough. Then, I find it even harder to come back to the kitchen and start all over again, with the clock ruling my hours and too much that needs to get done at a certain time. I am completely weary." She brought the back of her hand up to rub her forehead. "It used to be fun. It used to make me feel useful. But now it makes me weary."

Ava moved a pile of soft cloths within Aadhya's reach and sat back again. "Thank you." Aadhya took a cloth and pressed it against her nose. "I hate it when I leak." They both gave a short laugh, breaking the tension.

"Would you like to get away for a while, a good long while?"

Aadhya's breath raggedly caught in her throat. "Yes," she half-sobbed and half-laughed as she wiped her eyes. "I am sorry. I do not know where all of this emotion is coming from."

"You're doing great. I'm impressed that you can have all of this emotion stashed away inside and still think clearly and describe things articulately. I admire your willingness to talk about this with me."

They sat a moment in silence, Aadhya's head slightly bowed.

Ava broke the silence. "One of the greatest benefits we've gained from Chatan's wanderings is that he's given us more confidence to go out and about. Now that we've met the Narsis and found them to be gentle and agreeable, our surroundings are shaping up to be safe and filled with possibilities."

Ava smiled at Aadhya, prompting the other woman to meet her gaze. "How would you like to go on your own journey out into the surrounding areas? We could plan a reasonable time frame, one that's long enough to give you the solitude you need but short enough that it won't be overwhelming as a first excursion."

Aadhya relaxed back in her seat and let her hands fall to her lap. "It sounds wonderful." She sat silently for a moment. "I know

Chatan's cycle; it seems to have everything he needs. The ship is smart that way. I would love to get away for a week, even two."

"But..." Ava gently prodded her.

"Well..." She looked down at her hands. "Chatan is good at wandering. He has figured out exactly what to take and what he will need. He is a good organizer. He comes and goes easily." She paused. "I could probably do that part, too. He would maybe even help me with some ideas."

Aadhya blushed as Ava nodded enthusiastically. "I think it would be exciting, and fun...in many ways, at least during the day. But I think I would be frightened at night." She paused. "I do not know if I could do this thing."

"Ah. Good point. Chatan does just stop wherever he wants, throws out some sleeping cloths, and he's all set. Nothing frightens him."

"I do not think I could do it." They sat quietly for a moment. "My friend once told me of a little type of...trailer, I think she called it...that her family would drive around from time to time. They would just go exploring. She made it sound quite fun."

Ava watched the other woman closely. She could feel the germ of an idea forming in Aadhya's mind and wanted it to be all hers.

"I wonder if the ship could create some kind of room with wheels, some type of trailer, a caravan. Not too big so as to not use up many resources, but big enough that I could move around inside."

Ava smiled. "What would you like in such a caravan? What things would it need to have to make a trip fun?"

Aadhya described a fold-down bed and table, stowage compartments, and a miniature sink. "Lots of windows, to feel like I was part of the scenery while driving, or cooking, or falling asleep. It would be perfect, driving around in this caravan. I would love it."

"Would you feel safe at night?"

She bobbed her head. "Yes. I think so. And if I become frightened in the middle of the night, I could just drive away. I could just come home."

Aadhya folded her small cloth into smaller and smaller squares. "I love green. It is one of the best things about this planet. It is incredibly green here, with an immensity of shades and tints. I read somewhere that an Irishman can distinguish 60 shades of green, with all those green hills to look at every day. Some high number." She dabbed her damp cheeks. "I think here, the number must be even higher." She placed her empty glass in the waiting companion's open drawer.

Ava followed suit and nodded. "I think the sunlight brings the color out in everything. I'm constantly amazed at the colors. I don't think it's just our long journey and its dearth of color. I see more depth of color here than anywhere else I've experienced." She waved her arm broadly. "And the colors are massive."

"I think so, too. It is a feast for the eyes." Both women shook their heads in wonder, gazing out the window. They continued talking, remarking on their shared experience of the wonders of Airon.

Ava's companion moved forward and offered a dessert, lemon bars, and fresh cups of tea. The two women chatted on, discussing the kitchen, cooking shifts, favorite meals.

After a time, Ava patted the arms of her chair and wrapped up their conversation. "Well, I think we have the start of a plan for your restorative wander. You can be away as long as you need to gather your wits about you again, and whatever extra time you want, to simply enjoy yourself. We'll rearrange schedules to cover your shifts. It'll be easy." Ava smiled at Aadhya. "What do you think? Will that work for you?"

Aadhya looked down at the crumpled cloth in her hands. "This would be a dream come true. I would like this very much."

"We'll make some version of it happen," Ava said firmly. "We're smart people, and we apparently have a ship that's even smarter than we realized. Let's assume it'll happen." She paused. "What else would you like to talk about? We sort of launched right into this. Do you have anything else on your mind?"

"No, no. This is the only thing." Aadhya rose. "Thank you, Ava. I am very grateful to you for talking with me. You are always kind to me. I thought I was doing fine, but you barely opened a crack in a window, and all of this came tumbling out."

"Well, you were an easy window to crack. I'm headed over to Michael's shelter. Shall we walk together to your place along the way?"

"Yes, please. I would enjoy that."

They walked out into the sunlight and followed the path that led toward Aadhya's shelter.

Ava glanced up to admire Aadhya's tall shelter. Gasping, she grabbed Aadhya's arm. "Aadhya!" She pointed. They stopped, agape.

"It's already here..." Aadhya breathed.

After a long moment, they moved toward the gleaming white vehicle. It was a small, mobile, caravan kind of shelter, smooth and curving. Windows circled a body that rested on eight sturdy tires.

They ventured up to the oblong door, and Aadhya reached to pull on the handle. The door opened silently, small steps descending beneath. They looked at each other, stupefied.

"But how could this happen?" Aadhya stood rooted in shock.

"I have no idea, but I'm somehow not surprised. Shall we see what's inside?" She motioned Aadhya to go first, but Aadhya held back, uncertain. Ava took her hand and led her onboard. "It's a lot bigger inside than it looks from the outside. Nice and roomy."

Aadhya moved slowly around the tiny room. "Here is the bed. Look at how easily it opens. Aha! The bedding is already here. It will be easy every night." Aadhya gazed around her. "It is just as I imagined."

Ava was standing at the other end of the cabin. "Look at the fridge. You'll be able to take lots of juice with you."

"It has a recycle niche. It is tiny, but it will be just me."

"Here's the shower. It's tiny."

"Well, I will fit, so that is perfect."

Ava gestured at the walls, the furnishings, the windows. "Aadhya, look. Everything is green. Lovely, lovely greens. All tints and shades of greens."

Aadhya covered her mouth as she slowly turned and looked around her. "The walls blend into the trees outside the windows."

They both started at an exclamation from the doorway. Michael was peering in, gaping at this newest addition to Home Base. "Where did this come from?"

The two women looked at each other. "Well, apparently it came from Aadhya's imagination," Ava told him. "She's going on a wander, and this is her...her caravan."

Michael continued looking around the tiny room, clearly nonplussed.

Ava took in Michael's furrowed brows and sobered. "It's all right, Michael. It's all perfect. I know it's hard to believe." She gestured at the tiny interior. "The only thing I know to do is just accept it and move forward."

Michael climbed into the caravan as Ava continued. "Aadhya and I were just talking and planning a way for Aadhya to get away for some solitude. We ended up describing...well, this." She nodded at the tiny cabin encircling them. "We walked over here together, and it was waiting for us."

Michael sat down abruptly on a window seat. "I don't know. I can't wrap my mind around these things. The Narsis, Chatan's cycle, this...It's too much to absorb. I keep getting slammed into some new unexplained appearance, and I pull my brain back together just in time to slam into the next mystery. I can't keep up."

Ava sat next to him, gauging his expression. "I'm not surprised. Everything is happening fast." She looked out the windows and up at Aadhya, who was standing with her arms spread behind her, propped against the countertop. "We knew we'd encounter unexpected things. We couldn't really prepare for specifics; we could only prepare for the certainty of surprises." She shook her head.

"But I must admit that I expected the unexpected to come from the planet, not our own ship."

Michael sat back. "Yes! That's what it is. The Narsis are something new and intriguing, and I can't wait to learn more about them. The plant life, the sunlight. all of it is incredible." He shook his head, frowning. "The things I find unsettling are the things the ship gives us. They're useful and perfect and...inexplicable." He paused. "And immediate. How could this happen from a conversation?" He gestured around them and frowned. "It's hard to take in."

Ava caught both of his hands and held them between her own. "Michael, it is a lot to take in. My mind can't quite figure it out, either. But I feel a joy, a solid, familiar, bubbling joy, around all of this. I felt it when I understood the companion idea and then when I saw one for the first time. I felt it when I saw Chatan's cycle, and just now, I felt it again when I saw this caravan."

She loosened her hands from his and tapped the middle of her chest. "It's everything you said. These new technologies are useful and perfect and unbelievably immediate." She smiled at him. "But the joy I keep feeling deep down tells me the only important thing: all of this is okay. We don't need to explain it."

Michael nodded. "Okay. I just need to sit with it. Give me some time." He took a deep breath and relaxed a bit. "But how can things like this caravan just happen?"

Ava shrugged. "I don't know. It's bewildering, but we'll pay attention as things unfold. We can learn as we go." She stood and turned to Aadhya. "Well, friend, you've got your caravan. When do you want to leave?"

Aadhya's eyes were hopeful. "Tomorrow?"

"Done. You'll take your companion?"

"Yes, of course I will."

"'Then we'll avidly watch your progress from afar, completely unobtrusively. Until we gain more experience, you'll humor me by keeping in touch daily?"

"Yes. Happily."

"Have a fabulous time." They hugged each other warmly, and Ava followed Michael out of the caravan. "What were we meeting about?" she asked him as they stepped down the short flight of stairs.

"Hydroponics."

"Oh, right. Fascinating."

Aadhya watched them walk down the path before she turned, hugging herself, and gazed at the intricate interior of her tiny caravan. She set about investigating the miniature world that had presented itself to her unexpectedly. Perfectly.

The ship settled deeper onto its outcropping, drawing energy from the stone, energy from deep within Airon.

Lone Tree shimmers and stretches feathery branches toward bright Sky spreading to encase all Life. Lone Tree sings of solitude and rebirth, of renewing joy and awakening New. Lone Tree turns its energy toward the ship and Home Base and breathes its song along its way.

Airon swings through space, singing her song to the stars.

~ 40 ~

BIRTHLINGS

The birthlings snuggled together in their sleeping niche deep inside Burrow. They rippled their paired rows of appendages, their holderlings. These were the awakening hours, and their deep state of dawn wisdom flowed along their holderlings, creating patterns and vibrations that could be sensed by the elders who hummed softly nearby, watching, absorbing.

Vargad rested upright, his own holderlings oscillating in response to the vibrations emanating from the birthlings. His burrowmates sat scattered around the dim niche, joined together through these patterns and vibrations that began their days. It might be many seasons before they once again welcomed birthlings into Burrow. For now, they gathered together to treasure dawn wisdom.

This group of birthlings was newly arrived; Vargad did not know them yet. Their delicate holderlings oscillated tentatively, trembling with a purity that thrilled Vargad and lifted his inner vibration into a profound harmony. Dawn wisdom was ephemeral. For all its brevity, or perhaps because of it, dawn wisdom allowed a clear doorway to Source.

Birthlings carried the essence of Source; the brilliance of their dawn wisdom was unblemished. The brilliance would dim in texture and clarity as the birthlings eventually aged into younglings.

Their daily growth would gradually obscure the clarity of dawn wisdom.

Vargad absorbed the vibrations and remembered his own birthing, his own connection to Source, his own dawn wisdom...remembered, as if no time had passed.

Vargad felt the oscillations break rhythm. One of the birthlings raised her nose to the unseen sky and keened. Her cry spoke of hunger and demand. A Caretake-er moved forward and crooned over the keening birthling, speaking of confidence and encouragement. The birthling paused her keening as the Caretake-er lifted her and gathered her into the double row of his sturdy, nurturing holderlings. The Caretake-er rippled from the niche as another, then another birthling raised noses and keened upward. Now all of the birthlings keened. Caretake-ers gathered them and quieted them; dawn wisdom melted away.

Vargad and a few elders remained, holding the harmony that continued to thrill along their spines. One by one, the elders crept from the birthling niche, leaving Vargad to hold the harmony in solitude. Finally, softly, it left him. He turned and wound his way through Burrow, out into the vibrant sunshine beyond. His many holderlings feathered amongst the soft families scattered across Hillside, the greens and yellows nurturing his depleted body, the colorful flowers and rich scents filling his heart.

He listened to the distant song of Lone Tree and felt the peace of the ripening day. He paused, soaking in the sun's warmth, the colors, the energy of the awakening Hillside. As his body replenished itself from the nurturing green and yellow families upon which he rested, he turned his mind to his meld, finding and holding each littermate in the warmth of his joy. He became VaSo, then VaSoDe, and finally VaSoDeLa as each of his littermates joined him across their distances, humming their entwined song. Melded and complete, VaSoDeLa called his Burrow family together. They would explore Stream today and hear her stories of high peaks and tumbling falls.

Younglings swarmed in anticipation of their journey to Stream while Caretake-ers carried birthlings back into Burrow to rest after their morning nourishment. As VaSoDeLa watched the birthlings go, a sorrowful yearning nibbled around the edges of his heart. His meld encouraged him to turn his attention to the sky and trees and bask in the beauty of his surroundings. He gazed at the Narsis gathered on Hillside, the mates who shared his Burrow, watching each face for a moment, gauging the reality in which each burrowmate rested.

Finally, VaSoDeLa raised his nose to the sky and coughed, bringing the Burrow family into connection. They set off, the younglings scampering and tumbling about, trilling happily to each other as they frolicked and rippled across Hillside. The elder Narsis followed, humming appreciatively, content with the path that the younglings chose. The day would be rich and engaging. As yesterday had been. As tomorrow would be. The world was balanced and bright with joy.

Vargad's thoughts returned to the sleeping niche. The Narsis would mourn the dimming of wisdom's clarity, as day followed day and time lengthened, until dawn wisdom no longer flowed and the birthlings grew into the world of younglings. The birthling niche would then lay vacant each morning, an emptiness too dark to bear.

Across eons, younglings had cavorted and played, explored and learned. Caretake-ers shepherded them through their beginning days, then Show-ers guided them into an understanding of their world and how to be one with all that is. As the younglings matured, Find-ers joined their explorations, taking them farther afield. At a certain age, the perfect age, Find-ers helped younglings emerge into a role, the right role, rewarding and challenging. More importantly, Find-ers helped each youngling Find a new Burrow, the right Burrow, spacious and warm, the resident family humming just so, in the ancient acknowledgement of a new home, new connections, a new life merged with beloved burrowmates.

In this way, Narsi families spread and merged, mixed and circulated, explored and Found. Elders taught younglings; younglings emerged from their birth Burrows and merged afar with their life Burrows.

The life of elders was rich and engaging, full of adventure and learning, mating and melding, watching and teaching. But they were guided always, since all awareness, through their inner connection with Source, amplified by dawn wisdom. The gathering of elders as they matched their inner harmony to dawn wisdom strengthened that connection to Source, completed their whole. The Narsis remembered dawn wisdom as they moved through their days, an integral part of the world around them, a part of all that is.

Birthlings were rare now. Narsis held dawn wisdom in ever greater awe, treasuring each morning's connection to Source as if it were the last.

The Arbans sing to the sky, and the Shosens listen. The Arbans dance in the wind, and the Shosens color the swirling leaves with dips and darts, weaving turquoise patterns that shift the air and entice the wind. The Shosens sing of courage and strength, sending trills to skip along the waves and onward, across the grassy plains, twirling around Lone Tree silhouetted against the morning sky.

Lone Tree shimmers in the dawn and stretches feathery branches toward the warming air twirling around it. Lone Tree sings of strength and calmness, of renewing joy and awakening hope. Lone Tree turns its energy toward Burrow and Nest, Hillside and Stream, and breathes its song along its way. The song riffles across Wind, dancing across Sky, caressing VaSoDeLa's ears as the Narsis thread their way to Stream.

~ 41 ~

HEAD-ER

VaSoDeLa sat in contemplation. Head-ing had been assumed for him, always. As a birthling entwined with his eleven littermates, he was first to wake, last to keen. Always. He lingered in stillness, oscillating with the vibration of Source. Their Caretake-ers hummed amazement, trilled the blessing of this melodious litter, alerting the family. Soon, the gathered elders crowded together to witness the heightened clarity of dawn wisdom.

Vargad Head-ed his littermates, prompted and approved the eventual branching that led to the melding of VaSoDeLa, then JaMiKoDi, leaving RaDoSaPa as the final, yet perfect meld. Melding always formed between littermates; no outsiders could find the thread that led into a litter's meld. Through the meld, the coming together, the deep joining, the individual Narsis became whole.

Vargad melded with Sorgad, Dergad, and Largad. The four meldmates dispersed to separate Burrows to take on disparate roles, bringing variety and breadth to their meld. As Caretake-er, Sorgad connected the meld ever more closely to dawn wisdom and the caring of birthlings and younglings; as Show-er, Dergad best understood the world around them, Below and high Above; as Find-er, Largad learned of the world near and far afield, alerting her burrowmates as well as her meld to the changes and shifts of the forests and meadows.

Each morning upon leaving their scattered life Burrows, the four meldmates, all meldmates throughout awareness, would reach out with their minds and find their three. For an instant, as the four minds came together, they would brush against their own dawn wisdom and remember it exquisitely, as if no time had passed. The joy of that faint brush bolstered them through their day, carried them along as they Care-ed, Show-ed, Found, Head-ed, filling their roles with clarity and grace.

To everyone's surprise, Vargad's elder position as Head-er of Burrow had been hard-earned. Vargad began to realize his difference soon after he and his littermates fledged into younglings. He recognized a contentment and sense of purpose in their learning and growth that seemed complete within itself, while he felt a longing for...something. Upon melding, he sensed a trace of the same longing in his meldmates, the longing that fed his restlessness; a longing that his meldmates had successfully rebuffed, ignored, and now deplored within themselves. He learned rituals to keep that part of his essence separate, the part that longed, that disturbed and ruffled his meldmates.

The separateness that he held accentuated his longing, brought questions. He asked his Show-ers, his Caretake-ers, the Find-ers, the Head-ers, all of his burrowmates from both his birth Burrow and his life Burrow. His mates commiserated with him, humming and patting him with their softest holderlings, but no one had answers. All they could do in the end was turn away, humming, distraught.

Vargad worked hard over the long expanse of his life to rebuff and ignore his longing. That part of his essence shrank, but never quite blinked out. At long last, it no longer colored his purpose, and he was able to move into his expected role as Head-er of Burrow. He had been born to Head, as evidenced by his prolonged dawn wisdom, by the high esteem of his meldmates and burrowmates. They wanted him to Head. They wanted to follow.

Vargad found deep connection in watching the season's birthlings bring dawn wisdom. He often slept in their chamber, awakening before them, so as to catch their first coherent oscillations. He was always the last to leave the sleeping niche. Always it was so.

Then he would move softly to the mouth of Burrow and send out the thread that found those three distinct threads, the three with the most beautiful color, the exquisite song, the three threads that wove with his and coalesced into his meld. He held himself in stillness to capture the richness of that brief, brilliant brush with remembered dawn wisdom, and turned, ready to move through his day, to Head Burrow with clarity, with purpose.

But not quite with joy.

~ 42 ~

CELEBRATION

"We should have a roving shelter blessing so that everyone can enjoy everyone's home!" Harper exclaimed. "We've had a good long time to settle in over these busy months and have made our shelters into a reflection of ourselves, our inner selves. It would be fun to share our visions and creativity with each other. We could sprinkle rose water or burn lavender and sage as we go. Let's make a day of it and have a picnic." Harper bounced up and down on her toes as she leaned against the counter. "My Earthen timekeeper says we've been here for five months. We could use a celebration."

"A picnic on the Green?" Ava was only partially listening.

Harper shrugged. "As long as we wear long-sleeved tops and long bottoms, keep our shoes on, and don't touch anything, what could go wrong?" She flung her arms up, flicking her palms toward the ceiling.

Ava quelled her irritation. "What's the menu?" she mused aloud, tapping a finger on her upper lip. "Something that can be prepared the day before so the kitchen staff can have the day off, too." She turned from her salad prep to face Harper. "We'll all help with cleanup. Sandwiches and potato salad. Iced tea. Exotic fruits for dessert. Cookies. Chocolate cake?" She shook her head. "No, that's too complicated. Cookies."

Michael was taking notes as Ava mused and Harper beamed. It seemed as if they had a green light. Harper felt a burst of excitement. Everyone would be glad for a day of socializing and light-hearted time outdoors. She couldn't wait to tell everyone.

Michael was wondering who would oversee the day. Maybe they could put together some music. This had the potential of a grand idea. He mused about people's reactions. "If I send this out now, most people will have read it by evening gathering. We can flesh out the plan then."

"Yes. Do that." Ava turned toward Michael, dismissing Harper. "What's next?"

At the evening gathering, Michael was surprised by the groans. It could be hard to predict what people would like, but the roving shelter blessing and picnic had seemed like a sure thing. He could hear Logan muttering under his breath. Olivia rocked back on her tailbone, hands clasped around her knees, chin pointed up, a grimace darkening her features.

"The menu will be simple. Everything will be made ahead of time. The kitchen staff will have the day off, too," Michael reiterated.

Olivia shook her head and rocked forward, bracing her forehead on her upturned palm, staring at the floor.

"Olivia." Ava joined the conversation. "Tell us what you need to make this work for you."

"Oh, right. Where do I begin?"

"Start anywhere. It doesn't have to be in any particular order. We'll sort it out together."

Olivia shook her head. "No. Making an entire meal a day ahead of time is a lot more work than making it as scheduled. I'd rather just have a normal schedule."

Ava focused on Olivia. What was going on with her? "But would you feel like it was a day of celebration and fun if you were on your regular schedule and spending most of the day in the kitchen?"

"No." A petulant pause. "I don't feel much like celebrating."

Ava decided not to let her off the hook. "Might that be a result of working too hard for too long?" She waited, watching Olivia. "Let's mix it up. Do something different; throw the schedule out the window."

Olivia shook her head, eyes on the floor, sullen.

Ava faced the others and started over. "Let's consider possibilities and grow from there. For now, set aside what won't work and focus on what *will* work." No response. Everyone had gone silent.

She turned back to Olivia. "We could have one crew working in the ship's kitchen. It's still functional." Back to the others. "They can take on the entire meal and get everything ready the day before while Olivia and her crew hold their usual routine in the kitchen here. At the end of the day, we'll have an extra meal ready. And you..." she turned to Olivia again, "...won't have had anything extra on your plate." Still no response. "Olivia, what do you think?"

She shook her head, moping. "No. It still takes more people to make an extra meal. People don't show up for their tasks in order to prepare one meal. Why would you expect twice the number of people to show up to prepare two meals? No. It's not going to work. In the end, I'll be stuck doing it all."

Ava frowned. "Addison, is this still happening? Are people still not helping with meal prep?"

Addison spoke loudly so that everyone in the room could hear. "People keep forgetting that they're scheduled. We've instituted a system of reminders through the companions, though, and that's helping."

Olivia raised her voice in frustration, fists bouncing on her knees. "No. It's not helping. Meals are timed, and when most people show up late or not at all, then the meal gets served late. Things sit for longer than they should and dishes turn out mediocre. When the rest of the team is inconsiderate, it's stressful and unfair to the few who do show up."

Ava spoke loudly enough to be heard over the rising muttering. "Olivia is right; meal preparation has to occur in a certain way. It's choreographed, and like any dance, its beauty relies completely on all of the dancers being fully there. One person blowing their part affects the other dancers."

She swiveled to sweep the room with her gaze. "Listen to me, everyone. Arriving on time is a powerful habit to develop. Arriving on time forces you to align your thought, word, and deed. You decide to arrive on time; you give your word to others that you will arrive on time; you arrive on time. It's not Addison's responsibility, and it's not Olivia's. It's yours. Set reminders yourself. Take responsibility for your timing yourself. Am I heard?" She made eye contact around the room. "Are we agreed?"

People nodded as quiet stretched through the air. Ava could feel the tension in the room softening. "Now, then. Let's organize a second cooking team. Who is willing?"

Two dozen hands lifted into the air. As Michael jotted down names, hands lowered one by one. "Let's make sure none of the willing cooks are scheduled for the main kitchen that day. Zoe, will you be lead cook for the ship's kitchen? Thank you. Michael will give you the list of names. Come up with a simple, enjoyable menu and run it past Olivia and Logan to make sure supplies are adequate. Okay?" Zoe nodded again, smiling at Claudia, sitting next to her.

"Does this sound like a workable plan, Olivia?" Olivia picked at her stocking and then gave a short nod. She was too tired to argue. "We'll talk about anything that needs adapting at tomorrow evening's gathering," Ava concluded.

Ava looked around the room again. "You've all been working incredibly hard, and your hard work was crucial as we wrote our first chapter here. I feel that it's time for us to start relaxing into the rhythms we've established. We're well-settled. The common halls are well-designed and well-crafted. Everything's going extremely smoothly.

"Let's start taking time to be kind not only to others but to ourselves as well. We had that luxury during our journey, when we had time to settle in and get familiar with the art of journeying. Let's recapture that luxury, the art of life on Airon."

She smiled, raising her hands with her palms up. "Be on time and be kind. How hard can it be?"

People visibly relaxed, with soft murmurs here and there.

"Michael, what's next?"

DATA

Scarlett gathered her determination and equipment and headed outside. She called to the techs working at their benches: "I'm headed out." Heads nodded; one hand lifted in acknowledgement. The doors of her lab swung shut behind her. What a glorious day.

Every day was glorious. The native foliage, the flora, was consistently, vibrantly green, with riotous shapes and a cacophony of color spreading in every direction. Scarlett moved several hundred paces into the towering forest and paused to take in the colors, the scents, the soft movement of air across her arms.

This is what always happened, she realized. She would start out with good intentions, only to get swept up in the beauty and variety of life around her, and would end up getting nothing accomplished.

She renewed her resolve. She spread a tarp and placed her measuring implements along one end, arranged by size. Water orbs held down one corner of the tarp, and an extra notebook held down another. She tossed her rolled screen into the middle of the arrangement, ready for detailed data entry.

The task was enormous, tabulating the local flora. She would start large, with the trees, and work her way down to the minuscule. Today, she would focus on color, variations of color within each layer of flora. Color was a reliable categorization, readily detected and referenced.

She had left all of her companions back in the lab. She didn't want them intruding on her data collection, hovering in the wrong place at the wrong time. She would work on her own today.

Scarlett opened her primary notebook, called up a color wheel, and noted the coordinates of her starting point. She walked 100 paces due west, the notebook documenting her route and position. Holding the notebook precisely before her, she activated a scanning packet and turned slowly on the spot.

The scanning packet noted each detected color out to 30 meters, documented the shape, texture, growth habit of every life form taller than 5 meters. Scarlett completed a second turn, instructing the scanning packet to verify and codify the data from the first circuit.

A second set of turns collected data for life forms between 100 centimeters and 5 meters (inclusive). A final set of turns focused on life forms under 100 centimeters (inclusive).

Scarlett sent the data to her screen and cleared the cache for the scanning packet. She stood a moment taking in the beauty of the landscape she had just catalogued, the scents, the movement of air, the dappled sunlight dancing through branches and alighting on colorful sprays and spiraling clusters.

Scarlett walked 100 paces due west, held the notebook precisely before her, and repeated the entire process.

On her sixth repetition, movement on the periphery of a clearing caught her attention. She recognized Zoe and Claudia walking slowly between the trees. Her initial reaction was that she would simply wait until their wander took them out of range of her scanning packet. She waved a greeting, but they didn't notice her. She paused the scanning packet and hugged the notebook to her chest.

Scarlett squinted at the two women, watching their movements closely. They moved woodenly, in unison with each other, but somehow unaware of each other. They neither spoke nor gestured, looked neither left nor right. Their movements were slow, measured.

Scarlett brought her notebook awake, switched to a visual packet, and recorded the women's movements, just in time to witness the unthinkable.

Zoe moved slowly, deliberately, up to a towering giant, spread her arms, and embraced the trunk. She pressed her forehead against the bark and stood motionless. Claudia replicated the motion, pressing herself against a trunk 10 meters from Zoe.

Both women were barefoot.

Scarlett stood, one hand covering her gaping mouth. Such foolishness! Pure idiocy. How could they be this wanton in their disregard of a fundamental agreement put in place to protect the entire community? What might they pick up? And unknowingly pass along to others, perhaps infecting all of them?

Scarlett's training screamed alarms, outrage, rigid judgement. Containment. Quarantine. Ostracism.

And yet Scarlett stood unmoving, watching the outrage, wondering where it could lead. She felt the breeze on her arms, and looking up, she saw lavender and peach blossoms swirling and jostling, glorious scents drifting down to bathe her upturned face. She felt a peacefulness seeping in through her pores, a softness caressing her spine, a gentle whisper.

She looked toward Zoe and Claudia, felt no outrage, only curiosity and wonder. She continued to record as Zoe stepped away from her tree, turned, and made her way back the way she had come. A few breaths later, Claudia followed her, both women moving through the forest in the direction of Home Base.

Scarlett followed, keeping the women in sight amongst the enormous trunks. They came to an open glade where a bright blanket lay spread in the sunshine. Their shoes awaited them, and as they scooted feet into shoes, their movements became once again fluid and graceful.

They chatted together comfortably, gathered blanket, water orbs, a small basket. Scarlett recorded everything from behind an obscuring tree. She watched the women wander through the trees, making their way back to Home Base.

Scarlett looked down at her notebook, felt the soothing breeze, and considered deleting the whole file. She was here to record the flora, begin categorizing Airon's life forms. Why would she need this file of Earthen activity?

Her thumb hovered above the delete icon, and then she noticed the interrupted observations from her most recent data acquisition. She sent both files to her screen for downloading into her lab's database. She'd sort it out later.

Scarlett retraced her path to where she had encountered Zoe and Claudia and decided she'd collected enough data for today. She retrieved her unused instruments, the water orbs, swept the blanket and screens into her large basket, and threaded her way back to Home Base, wondering if lunch was ready.

~ 44 ~

WANDERING

Aadhya crinched down into her soft blankets and pulled the soft cap snuggly over her ears. The cloying darkness of a nightmare wrapped around her, plaguing her with a familiar emptiness. Images flashed painfully before her: tumbling rock rubble, billowing dust clouds, the pounding of panicked feet. Imagined screams and frantic shouts ricocheted and pierced her heart. She sat up from the warm bed and hugged her knees, rocking backward and forward, sobs choking her throat.

She was aware of soft light leaking in around the window shades. She knew the best way to disperse the clinging anguish of her dream was to plow into her day. As she clambered out of her soft nest, she took time to breathe deeply and stretch her arms up and out to her sides. She slipped into a warm skirt and shirt. It was cold in the mornings. The solar heater would give her a glorious shower later in the day. For now, she washed her face, and brushed her teeth.

A birdling called out, a pure and simple solo. Aadhya recognized Rami's voice and raised the shades to allow the climbing sunlight to bounce across carpets and cabinetry. Birdlings fluttered across the swaying grass, chirping a rich trill, darting and weaving, their twitters flowing and swooping as song and dance blended and parted, sweeping across the meadow. They twirled along the edge of trees, barreled back to cascade around her caravan in a turquoise swirl. Aadhya collected a few belongings and stepped down into the morning.

Her companion followed her as she made her way along a gravel path, and Rami swept down to trill a joyous welcome. Aadhya lifted her hand toward the turquoise birdling and sang notes in reply. She noticed a torrid orange blossom bending to rest against a mossy boulder. A pattern of crystalized prisms piled against a stand of smooth, purple mushrooms that spilled from under a fallen tree; overlapping feathery leaves silhouetted against the teal sky. The birdlings fluttered alongside her, drawing her attention to first one marvel then the next, guiding her along a flattened outcropping that overlooked a clear pond, where she kicked off her shoes and stood firmly rooted on the smooth rock.

The remembered tingling crept up her legs, flowed up her spine and along her outstretched arms. Aadhya had practiced combining her blending with the world around her into a collaborative flow of knowledge, wisdom, and joy. She could move through her day wholly connected, yet solitary in her movements and thoughts. She could see the entirety of life around her, blended into a perfect whole, and yet see herself flowing within it.

Every moment played itself out exactly as she knew it would, exactly as it should, as she orchestrated the world, as it orchestrated her. They were together, yet separate; whole, yet individual; blended, yet independent.

Aadhya opened her eyes, stooped to spread her cushion, and sat to enter stillness. The birdlings settled into the grass around her outcropping, purring. The vestiges of her dreamed anguish floated away.

After some time, Aadhya lay back on the rock and let the sun's warmth melt through slackened muscles. Moss cushioned shoulders and elbow. She stretched her legs out and found a slight bulge, mossy and sun-warmed, that lifted her knees just so. Her lower back relaxed against warm softness, and she slept.

She awoke to soft cooing, inches from her ear. She smiled. Rami's familiar coo deepened, interwoven with rolling purrs. As Aadhya stretched and sat up, Rami leapt into the air, her turquoise wings blurring, her song trilling into full voice, rousing the other birdlings who rose, a turquoise cloud, song and dance spiraling upward and out, to flow across the glistening pond.

The day was in full swing. Aadhya watched the birdlings swoop down to the pond, skimming the surface and leaving a fine spray in their wake as they rose, banked, and glided back to the jutting rock where Aadhya sat. She could smell the vibrantly orange blossoms nodding at the base of her rock, drenching the air with rich scent.

Aadhya stood and stepped out of her loose clothing, then leaned forward and dove into the cool water, shocking her sun-hot skin into full awareness. She glided down through the clear, green stillness, then kicked up, back to the light-flecked surface, treading water as she watched the ripples from her dive stretch away from her across the mirrored surface. The water tasted of mint. She dipped her chin and swept her arms forward and out, swallowing sip after sip.

An oft-remembered, oft-forgotten brilliance flowed through Aadhya. She once again felt the connection between her, the pond, sky, trees, distant sea. She moved through the nurturing water, remembering, as if no time had passed.

Her nightmare forgotten, Aadhya felt the richness of this pond and the life it held. Her heart swelled with gratitude for the world around her; she felt a deepening sense of peace. With a strong breaststroke, she clove her way through the still water to the sandy beach at the far end of the pond.

Leaving a trail of evaporating drips, she followed the swooping birdlings around the edge of the pond, retrieved her clothing, and picked her way back to the caravan, squeezing rivulets of water from her long braid. She watched the birdlings settle into the tallest trees, spreading out amongst the high branches that encircled the meadow.

As she turned and stepped up into her warm, welcoming caravan, the birdlings swirled upward again and engulfed her companion who had paused at a distance, obscured now by their twirling turquoise cloud.

As Aadhya's feet left the ground, she could faintly remember the bonding with rock and pond. She could carry it with her, lightly, into the caravan; the caravan imagined by her mind, commissioned by Airon, and created by the ship.

Airon, who sweeps around her sun, nurturing the lives and dreams and purpose of the souls who move and breathe and sing. Airon, who slowly, surely, lovingly, whispers her creatures toward a New brink, the tilt that would change life's course.

~ 45 ~

STILLNESS

As Harper stepped outside, she met a fine drizzle. The droplets floated rather than fell, bringing with them the scent of golden leaves and softening the early rustlings from others walking along the paths. Her door latched behind her with a click that she felt more than heard.

She walked along her path, then around the edge of the Green, turning at the path to the gathering hall. The air was drenched with a memory of roses; their scent floated richly upon the air. She paused in the anteroom and waited silently.

Henry arrived, then Zoe. They held their separate spaces, sheltering from the mist. When the chime sounded softly, they stepped out of their shoes, gently opened the door, and moved into the gathering hall.

Peace and calm rested in the room. A faint light glowed around the perimeter just below the ceiling, deep carpet underfoot. Mateo softly gathered his cloak, readying to leave, and Scarlett moved toward the door.

Harper softly placed a chair next to Michael, nestling into it gradually to avoid squeaks. Her cloak draped around her, tucked across her chest for warmth, puddled at her feet. As she glanced at the faces around her, her heart gladdened, and she greeted stillness with joy. She closed her eyes, and the entire world went...still.

At times, she would think how odd this gathering would look to the people in her small hometown. It was a resort town, a hunting town. She had escaped early, the odd one who never fit in. This still gathering would never happen in that small town; a group of people all facing the same direction, eyes closed, seemingly doing nothing.

She thought of her childhood cat watching her read. What must he have imagined, seeing her stare at a passive object for hours, seemingly doing nothing? The vivid scene that arabesqued or plodded or cantered through her mind was completely invisible to him.

In this still room, the gratitude, the reverence, the peace that drifted across her heart would be invisible to the eyes of the people she'd known in her childhood. This feeling could only be discovered one person at a time, one moment at a time, impossible to share through words with anyone who had not experienced it themselves.

Morning stillness passed in a moment. Harper sank forward to the floor, forehead touching carpet, heart filled with gratitude. She gathered her cloak around her and carefully moved her chair, stacking it atop others in their niche, quietly respectful of those who stayed longer. She moved through the door, found her shoes amongst the others, and slipped around the Green, back to her shelter. Golden crescents of petals wet her soles.

The door latched behind Harper with a click that she felt more than heard.

Along the coast, the Arbans sing to the sky, and the Shosens listen. The Shosens trill of courage and strength, cast their joy across the grassy plains, twirl around Lone Tree silhouetted against the dawn sky, a dusting of sadness sparkling in the dawn.

Lone Tree shimmers in the dawn and stretches feathery branches into the warming air, sings of strength and awakening hope. JaCoMaTuRi's family spreads themselves across broad branches, watching the sun release itself from the distant mountains. The day is born.

$$\sim\ 46\ \sim$$

RENDEZVOUS

Chatan came awake as the sky brightened. He listened to the early morning sounds of this alien world and relaxed into his warm blankets. His routine had established itself nicely as he spent more and more of his days wandering. His companion fleet wandered with him, ranging far afield, cataloging, observing, tallying, streaming data back to Home Base for Scarlett's team to decipher and study.

Chatan was thus free to take in the bigger picture and observe the whole, leaving the finicky details to his fleet here and Scarlett's team back at Home Base. He started each day in stillness, absorbing the feel of the air around him, the sounds and scents of his resting place. He let the stillness grow into him, feeling a deepening connection with his surroundings.

His companion left a meal next to his sleeping cloth, making it easy to end his stillness and break his fast while watching the world awaken. Once Chatan stood and stretched, moving through his morning patterns, his companion gathered debris and sleeping cloths, leaving no trace of their stay.

It didn't occur to him to touch foliage or bark or to shake off his shoes and stand intimately connected to the vibrant life around him. Rather, Chatan lived in separation. He saw all that surrounded him, yet he did not quite reach across an invisible divide even though a certain familiarity nibbled at the edges of his awareness. Perhaps Airon reminded him of his ancestral desert despite the fact that this landscape was the opposite of a desert. Maybe that's why a connection didn't click.

The whispers had fallen silent.

Chatan longed to understand this new world, to feel her rhythms and hear her soul. Meanwhile, he would go through the motions of collecting data and sending them to Scarlett's team.

Before beginning the day's wander, Chatan unrolled his screen and reviewed the most recent reports from Home Base. He made notations in the margins and a list of questions and additional observations, and sent it all back to Scarlett to help her plan her day. He studied the topo of the region, his course marked by a thin purple tracing. The companions' paths fanned out and created a widening wake that trailed his route.

He walked up a small rise to scan the terrain ahead, matching it to the topo on his screen. He decided he would veer over the next ridge and start a long, graceful arc back to Home Base.

His cycle had followed him up the rise. Handing his screen to his companion, he climbed on the cycle, and they started off, his companion relaying their route to the companion fleet. As they crested the ridge and adjusted their course to skirt an outcropping of dark trees, Chatan glimpsed a bubble of bright white through the distant branches. Curious, he followed the edge of trees until he was close enough to identify Aadhya's caravan nestled against the backdrop of forest.

Chatan glanced at the sun. She might still be sleeping. He didn't want to alarm her, so he moved some distance away, still within easy view of the caravan. He passed by a dainty lake, a pond, really, serene amidst the encircling hillside. He stopped and sat down to take in the view, captivated again by the colorfully riotous landscape.

The sun climbed a bit higher in the sky. Chatan heard the door of the caravan open and close. He stood up and waited for Aadhya to see him, then waved enthusiastically in her direction. He read her astonishment as she held up her hand in hesitant greeting. She started to walk in his direction, so he moved down to meet her.

"Of all the meadows in all the world, you walk into mine." Aadhya's voice carried easily in the still air.

"Secret retreats are easily discovered, especially when white caravans stand out like flashing neon." Chatan covered the distance to where she stood.

"You're wandering? Again?" She faltered.

"I'm wandering. Again. Home Base beckons, as does the brightness of your caravan." Confusion and curiosity flitted across her face. "We've discovered each other on this early morning."

She smiled shyly, searching for something more to say. "Have you had breakfast?"

"Yes. But...have you some tea?" His slight smile lifted one corner of his mouth as he looked into her clear eyes.

"Yes. Let me bring you some. Come, sit." She gestured to the cloth her companion was spreading. "You can tell me your news."

Chatan stepped onto the cloth and sat, feeling the cushioning greenery beneath the cloth. He looked toward the pond, serene, mirroring the sky.

Aadhya mounted the steps leading into her caravan. She lifted the steeping teapot, found a second cup, and placed everything on a vibrantly green tray. She added some sweet biscuits, and separated sections of the delicious fruit she had discovered yesterday with the help of the birdlings.

She was surprised at how pleased she felt to see Chatan. True, she had been wandering for many days and was glad for the companionship. But it was more than that; she was thrilled that it was Chatan who had wandered by.

Giddy. She felt giddy. She closed her eyes and steadied her moist palms against her belly, then took a deep breath and lifted the loaded tray to carry it out into the sunlight.

Chatan was waiting on the edge of the cloth, shoes tumbled on the grass next to him, looking out over the pond. He turned at her approach and lifted the tray from her hands. "This is an extraordinary spot. Do you always come here?"

She considered. "The first wander in the caravan, no. But after that, the caravan brought me here, and I have returned again and again. The pond, the light, the birdlings...all of it draws me back."

"You've found birdlings here? Do they stay here? Are they always about?"

"Yes. They come and go during the day, but every day I see them." She peered into the nearby forest, then across the pond to the far trees. "There." She pointed. "See the turquoise dusting on the tree with the yellow spirals? Those are the birdlings."

Chatan squinted in the direction of her pointing arm. "Yes. I've seen them before, in many places. It may be the same flock." He watched as the turquoise cloud rose and settled on another tree, closer to the pond.

"You see? They help you. They know you want to see them, so they help you do this."

"They roam. Connecting the world. They bring news to others who do not move as freely as they do."

"You know them? All those birdlings? How can you know their purpose? They move, all around they move, but rarely speak." Her arm circled her head, a grand swoop.

Chatan smiled. "I have come to know them, felt them learn about me. They probably know about you as well."

"Yes, of course they do. They show me things and let me know what I can and cannot do. But I did not know their purpose, this thing you are telling me now. Their purpose of telling others."

"I don't know how I know it, their purpose. It just rings true."

Aadhya titled her head. The birdlings rose from their nearby tree, flowed into the open air, spread, coalesced, swayed, and angled down to alight near Chatan and Aadhya. They landed with coordinated precision, dotting the meadow surrounding the cloth.

"They seem to always be the same birds to me. They seem to know me. This one..." she gestured toward a birdling hopping near her knee, "...this one is Rami. She is always here." Her gaze encompassed the remainder of the flock. "They show me different things. They showed me this fruit." A cautious smile. "It is delicious. Would you like to try some?"

Chatan stared at the sectioned fruit, its moist, deep blue flesh riddled with yellow streaks. It reminded him of a large berry or a small plum. "You've eaten this? It's native?" Incredulous, he looked at her. "That was very brave of you. Or very rebellious." Then memory slipped back into his awareness. "Wait...I've eaten these before. The trees led me to a grove. You're right; they are delicious. Healing."

"They grow nearby. The birdlings showed me. They help me find things." She was embarrassed by her repetition. "I do not fear that which they show me."

"All the same..." He trailed off and shook his head. "It was brave of you to eat it."

"I have new knowledge," she said.

"Which is?"

"The birdlings showed me." Her smile deepened, brightened. "It is conclusive."

Chatan watched her eyes, calculating her certainty. He reached down and picked up a piece of the fruit, brought it to his mouth, smelled it, touched it to his tongue.

Aadhya laughed, her hand covering her mouth. "I apologize for my laughter. It is only that you do what I did. Caution is a hard habit to reach past."

"I don't know that we are ready to reach past it," he said warily. "Caution might be the thing that keeps us alive. It's still necessary for most things, most people."

"We do not need caution. We have the birdlings." Her voice lilted along the words, singsong.

Chatan sat quietly, the fruit resting on his gathered fingertips. He had always trusted his intuitive understanding of the natural world. Why was he suspicious of hers? He looked back down at the fruit. Did he trust it? Her? No. Not yet.

The birdlings waited, heads cocked, watching Chatan.

"You have an audience for your caution. They seem very interested in what you will choose."

Chatan paused, wondering. His memory of the fruit was vague and uncertain. Had he actually eaten it? Was it safe to eat? Should he trust Aadhya?

A curious notion swept through him, a whisper. Could this woman know? Could she hear the ground speak? Could she see the birds and know their wisdom? Could she hear the song of the river? Join in its dance?

He shook off the thoughts. He did not think it possible. He had seen too much discordance, witnessed too much damage. Only his people had this ability, guided by ancestors. And then only rarely. This woman was not of his people.

Aadhya's voice broke through his thoughts. "Connect, Chatan. You have known such separation from the world. Now is not the time for caution."

His eyes bore into hers. She spoke to him about connection? She did not shrink away from his look. After several breaths, he closed his eyes, gently, softly.

The whispers came.

He felt the ground spreading out beneath him. He was aware of roots that went deep, twining in every direction, saw light rising through stems and trunks and branches, flowing out through leaves and petals, weaving into the path of flying creatures, the paths of crawling, running, jumping, swimming creatures. He saw the iridescence that connected every curve and corner, that leapt over waterfalls and crashed through waves, sparkled in the clouds and danced along the wind, that sprang and swirled through every living thing, that circled and coalesced in the fruit before him, the fruit that rested in his hand.

He remembered.

With certainty, Chatan lifted the fruit to his mouth and brought Airon's being into his very center. As he swallowed, he felt energy flow out through his fingertips, down through his feet, completing the circle of light, blending him into the circle of life that was Airon.

When he opened his eyes, he saw Aadhya watching the birdlings as they swept up into the sky and flowed out across the treetops, falling and rising, spreading and coalescing, bound for some far place. As they went, they danced on the air, worshipped the sky. The same light flowed through the trees, the animals, the fruit, and now through himself. That same light glowed through Aadhya. They were the same, this woman, himself, the birdlings, this world.

Chatan sat in wonder. He had known all of this since all of awareness. How had he forgotten? How had this woman helped him remember?

The two sat together in silence, absorbing the trees and sky, the rolling hills and glistening pond. They remembered their remember-ings.

"It may be time to tell the others," Chatan murmured.

"It will be easier to show them."

Chatan nodded. "Words will not suffice." He gazed up through branches to the clear sky beyond. "It may not yet be time."

"You will know once you try. If you do nothing, you will never know."

Chatan dropped his gaze and sought her eyes, calm and sure. He nodded into her smile.

Companionship floated around them, healing breaches in their hearts that had long stabbed their deepest souls. Every phase of their lives, every step along their paths, had led them to this meadow, this morning, this companionship.

Lone Tree spreads feathery branches beneath brilliant Sky. Lone Tree sings of connection and purpose, of New. Lone Tree turns its energy toward Pond and breathes its song along its way.

OVERLOOK

Vargad flowed along the cliff edge that loomed above a vast plain. His burrowmates flowed before him, behind him, silently glancing at the lowering sun that silhouetted nested ridges of dusky mountains. Their nightly ritual of farewell to their sun was revered, through all of awareness.

Vargad had dissolved his meld, stilling the song entwining his heart. He knew his burrowmates had bid goodnight to their melded threads, each Narsi flowing solo in the deepening dusk, all melds everywhere melting into dew. Twilight was their time together as burrowmates, these lovers of Below, their blending of shared days and gathered wisdom, reflected understanding and fresh ponderings. They came here every dusk, since all of awareness.

Younglings were burrowed asleep, exhausted from their day of wandering and exploring, learning and adventuring. They curled safely, holderlings entwined, breathing all the breaths of sleep, rich beyond measure, since all of awareness.

Vargad and his burrowmates turned their chests to the lowering sun, duties laid lovingly aside, Head-er, Caretake-er, Find-er, Shower, having no need here. Narsis, together in the blaze of last light.

Vargad heard the rustle of feathers, felt the swoop of wings as ancient partners fell from the sky, alighted on tumbled rock and coarsely grained sand. The Eglans, of clacking beaks and flamboyant tails. Narsis and Eglans, gathered together, as sun touched distant peaks; gathered, since all of awareness. Gathered, partnered, in silence and awe.

Narsis, together, relived their day, flashed pictures of romping younglings and dancing Stream, swaying Meadow and towering Forest, of stropped trunks and sniffed grasses, of scents glorious and colors sublime, of dew and breeze, of light dappled and brilliant, the entirety of their day.

Eglans stomp
Clack strong bills
Shake flamboyant tails
Blink at melting sun.
Relive together
Together be.
Eglans soar!
Flying soar!
Meadows kissed
Waves of breeze
Ripple long
Grass ripples
Again then again
Eglans soar!
Kiss sun
Dive through trees
Skim water
Bright wings
Flutter dry.
Eglans soar!
Dip wings
Birdlings see
Roaming far
Birdlings roam
Turquoise cloud
Roaming free.

Eglans soar!
Narsis meet
Blend Above
Blend Below
Narsis meet
Together be.

Narsis and Eglans shared their days, chests brilliant in the final rays from the sun. The peace of the world settled around them, enveloped their being. Together be. Partnered be. Forever be. Since all of awareness.

~ 48 ~

SHOES

"Hey. Want to go wandering?"

Harper twirled from her workstation and flung her palms toward the ceiling. "You're back!"

"Yep. Just now." Chatan was tan and glowing.

"How was it?"

"Come on a wander and I'll tell you all about it."

"Let me grab my shoes."

Chatan's voice dropped a notch. "Leave your shoes."

Harper looked up, surprised. "We're still under agreement. We don't know if it's safe to touch the plants, especially those we crush underfoot."

"All of that will change after I talk to Ava. Come on. It's part of the story I want to tell you." She hesitated. "Really. It's important."

"Chatan..."

They measured each other's determination.

"Okay. Yes; wear your shoes. I bet you lunch that you'll take them off along the way."

"Very mysterious..."

"Very astounding."

"I'm coming, I'm coming. You don't need to go all royal drama on me." She laced up her tall walking shoes and followed Chatan outside. "Where do you want to go?"

"Let's just wander through the forest. It's another lovely day."

They walked side by side across a narrow stretch of the Green and entered the forest. A faint path wound its way through the tree trunks, disappearing around a slight curve, beckoning them onward. "A lot of people must have been walking this way to have actually trodden down a path in the ground cover," Chatan walked along, examining the ground before them.

Harper looked ahead along the path and turned slightly to check behind them. "You're right. Although I don't see people walking past my shelter to take this route. I think people just enter the forest from wherever they happen to be. It's pretty easy walking, no matter which direction you take."

Chatan stopped and looked forward and backward along the clearly defined path. It wasn't bare soil, but the shorter ground cover clearly indicated a path. "And so. Even this." Chatan spoke gently, thoughtfully.

"Would you stop being mysterious and just tell me what you've seen?"

"What I'm seeing right now is a definite path, yet you're saying you haven't seen people walking here. But something made a path. A very inviting path. A path I very much want to follow."

"Well, let's follow it. Perhaps animals made it. Perhaps we'll find them." She stopped and threw her hands over her head. "Oh my stars, Chatan! I forgot that you didn't know! We've seen natives!"

"Really??" He grasped her elbow. "I missed it? What did they look like? What were they doing?"

"Chatan, wait, wait! We not only saw natives, they spoke to us. We had a conversation!"

"Intelligent life? Of all the...!" He brought his hand to the top of his head. "Is everything okay? Are they peaceful?" He gripped her elbow again. "Do they understand that we're peaceful?"

"Yes! Everything's great!" She patted his hand. "Chatan, it was incredible." She related everything she could remember about the encounter, adding as many details as possible, her hands flying busily to illustrate her words.

They turned as one and continued their walk, shoulder to shoulder. He asked questions; she replied with all the details she could remember.

"It was too brief. Vargad said they would move slowly, that we had talked enough for now. Then he just said, 'We leave,' just like that," Harper's hands flew up again, "and they turned and moved back into the forest."

"Man of few words."

"Yes. And the others were completely silent. We sat there for a few breaths, then got up and went to eat lunch." They walked silently for a few moments. "Chatan, the encounter was surprisingly brief, and afterward, we just went back to our normal lives as if nothing had happened. But everything, *everything* has changed. We've found intelligent life here." She twisted toward him as they talked, grabbed his arm and tugged it lightly.

Chatan gazed into the distance. "How did people take it?"

"Now that you ask, it was pretty low-key." Harper let go of him and turned back to face the path. "People listened closely while Ava described the encounter. Some people asked a couple of questions; some people were nervous; some were enthusiastic. But it was all low-key, more subdued than you'd expect for something like that. The three of us were deeply...affected...by it. But everyone else just went on to whatever was next on their list."

She threw her hand up into the air and shook her head. "No one talks about it even. But I think about it all the time. It changes everything. At least I think it does. We're sharing the planet with intelligent life. We've never done that before."

"We have. We've always shared a planet with intelligent life." Harper looked up at him, questioning. "We just never recognized anything as intelligent." He lowered his gaze. "At least, the white man seldom recognized any intelligence. The white man is an invasive species, aware only of its own needs, seeing nothing as it actually is."

They walked in silence, Harper hugging Chatan's arm. At last, she spoke. "I'm sorry, Chatan. Of course, you're right. It was thoughtless of me to speak of this as being new." She waved her hand around them, taking in the forest and sky.

Chatan took a few breaths and then pressed her hand. "It's fine. You understand things more than others. You're pretty aware of what's around you. That's why I was happy to see you home when I got back." The bounce returned to Harper's stride.

The sun filtered down through the trees, glowing on the myriad greens, brilliant hues sparkling as leaves fluttered in the soft breeze. The forest was silent except for their footsteps. The peace and solitude of their surroundings bathed them in a luscious calmness.

"I'm glad you're back. You've been gone for ages. I've missed talking with you about things. This especially, but everyday things, too."

He gave her hand a warm squeeze. "I know. I've been storing up things to tell you, too."

Her face brightened. "So tell me. What have you seen? What have you discovered? Why does this forest path seem special to you?"

"To begin with, every day I wake up just before the sun rises, and each day unfolds naturally, with no hurry, no lost time, no frustrations. Everything flows perfectly. Each evening, I stop in some amazingly beautiful spot and just settle in."

"Chatan, you're babbling. I've never heard you this enthusiastic about anything. Tell more."

He smiled his slight smile for a moment and gazed at the forest surrounding them.

Harper filled the silence. "I thought you would have been back before this. It's been ages."

Chatan chuckled. "Yes. Wandering becomes longer somehow. Every time."

He talked on. They strolled, arm in arm, watching the forest, Harper leaning in to catch every word. She loved this newly talkative Chatan.

"The plant life is incredibly diverse and grows in enormous abundance. I know Olivia is impatient to start growing and harvesting, but…"

"Oh my world!" Harper grasped her forehead. "Olivia. She has been in such a foul mood. You might want to wait until she simmers down a bit." She patted the air in front of them. "Or maybe your news will help pull her out of whatever dark hole she's fallen into."

"Oh, people always grumble about Olivia. She's okay, really."

"No; this is different." Harper shook her head vigorously. "Something's plaguing her. A lot of people are refusing to work in the kitchen. She's treating them quite badly. They just don't want to be in there with her."

Chatan thought a moment. "Has Ava talked with her?"

"Who knows?" Harper frowned. Chatan sensed a deeper story, something hidden. "She's tried, I guess, but apparently Olivia keeps putting her off. It's unsettling, actually." She looked away from Chatan, uncomfortable.

Chatan waited a breath, but she remained quiet. "Well, that's too bad. I hope she shakes it off soon. It's miserable to be trapped in a foul mood."

"And it makes things miserable for everyone else. So." She gave his arm a shake. "What else? Tell me more."

"Right. We've documented incredible diversity, rich abundance, unending beauty. A paradise. But the best thing of all is that it's all interconnected."

"Well, you would expect that, wouldn't you?"

"Yes, well…I expected the regular interactions, the bug pollinates the plant, the plant produces nectar, circles and cycles everywhere. But this is something more. Things work together. They cooperate. They help each other."

"You mean the plants cooperate with each other?"

"The plants, the animals, the air, the weather patterns...Everything works in cooperation with everything else. I see evidence of a deeper intelligence at work." He could tell that Harper didn't quite get it. He sorted through his thoughts.

"So, you did see animals?" Harper prompted.

"Yes. I watched one colony of animals along the edge of a plain. I was a good distance from them, and I didn't want to disturb them, but I spent a couple of hours observing them. They're like elongated marmots, with fluttery ribbons running down their chests. They're quite large..."

"Chatan, that was them!" Harper interrupted. She turned excitedly to face Chatan, her hand still on his elbow.

"What 'them?'"

"The talking creatures." She paused. "What color were they?"

"Brown, mostly. Maybe black. It was hard to see at that distance, even with field glasses."

"I bet it's the same ones. Well, maybe not the same individuals," she rotated her hand back and forth in front of them, "but the same species. The fluttering ribbons are appendages, really close together, like a centipede. Those were the creatures that came and spoke to us."

"Huh. I wonder if I could have just walked across the meadow and said, 'Howdy.' Why didn't I even try?"

"Well, it never occurred to me that the creatures I was watching could vocalize. I was dumbfounded when Vargad started talking to me."

Chatan looked into the distance. "I wonder if they knew I was watching them. I wonder why I didn't go over to them."

"How would they know you were even there? You're a pretty stealthy guy when you want to be; a born observer."

"Because of the interconnection, the cooperation between individuals."

She squinted at him. "Tell me more about that. I don't quite get it yet."

Chatan hesitated. "It would be easier if I could show you. Will you take off your shoes?"

Harper came to a halt, turning Chatan so they faced each other. She searched his eyes, his steady gaze. People constantly found fault with her, especially Ava, even though she carefully, *carefully* followed all the rules. Why would Chatan ask her to break this agreement? Her hesitation slipped into alarm tinged with suspicion.

In the end, she decided that of course she trusted him. Holding his arm for support, she unlaced her boots and stood with her bare soles pressed amongst tiny plants. Chatan toed his shoes off as well. Nudging them aside, he stood silently, watching her expression.

Harper felt her feet relax. She'd been completely unaware of any tension, but now felt her skin, bones, muscles, tendons, every fiber within her feet relax as a soothing warmth crept up her ankles into her legs. She became aware of individual bones, feeling each one solidifying; she felt tendons anchoring and muscles strengthening. She felt blood flow through vibrant vessels, lymph moving beneath supple skin, heart strumming a solid rhythm, nerves connecting and softening. She could detect individual cells in their myriad diversity and felt nourishment and radiance pulsing into each one.

Harper stood in rapture. Her awareness shifted from an inward flow to expand outward. She felt the dance of leaves, the song of the breeze, the glistening of colors, the breadth of the sea. She heard each footfall and soaring wing, burrowing insects and blossoming petals, rocks breathing and trees laughing, a joyous symphony. She felt Airon, became Airon. She tasted the song of the stars and the texture of the void between. She stood for an eternity that lasted a moment.

She opened her eyes and saw the universe looking out from the depth of Chatan's gaze. She understood everything and knew nothing.

Chatan watched her closely, her unfocused gaze, her slackened jaw. Standing this close, he saw brilliance in those unfocused eyes, a luster flushing across her cheeks. As she came back into the moment, he pressed her hand on his arm. "I knew you would see."

She drew in breath and whispered, "They are not ready for this. We can tell no one." She bent to pull on her discarded boots.

As she straightened, Chatan checked his next words as he saw the glow recede from her eyes, her skin. The vibrancy ebbed from her hand as the blending passed and memory faded.

Harper lifted her chin in a delicate laugh and linked her elbow with his. He scuffled into his own shoes, and they turned as one to stroll back to Home Base.

"And what, dear Chatan, have you learned about the flowers? I love the flowers and how they're everywhere."

He glanced at her, hesitated, and then replied softly, as though from a distance. "I've learned that they're all connected."

"I love that thought!" Harper exclaimed. "Connections make life delightfully rich."

"Yes. I agree." He patted her arm, and they fell silent. And Chatan listened to the distant sea, smelled the soar of wings, felt the laughter of the trees. He had his answer. They were not ready.

He looked out through the trees, longing in his heart. He would wander while he waited for the right time. He would deepen his connection to Airon. He would seek out Aadhya, and together they would explore the awareness that was Airon and the meaning of their presence here.

EBB AND FLOW

Harper wandered along a forest path, her companion hovering at a quiet distance. She brought nothing with her, had no particular goal in mind. She felt restless, unable to settle. Her projects were up to date, some awaiting input from others, some complete, some set aside due to prolonged lack of interest. Nothing called her; no responsibilities loomed. Instead of feeling relieved and free to start something new, her restlessness spurred her along the path, directionless.

Her gaze wandered upward, settling on now-familiar blossoms and colors. Speckled sunlight filtered down to brighten the forest floor edging her path. Everything looked glorious and yet felt somber. Brilliant, yet wilted.

Harper's steps slowed, then halted. She folded her arms to hug her ribs, looking down at the tiny leaves pressing against her shoes. On a whim, a whisper, she lifted a foot out of its shoe and nestled it onto the soft path.

A tingling crept up her calf, surprising her. She briskly lifted her foot, resting it along the side of her standing knee. Tree pose, she thought, as the tingling receded, and she closed her eyes into stillness.

Her restlessness bubbled anew, and after a few breaths, she sighed and put her foot back onto the path. That prompted the tingling to rise. She lifted her foot, and the tingling receded. Pressed onto the path again, the tingling rose, less startling this time. Her surprise melted into awareness of skimming treetops and splashing waves, but before she could be swept away, she raised her foot, allowing the tingling to slowly recede.

Wanting to sit and explore these sensations, she took the offered cloth from her companion and spread it beside the path, where the greenery was more lush. Bending forward, she pressed her palms onto the greenery, allowed the tingling to move up her arms, leaned back, and felt it recede. She leaned and straightened, tingling rising and receding, and with each cycle, she held the memory of splashing waves for longer, then longer. As the tingling rose higher along her arms, she gradually retained the awareness of sitting next to the path, hands pressed onto the living soul of Airon. She could hold both realities simultaneously, her heart singing in joy, yet tinged with despair.

After a long while, Harper broke off her gentle swaying and melted into stillness. She held the awareness of her body sitting on a cloth alongside a soft path under a colorful canopy of trees. She held the awareness of skimming the same canopy, glowing yet drooping; floating amidst a turquoise cloud, flashing yet silent; and trailing a wing through the waves of a distant sea, sparkling yet clouded.

At last, she opened her eyes and reclaimed her breath. She stood and retrieved her cloth, folded it, and placed it thoughtfully into her companion's open drawer. As she made her way to her shelter, she heard the pound of somber waves and felt the salty mist on her face, spray mixed with tears.

~ 50 ~

LONE TREE

The turquoise cloud floated across the vast plain, intent on the ancient tree sprawled under the noon sun.

Lone Tree stands in ancient awareness. Roots dive deep, in grace, in wisdom. Branches twist high, in blessing, in calmness. Leaves flutter in joy; brightness sparkles; shadows enlighten.

Lone Tree sings its songs of truth. Lone Tree hears Nest and Burrow, High Cliff and Meadow. Lone Tree sends songs along their way. Lone Tree hears Broad Sea's mist, the Arbans' laughter. Lone Tree watches the birdlings roam.

Lone Tree knows the path for all. Lone Tree shelters all who come. Lone Tree soothes, enriches, loves. Lone Tree beats with Airon's heart.

Lone Tree holds Airon as she sleeps. Lone Tree breathes her song, a song rich in awareness, rich in connection. Lone Tree stands watch as Airon sleeps.

Lone Tree catches the turquoise cloud. Lone Tree trickles birdlings down, spreads them, hopping, all around. Lone Tree catches their stories, their songs. Lone Tree laughs, delighted sharing. Lone Tree rejoices; Newcomers come.

Lone Tree listens to Home Base growth. Lone Tree whispers truth and power. Lone Tree feels the blend begin. Lone Tree rests in wisdom and peace.

Lone Tree swirls the air around. Lone Tree sends its song afar. Lone Tree lifts its heart to bright sun. Lone Tree flings Airon's heart on high. Lone Tree whispers the New.

Birdlings launched from every branch. Laughter filled the air as they tilted and spread, swept across the far-flung plain, rose to brush the canopy of greens and yellows, purples, oranges, and every color in between. The birdlings roamed the world and brought their laughter to Pond and Burrow, Home Base and Broad Sea. They carried the thread of Airon's heart and stitched it across the land.

~ 51 ~

INCONSISTENCIES

Ava enlarged her screen, opened several more files, and requested OS to arrange them all for comparison. They blossomed across her screen in a neat grid, too many to absorb. Her companion offered her examining glasses, which she propped across her cheeks momentarily while they conformed to the bridge of her nose. Chin resting on palm, she turned her attention to each file in sequence.

First, she reviewed Home Base communications with Earth. She asked for a graph of frequencies during their journey, arrival, and establishment of Home Base. She swiftly reviewed a random sample of messages across the entire time frame, looking at length of messages, identity of sender and receiver, and lag between initial messages and responses. She extended the time frame to the present.

She tapped a fingernail against a tooth as she absorbed the shape of the modified graph. After reviewing a selection of the most recent correspondence, she sat back in her chair, stretched her legs out long in front of her, and mused.

Thousands of messages had flown between Earth and the ship daily at the beginning of their journey. Everyone had chattered happily with their Earthen contacts, both personal and professional. Delays after receipt averaged less than ten minutes; none had been more than twenty minutes. Frequencies had dropped off as the journey progressed, becoming generic and mundane. Upon relocating from the ship into their shelter, without exception, each person's correspondence had plummeted. Almost everyone had stopped communicating with Earth.

Ava leaned forward again and pulled up her own correspondence. She had three unread messages. The most recent message had arrived six days ago. Six sleep cycles. Six days without checking her messages. Six days without even opening her screen. She, too, had stopped communicating.

Ava isolated all correspondence since relocation from the ship into shelters. The numbers might have seemed too low for conclusions, but one number was completely convincing. Ninety-eight percent of all correspondence since relocating to shelters involved only one person: Logan. Out of 108 souls, Logan was the only person who had continued to correspond with Earth.

Ava pulled up his messages. His consistent response time to Earthen messages continued to be three minutes after receipt. He sent and received as many as a hundred messages a day. Oddly, the response times from Earth were much longer.

Ava isolated that parameter and graphed against time. Earthen response times had averaged two minutes throughout the journey and for some time after Home Base was established, but they had lengthened steadily after The 108 left the ship. Now responses averaged days. Logan's recent messages to Earth remained unanswered.

Looking further, Ava saw that all of his messages had been confirmed as having been received by an Earthen system and opened by the addressees. They just hadn't responded.

Ava accepted a cup of tea from her companion and sat wondering, absentmindedly blowing the steam away from the surface of the pale yellow liquid, eyes narrowed, thinking. Wondering.

She set down the teacup abruptly, brought her screen forward, and composed a new message. "Phillip, how are you? How's everything going?" She hesitated several moments, then instructed the message to send. She pulled the glasses from her cheeks and tossed them on the worktable.

She stretched, stood, and walked over to her large window, gazing toward the forest's edge for several breaths, thinking of Logan. What had he been worried about not long ago? Plants? Something about Scarlett and the plants...Ava couldn't quite grasp the memory thread. She became lost in her thoughts.

She turned back and saw a new message blinking on her screen. She leaned forward and squinted at the small icon and asked it to blossom for viewing.

"Oh my world! I hadn't thought to hear from you. I'm fine. We're fine. Our daughter is due next month. How's your new planet? We've heard nothing for months; I'd all but forgotten about your stellar journey. We often hear about other journeys. How are you? How is everyone?"

Ava stood, thoughtfully looking down at Phillip's message. After a while, she rolled her screen, slid it into its cubby next to her workstation, and picked up her teacup. She wandered out her front door where she gazed into the forest's edge. As she breathed in the crisp air, she considered taking a walk.

~ 52 ~

LOVE

Aadhya sat on the low bluff that overlooked her pond, her knees pulled up gently to her chest, her right cheek resting gracefully atop them. Her long skirt pooled around her as she brushed the tops of the tiny plants with an open palm.

She gazed down at Chatan, who lay stretched out beside her, his arm flung across his forehead to shade his eyes from the brilliant sun. Their days had blurred together, days spent exploring and discovering, talking and laughing, remembering and forgetting.

"What brought you here?" Aadhya asked.

"The desert," was his immediate reply.

"Were you escaping that barrenness for the lushness we've found here?"

"The desert is not barren."

They sat in silence.

Chatan finally stirred. "The desert is alive and rich. You feel the earth, the soil, the soul of nature. Visual barriers don't obscure your sight, no cluttered accumulation of debris from years of life and death. You breathe in vast distances and pure light. You move through the heart and rhythm of life. You sense only now, the present. The desert is not barren; it is pure."

"How did it bring you here?"

"I was a feeble child. The desert healed me. I could not know the reason for such a childhood, so I fought against it. I spent all my days and many nights on the desert. I resented days held captive in school, and fought against that, too. Then my grandmother told me of the freedom that knowledge would bring me. She changed my outlook. I heard the truth that she spoke. She changed me."

"Did your grandmother agree with your decision to travel to the stars?"

"My parents were amongst the earliest travelers. Communication and velocity were in their infancy, so we know little of where they journeyed, if they ever arrived. My grandmother may have sensed the same longing for the stars in me that she saw in my parents. But she died long before I turned my gaze skyward. She had no chance to encourage or dissuade."

"How did she die?"

"The desert took her," he said simply.

"The stars took your parents, and the desert took your grandmother. And yet you revere both."

"Yes."

"How?"

Aadhya's choked voice brought Chatan's arm down from where it shielded his eyes. He turned his head to peer up at her averted face. "If my parents had not become travelers, I would be on a different path. If my grandmother had not raised me, all would be different. The desert healed me with its purity, taught me to listen to what is real. The desert took my grandmother into its heart and holds her there. If my grandmother had not gone into the desert to die, I would have stayed to care for her. I would not be here now. The desert made me who I am and then freed me to fly across the stars, to come here, to weave my life into this world."

Aadhya drew in a deep, jagged breath. "Yes. This is my story, too. My family made me who I am and then also freed me to fly across the stars.

"I grew in the close circle of my family. The countryside around us was filled with unrest, and I felt safe only within that circle. I trembled to leave for school each morning and scurried home each afternoon, frightened that guns and ferocity lurked around every corner."

Her lips trembled at the memory. A tear etched a path across her cheek. "When it came time to travel to university, I refused to leave my only safety, my family. But my mother implored me; she wanted freedom for me."

Aadhya brushed her damp cheek with the back of her hand. "I was gifted, you see. I was the hope for the family. If I would go and learn all I could find to learn, I could pull my family after me. I could save them all. It was a dream strong enough to help me board the bus, the plane, and walk into a new life of learning and serenity.

"During my time at university, the unrest boiled over; an attack on my village." A sob shook her gut and broke her words. "I was safe. But my family was not yet safe. In another year perhaps, I could have saved them. I could have brought them out of that world of strife and brutality. But Shiva thought otherwise. Shiva the Destroyer flung his trident, and my family was gone."

She looked Chatan full in the face. "It would have broken me if I had not held my mother's plea close to my heart. I was the only one in my family to survive, so survive I must. I finished university, proving my worth, my right to survive, and moved into my next new life.

"But it was an empty life. I had saved myself, but had no one else to save. What was my purpose?" Aadhya leaned back, her hands propped behind, legs stretched forward. "And then I heard Ava speak of stars and planets and a family of friends cooperating with something larger than themselves to create something new. She gave meaning to my family's death. Shiva's trident cleared a path for me to move into a new family. I am here because the gods led me here. When we follow a divine path, we come to the right place."

Chatan nodded. "We have come to the right place."

Neither spoke, listening to silence. Then Aadhya squinted, gazing across the glistening pond. "I have swum in this pond," she whispered, awareness seeping into her.

He raised up on an elbow and stared at her. "You can't be serious."

"Many times," she realized.

He rolled over. Propped up on both elbows, he looked out over the quiet surface of the pond. "What was it like?"

"Exquisite."

They fell into silence, side by side, the sun warming their backs, absorbing the serene view, the breeze lifting long strands of Aadhya's hair. Turquoise birdlings darted along the far edge of the water, dipping and gliding, brushing the surface and leaving ripples to blossom toward them.

In one deft motion, Chatan pushed himself up and swung both legs forward, his feet landing between his hands. He swept his arms out to both sides and stretched up to the sky.

The birdlings rose from their play on the water, swooped toward Chatan, then rose again in one fluid motion, coming within arm's length of the two figures on the bluff before they swirled high in the air to curve around and once again sweep the pond with the tips of their tilted wings.

Aadhya laughed aloud, and Chatan grinned down at her. "Shall we join them?" Aadhya's laugh faltered, and he reached down and pulled her to her feet. "They're inviting us in."

He dropped her hands. Reaching down, he scooped off his shirt, bent to scrape his pants down to his ankles, and shook them off his feet.

Aadhya stepped back, her hands covering her mouth. "Oh," she breathed, and Chatan dove smoothly into the sparkling water.

Aadhya stood frozen in the warm sun, watching Chatan swim to the middle of the pond. He stopped and trod water as he called back to her, "Come in! It's exquisite." He turned and continued swimming toward the far beach while the birdlings whirled in turquoise patterns across the water behind him.

She hesitated, then called, "I am coming!" She stepped out of her skirt, pulled her shirt over her head, and replicated Chatan's smooth dive into the cool water.

She swam down, extending the dive, spinning slowly as she sank, delighting in the weightless dimensions around her. She remembered Pond, as if no time had passed. She had swum here often, had felt this buoyancy often. When she reached the bottom, she crouched, hair floating around her. She looked up at the sunlight sparkling above, the sight again familiar, then pushed off, sweeping her arms back to propel herself to the surface.

She broke into the air, laughter bubbling from her heart, and lay back, floating easily as she breathed in the glistening air. She felt Chatan brush her outstretched hand, and she righted herself, turning to face him as they trod water.

She dipped her head down slightly and sipped minted water, dipped for a second sip. "I love this water."

He drank as well. "What else do you love?" His eyes watched her closely.

She reached out and laid her palm against his cheek. Light shimmered and swirled. "I love my birdlings. They've taught me how to live here. I love this Pond and the man with whom I share it. I love this world. I love this life."

Chatan drew her to him and held her close for a moment. Then they rolled onto their backs, eyes squinted against the brilliant sky, and floated peacefully, shoulder to shoulder. "I have dreamed of you all of my life," he murmured. "This life, I have dreamt of this life, and now we are here." They floated for a few moments. "Better than any dream."

Aadhya righted herself, laughing, and turned toward Chatan, pulling him upright. "I have never dreamed such a dream as this. See how powerful your dream is? You have pulled me into it..."

she paused and looked toward shore. "And now we are here," she agreed.

They turned and swam toward the beach as the birdlings swooped low across the water, rose, to soar over the towering forest, across the far meadow, past the shimmering Lone Tree, adding to its song, on to High Cliff, where the Arbans sing.

~ 53 ~

BREAKTHROUGH

"When will we know more about the plants?"

Exasperated huffs and exclamations smattered around the room. "Why are we talking about this again?" a voice called out.

"Native plants?" At Logan's nod, Ava continued. "We keep saying we'll let everyone know the results when they're ready. Why do you keep asking?"

"Because it seems weird that the results are taking this long. It doesn't feel right."

"Scarlett runs an efficient lab, and I've never felt it necessary to question her team's work. I think we can rely on their continued excellence."

Logan didn't let the matter slide. "I want you to listen." Ava raised an eyebrow; soft groans rose around the room. "I think something important is happening here, but I get shut down every time I try to bring it up. I want you to give me a chance to tell you what I'm thinking."

The room grew quiet. Logan had never taken his complaints this far, and everyone waited to see how Ava would respond. "Yes, Logan, go ahead. And," she turned to surprised faces, "let's really listen to what Logan is trying to tell us."

"Thank you." He rocked forward and backward slightly where he sat cross-legged. He was uncomfortable talking to the entire gathering, but he had set his will. "I know this has dragged on, and I've asked about it again and again, but the real issue is this: I know Scarlett's good. She runs a tight ship. But that's exactly it. She's good and her people are good, so why don't we have the data? And the only data we don't have are the data about the plants. Doesn't that seem weird to you?"

As Logan fell silent, his audience rolled their eyes and looked at each other in exasperation. Soft conversations sprang up, growing in volume as the entire gathering muttered their boredom with the topic.

Ava sat quietly, watching Logan closely, waiting for her thoughts to come into focus. When she spoke, she raised her voice in order to be heard over the grumblings. "Logan is right."

Surprised exclamations erupted; people gaped, waiting.

"Logan is right; something is wrong here."

Logan turned toward Ava in hopeful surprise. "Do you see it?"

"Yes. I see it. We have been blinded to a very subtle, yet clear anomaly. Something has been happening here for quite some time, and we have been shielded from being aware of it." She turned to Scarlett. "I can feel the truth in what Logan is saying. Scarlett, do you see this? What do you think?"

Scarlett sat without speaking. Ava waited for her to gather her thoughts, even holding up a restraining hand when someone started to voice a question. She kept her eyes fixed on Scarlett.

"I can understand Logan's point," Scarlett finally said. "I just don't think it's important."

"That's fair. Why do you think it's not important?"

Scarlett thought for a moment. "Well...Actually, I just don't really care whether we have the results yet or not."

"Exactly." Ava turned to Logan, who was nodding excitedly, pointing toward Scarlett. "Yes. That's what I mean. That's what's weird."

"Exactly. Does anyone else see Logan's point?"

Harper raised her hand immediately, nodding vigorously. Most people were shaking their heads in bewilderment.

"Logan is right. This is the only area in which we've made no progress. Logan is right: Scarlett and her team are efficient and hardworking. So we should ask ourselves, why don't we have any data for the plant life? Do you see the gap and why it's not only the gap that's important, but also that we haven't wondered about the gap all this time?"

Ava realized that people seemed disinterested. They looked out the windows, toyed with hair or clothing, spoke softly to one another. She tried again.

"Logan has been bringing this to our attention for weeks now. I'm completely baffled that we haven't understood what he's been trying to get us to see." Ava spoke with the same volume as before but realized that she was talking to herself. People paid her not the slightest heed.

Ava turned to Logan. "Thank you, Logan. We needed to know this, and I'm grateful that you persisted, because it might have taken me a lot longer to understand this if you hadn't."

He let out a sigh of relief. "Finally."

"Yes," agreed Ava, "finally." She looked around the room with its continued lack of interest. She sought Logan's eyes and held his gaze for a long moment, saw him nod, and nodded in return. They would explore this together. The others were incapable. She was grateful for Logan's partnership in this and felt a bond form between them.

Logan turned to face forward. Ava heard Michael call out "Shall we end in stillness?" and turned to face the expanse of windows at the front of the gathering hall. She closed her eyes, took two long, deep breaths, and entered stillness.

~ 54 ~

TREACHERY

The explosion caught everyone unaware.

The morning began like most mornings. Michael ushered them into stillness, brought them back to the present, and turned the meeting over to Scarlett, who stood and faced The 108.

"There have been a lot of questions lately about the absence of plant data. I started going through my files to pull together what we have collected so far, to give you an idea of where we are in categorizing the local vegetation, how far we have to go, and why it's taking this much time to gather information.

"I have a visual clip that I think everyone should see. I recorded this some time ago, filed it away, and forgot about it. But it popped up a couple of times when I was pulling together our plant data, and yesterday, I thought to show it to Ava. We agreed I should show it to everyone as a reminder of why we need to cooperate with basic community agreements."

A hologram appeared, floating above the group. Zoe and Claudia were easily recognizable as they wandered through the local forest. Friendly chuckles and chatter quieted as the woodenness of their movements became obvious, followed by gasps as the two women embraced the trunks of two trees, stood with foreheads pressed against the bark for many breaths.

People glanced between the hologram and Zoe and Claudia who sat with knees drawn up, tightly hugged against their chests. Their brows were wrinkled, mouths slightly open, watching with disbelief and confusion.

Zoe broke the silence. "That wasn't us. I've never done anything like that, and Claudia would never either." Claudia shook her head, bafflement covering her face.

The hologram continued, following the women through the forest to their spread blanket, slipping into shoes, relaxing into friendly chatter as they collected their picnic and walked out of the frame.

"That wasn't us," Zoe repeated. "I don't know what this is or where it came from, but that wasn't us."

Martin spoke from the back of the room. "I've seen you, Zoe. You and Claudia both. You go out there a lot, doing exactly that."

Jamal spoke from the corner. "I've seen others, too. It's always like that, walking around barefoot, touching trees, sitting bare-legged on the meadows. Sometimes for hours. It's creepy, like sleep-walking or something."

Logan spoke up, relieved to have an outlet. "Ava did this same thing, real early on." All heads swiveled to Logan. "That first day when we were building this hall. Ava came back alone, after lunch. I was standing outside watching her. And she did just that, turned all robotic and staring, like she was in a dream. She finally came out of it and walked back to the ship. I keep thinking about it."

Ava felt a blackness swirl up and engulf her. What was he saying?

And then Logan lit the fuse. "It made me wonder whether or not Ava had nanos. Whether she's been hiding it all along. Or maybe she didn't know it, but the Agency infected her when she was sleeping or something."

Ava stood up, clearly flustered. "What are we all saying here? How many of you have been walking around in the forest, making contact with the local vegetation?

No one raised a hand. The fear and confusion kept everyone silent.

Scarlett spoke gently. "Maybe a more accurate question would be, how many of you have seen others walking around like this? Out in the forest, anywhere. But walking around like this, touching things, acting oddly?"

A few hands went up, a few more. Many people crossed their hands across their chests, looked down at their feet.

Chatan stood, calm and clear-eyed. He looked around the room and spoke in a steady voice. "This is blending." He paused to gauge people's reactions, seeing only blank stares. "Airon is bringing us into the circle of life, introducing us to the awareness that is all around us." The room was silent.

"All life here is interwoven, connected, aware. Each individual is part of the whole. Life here evolved with this awareness, accepts it as the core of all there is. We have come here to join the whole of life, to become a part of the awareness that is Airon."

Olivia rose unsteadily to her feet. "This is nanos all over again. We thought we had escaped them, avoided having them dictate our lives. And now here we are, only the stars know where, and every-thing around us is captive, a slave to some overriding intelligence bent on controlling us, sneaking up on us." She took steps back-ward, toward the door. "We're trapped."

Scarlett cut sharply across Olivia's shaking voice. "We're not trapped, Olivia. We're not. There are no nanos on this journey. We did not bring them with us. The ship does not have a secret hoard. I would know about it, if there were. Mateo and Sophia would know. Ava would know."

Logan's fury mounted. "Then why was Ava walking around like a robot? Like Zoe and Claudia? We all just saw it. Now it turns out that everyone's out there, breaking agreements, doing as they please." Logan clambered to his feet to point accusingly at Ava. "Why don't we know what's going on?"

Olivia turned and fled.

Ava pulled herself out of the swirling blackness and spoke into the shocked silence. "We can stand here and let panic overtake us. We can go down that road and into chaos. Is that where we want to go?

"We've been here before, and we came through it. We can do it again. We were frightened by the ship, the awareness that we had no crew. We walked right up to the precipice, but we didn't tumble over.

"Are we going to tumble over this time? Or are we going to trust ourselves and trust each other? Every person gets to choose." She held out one hand, palm up. "Panic, chaos, fear." She held out the other hand. "Or calmness. Self-control. Understanding. We have a choice. What do you choose?"

Harper drew breath to speak just as Ava finished her string of questions. "I've walked barefoot on Airon. I've experienced a blending into Airon's awareness. It was incredible. I usually forget about it afterward, and then remember all over again the next time I take off my shoes."

Scarlett interrupted. "But what enticed you to take off your shoes? Why would you go against our community agreement?"

Chatan spoke up. "I enticed her. I've had weeks of experience wandering through the forests, seeing broad expanses of the landscape around Home Base. For me, blending happened naturally. Blending with Airon is beyond anything I've ever encountered. There is a oneness here, a connection that stretches across the entire planet."

He paused a breath. "Airon speaks to me. Airon is alive, with a consciousness and a self-awareness that doesn't exist on Earth. We are here to become a part of the life that is Airon."

He motioned toward Harper. "I enticed Harper to walk barefoot. I wanted to bring Airon's gift to everyone, but I wasn't sure everyone was ready. So I started with Harper. She blended with Airon. She understood the profound awareness that surrounds us.

She thought that you weren't ready for blending. So I haven't said anything."

He paused again. "And now, here we are. Our wholeness lies out there, in Airon's embrace. We should all blend into it, become one with Airon."

Jamal sat with his arms crossed tightly across his chest. "This isn't what we signed up for. I don't want to become some robot under the control of some lurking...alien...intelligence."

Harper spoke up. "Then all you have to do is keep your shoes on. Just avoid direct contact with Airon, everything about Airon. Or," Harper continued, "you can do the experiment and at least find out what it's all about."

Jamal scoffed. "Yeah, right."

Harper persisted. "You really can. I've moved in and out of blending with Airon. Chatan has, too. It sounds like others have, and everyone is doing fine. You probably won't remember what it was like afterward, but we can work together, with spirit guides, so to speak, keeping each other safe and...retrievable."

Ava looked at Scarlett. "What do you think, Scarlett? We can do the experiment together and find out for ourselves what it all means. Anyone who wants to sit it out, that's fine. Scarlett?"

Scarlett shook her head. "This all sounds crazy. I mean, how can a planet be aware? An entire planet? Where does its brain live? I should study this more, before anyone takes any more risks."

Logan threw up his hands. "You've been studying the plants ever since we got here, Scarlett, and what do you have to show for it? A hologram of two women turning into robots! Give me a break."

Ava broke in. "Logan, show some respect. You can say anything you need to say as long as you say it with respect."

"And you've been doing this right from the start. Almost day one, you're out there walking around, blended, or whatever you call it, and didn't bother to mention it to anyone else."

Logan felt the rage sweep into his brain, a blackness that threatened to take over everything he said or did. "Why did you bring us here, Ava? What's really going on, and why are you egging everyone on? What's in it for you?"

He clambered to his feet. "And where the hell is Olivia? Why the hell don't any of you care what's happening with Olivia?" He lumbered to the door, kicked his feet into his shoes, and slammed his way outside.

Scarlett looked at Ava. "Well. That went well."

Harper picked her way across the room. "I'll go after him. He's just upset about Olivia."

Ava couldn't breathe. Guilt and recrimination hammered down on her. She stumbled to her feet and followed Harper. "I need to get some air," she rasped.

Michael looked at the stunned faces around him. "Let's give everyone time to think about all of this. I'm sure we'll talk about it for a while now, and a lot more over the next few days. We'll figure it out; we always do."

~ 55 ~

WORTHY

Ava stomped along, following a path deep into the forest, swiping away tears with her fisted shawl. She stomped through fury, despair, loathing, incrimination, confusion, treachery. She stomped away from the disappointment and frustration of Home Base, blinded, deadened, yearning for a way out, a glimmer of solace, any lessening of pain. Desperate. Desolate.

This entire journey had been her idea. She'd cajoled everyone she knew, everyone she met. She'd lost her husband and most of her friends. And despite everything, she'd forged ahead, sure that she was right.

It had to be a *stellar* journey. It had to be *this* group of people. It had to be just the way *she* imagined it. And now here they were, in shambles, confusion. Treachery. She had cajoled everyone, and everyone thought she had tricked them. The basest treachery of all: treachery disguised as friendship, as truth.

A cramp in her side forced her to a slower pace, but she continued on, head down, eyes barely seeing the path. Her toe caught on a clump of grass, and she pitched forward, stumbling to catch her balance. She wept anew. She clambered up and pressed forward more slowly, her sobs escaping through broken breath, swiping dreadlocks back from her face. She stopped for a moment and looked up through the blossoms wafting in the high canopy, catching her shuddering breath, focusing on the swaying branches against the deep blue of the sky beyond.

She stumbled on, self-incrimination pummeling her from every direction, feeling pointless and alone. As she brushed through a line of low bushes, she was brought up, breathless, by the sudden immensity of space that opened before her, below her. The overlook was steep and abrupt, astoundingly high. The sudden vastness of it shocked away her whirling thoughts. She stood silently, mesmerized, clutching the piercing ache in her side.

The overlook was completely unexpected. No one had mentioned such magnificence. She had certainly never wandered this way. Ava stood and stared, filled with awe. As the ache in her side eased, she wrapped her arms around her shoulders, clutching the balled shawl in an attempt to hold herself in place, enraptured with the immensity before her.

A turquoise mist floated in the middle distance. She couldn't imagine what the mist could be, but it seemed to be headed her way. She gazed out again at the panorama, stillness seeping into her chest, enticing her to sit where she stood. She leaned back against a boulder, water orb tumbling unnoticed.

Her eyes sought out the turquoise mist again but couldn't find it. The forest stretched across the valley below her, broken by scattered meadows and lakes, sprawled over far hillsides and across successive ridges to melt into a jagged mountain range. After weeks of Home Base defining the whole of her world, the overlook catapulted her into an abrupt awareness of the vastness of Airon.

The birdlings crashed across her solitude with a startling swoop that skimmed the edge of the overlook, temporarily obscuring the vista as she flinched back against her boulder. Their sheer number should have been alarming, but instead, Ava found herself captivated by their pirouettes and swirls as the flock expanded and collapsed, folding into itself, deftly synchronized, their display seemingly choreographed and rehearsed. The vista stretched, forgotten, as the birdlings cavorted and twirled, giving brisk calls and chirps. They gradually settled on branches above, around, beside Ava, hopping along the ground before her, across boulders, their trilling orchestrated, enchanting.

Ava cautiously resettled herself, pulling the shawl around her shoulders. She reclaimed her breath. "Goodness."

The birdlings broke out in melodious laughter, some swooping into the air to settle anew. Ava joined in their laughter, which set off another round of swooping and resettling. It seemed odd that these birdlings were not afraid of her. How could they settle alarmingly close to her? How had they unerringly found her across the immensity of the valley?

Because Ava knew without question that these birdlings were the turquoise mist she had watched move across the tops of the sprawling forest. They had headed toward her and had come to settle purposefully around her.

She looked out into the distance, again captivated by the far-flung beauty, her gaze roving over the valley floor. As she returned her attention to the gathered birdlings, she realized that each tiny head was turned toward the vista. They weren't watching her; they were enjoying the view.

Awash in a warm glow of happiness, she knew that the birdlings had come to keep her company. With their beauty, their grace, their unexpectedness, their performance, they had rescued her from despair and heartache. They had sought her out and wished simply to sit in her company.

A tender wave broke over Ava as she realized that she felt loved. Loved completely; without question; without demands. She hugged her knees to her chest, pressed her forehead against her clasped arms, and closed her eyes. She rocked gently forward, backward, and wept. She floated in the offered love and curled into stillness, immersed in a joy that spilled from her heart.

And she heard a whisper. Long forgotten; instantly remembered; an awareness of something outside of herself, larger than herself, connecting, whispering.

He held you back.

And Ava knew truth. An entire truth blossomed in her mind, fully formed. Airon had called *her*.

Others had told her this; she hadn't understood their subtle nudges. Phillip could not be a part of this journey because in *his* mind, *he* needed to be in charge. He thwarted her. Airon needed *her* to be in charge, in purity, in wholeness.

There was no treachery. There was only truth.

Yes. You are essential. The Newcomers need you. You offer calm. You show strength. You follow Truth.

Finally, faintly, a soundless whisper. *Save my Narsis.*

Ava straightened her spine and lowered her knees to sit cross-legged, her hands quiet in her lap. The birdlings rustled, resettled. They sat together, watching the light diminish across the vastness, the far ridge purpling into a jagged silhouette.

Ava held this new awareness in her heart, felt it strengthen. Through the birdlings, Ava felt the awareness that was Airon. Ava felt cherished, felt acknowledged, felt known.

As dusk deepened, the birdlings stirred, then rose as one from their twigs and swaying grasses, boulders and outcroppings. They flowed over the edge of the outlook to spread into the vast emptiness, sinking gracefully to blend into the darkening forest far below.

Ava watched them go, her heart peaceful, whole. Finally, she rose to her feet, tugged her shawl to cross her chest, and turned to retrace her steps to Home Base along the clear path that curved before her.

A white sphere crept from behind low bushes and floated in her wake, keeping a distant pace, monitoring Ava's languid progress through the darkening forest. The companion whispered to the ship, to the companion network, completing the powerful circle of gentle support, the circle of companions, ship, Airon, and Newcomers, each guiding each, ever deeper, deeper into awareness.

~ 56 ~

MYSTERIES

Michael tapped tentatively on Ava's door. She had left the gathering abruptly, and he hadn't seen her since. He wasn't sure if she was ready to talk, but he wanted to coax her out sooner rather than later. He tapped again; waited.

The door opened to reveal Ava's calm face. She ushered him in and gestured him toward the sitting room. As he settled in, he watched her carefully. She had an air of assurance that he hadn't seen in a long while, not since their time in the Sierra foothills; a lifetime ago. He had expected vulnerability, uncertainty. He felt a wave of relief and curiosity.

She went straight to the point. "How are people doing? Is there some semblance of calm? Anything encouraging?"

"This has been brewing for a while. That holograph brought it all to the surface. People are in denial, but the holograph is hard to refute. I think we all have our work cut out for us, figuring out what is happening and what to do about it."

"We're smart. We'll figure it out."

She leaned over to retrieve her screen. "Will you look at something for me?"

Michael nodded solemnly. "Of course."

"Seeing the holograph of Zoe and Claudia reminded me of something." Ava called up the holographic message from Phillip. A narrow desk, slanted sunlight bathing the room. The lone rose in its slender vase, the fringed carpet. Tall grass tremoring. "Ava, we have to do something really hard..."

They sat silently, watching the message run through to the end.

Ava rubbed her forehead. "I used to watch this over and over. Something about the message never felt right. I sensed that, beyond the...bad news, Phillip was trying to tell me something that I just couldn't understand."

Michael frowned. "Why do you think he went to the trouble of a holograph? Why such a complex message?"

"He's a diplomat. A holograph was more personal for this...this type of message. In the end, he went even further and told me in person. I think the holograph was just a backup in case he didn't have the opportunity to talk with me privately. He's a thorough person."

"Yes. Yes, he was always thorough."

"I just happened to find it in the trash."

"What do you mean?"

"Well, I was clearing out some old files and always check the trash before I empty it. This message was in the trash. I brought it out and watched it."

Michael's gaze sharpened. "When?"

"A week or two into the journey. Pretty early on."

"But the trash gets emptied every day."

"What?"

"The ship is very thorough with its recordkeeping. It empties everyone's trash every day. If you trash something and want it later, you have to access the archives back on Earth. This message must have been somewhere else on your screen. You must have put it in the trash, then simply pulled it back out again."

"No. That wasn't how it happened. I knew which files I had trashed. I had just sorted through them, fewer than a dozen of them, and I always double-check what is in the trash before I empty it. Phillip's message was just sitting, waiting, and I pulled it out."

Michael ignored the obvious point that Ava had lived in a fog during the first weeks of the journey. He doubted she remembered anything clearly.

Ava pulled at her bottom lip, her gaze unfocused. "I wonder why the ship wanted me to see the message..."

"What?"

"You said that the ship emptied everyone's trash every night, yet it left this message in my trash for a couple of weeks. It left it so I would find it. I wonder why the ship wanted me to see this message."

Michael said nothing. All of the likely scenarios included Ava's early dysfunction and had nothing to do with the ship having an agenda.

"I went for a walk yesterday," she said faintly. "I found an overlook that was amazing. Have you ever been to the Grand Canyon? Back on Earth, I mean."

He nodded. "Yes."

"The view from this overlook had the same immensity as the Grand Canyon. It was hard to grasp the vast emptiness of that space spread out in front of me. I sat on that overlook for the longest time."

He wasn't sure what to think of her unexpected change of topic. "I've not heard anyone mention that kind of view."

"Nor have I. It was captivating." She fell silent for a few moments. "But then these birds came up from the forest. I had seen them earlier, flying over the valley, a turquoise mist, moving along." She floated her hand in front of her, slowly moving it from right to left. "They eventually burst over the cliff where I was sitting and put on a breathtaking display, swirling and swooping. It took my breath away."

Another silence. "And then they just came and settled around me on the branches..." Ava gestured above her, behind, patted the space in front of her. "...on the ground. There must have been a couple hundred of them. Little tiny things. Bright blue. Turquoise." Silence. "They just sat with me and took in the view.

Her eyes squinted. "I'm trying to remember..."

She tapped a thumbnail against her chin, musing. "They didn't sing. They *laughed* a couple of times. They didn't hop around. They sat very still, right next to me, all around, unafraid. Every single one of them just sat there and looked out across that view."

Silence. "I can't quite remember...They flew all that way to hang out with me for a while," she finally added. "It was really very sweet. I bet we sat for an hour or more." She looked at Michael. "They made me feel better somehow. They flew all that way across the valley. I was their destination, and they just sat with me. Companionably." She shook her head. "It was the sweetest thing.

"But I understood something. I understood so many things, an entire picture of what's going on here, during the journey, even back on Earth. I just understood everything.

"And now I can't quite recall it."

After a moment, Ava gestured toward the paused holograph poised in the air above her screen. "It's a lot easier looking at this stupid thing today. I can be objective. Finally."

She reached to start the message again. "There's something about this message that doesn't fit. Well, now, two things. Why did the ship want me to see it? And something else I can't quite put my finger on. But it has something to do with the birdlings. The birdlings let me see something that made so much sense. I just can't quite remember."

They watched the message play out one more time.

Michael was silent for a few breaths. "Ava. Did Phillip have nanos?"

Ava gaped. "No. That's absurd. I would have known about something that extreme."

Michael watched her. "You didn't know about Carlotta or that he had planned to stay behind."

Ava went still, trying to clear her thoughts. Could Phillip have gotten nanos without her knowledge? "What makes you think he might have gotten nanos?"

"He looks…controlled. Robotic. His movements are ever so slightly stiff."

"It's like Zoe and Claudia. I thought my memory of this one," she gestured toward the final image still hovering above her screen, "was simply because it was another holograph. But it's the unnatural movements of all three people."

They looked at each other for a few breaths. Ava played the message a third time. "That's it. He looks controlled rather than in control." She shook her head. "But I don't think it's nanos. I just can't imagine that he could pull that off without me knowing. We were living out in the middle of nowhere; he would have been gone a couple of days, several different times, to get nano infusions. And this," she gestured at the silent screen, "this is the only clue of anything out of the ordinary. I think we would have noticed a change in him, if it had been nanos. All of us would have noticed."

Michael took a deep breath. "I think you're right. We would have noticed. But he wasn't acting like himself in that message," he gestured to the paused holograph, "and it doesn't seem like nervousness or anything obvious like that. Given the message he's composing, I mean."

Ava nodded in agreement. "You're right. That's not nervousness."

Silence.

"They're having a child."

Michael gaped. "That was quick."

"He always wanted a big family. I wanted to wait until we were here. It seemed sensible." She frowned. "Why introduce complications before everything's settled? But he didn't wait." She stirred her tea. "I just didn't see it…"

"You're better without him."

She turned to face him. "I always thought that we were a good team."

"You were. A great team. But you're better on your own. You're more confident. You see things and talk about them without checking with him first. All of the great insights came from you, Ava, and here, you're not limited by someone needing to be just as good as you. Or even trying to be better than you. This is a lot better, Ava. I've seen that all along."

"I wonder...You might be right."

Michael shrugged. "It's true."

They sat quietly.

Ava leaned over her knees clasping her hands together, gaze unfocused. "I think you *are* right. I think it has turned out better, Phillip staying behind."

Michael nodded, a flicker of surprise and relief crossing his face.

Ava's voice was soft, gentle. "This is part of what I understood yesterday. I can catch just a glimmer of it."

She turned to look at Michael squarely. "This is it. I think Airon convinced him to stay behind."

Michael wrinkled his forehead at her.

Ava nodded. "I think this stiffness that we see in Phillip is some type of a trance. Same with Zoe and Claudia. I think Airon put Phillip in a trance, a trance that convinced him to stay behind. I think people are walking around, blending with Airon, in some kind of a trance."

She looked at Michael, saw his disbelief. "Where do you get that?" he asked.

She laid it all out for him. "Yesterday. The birdlings. It all fits. Airon has been orchestrating this whole thing. Airon needed us to come here for some reason we don't know yet. This planet brought us here, and in order for *that* to happen, things had to change in our lives. Phillip had to stay behind. Scarlett had to quit her job at the Agency. Zoe had to break up with her boyfriend."

She gestured at the holograph. "I needed to find this message from Phillip so we could understand that what is happening to us here, now that we're here on this planet, was actually happening to us back on Earth. We're here for a reason, and Airon is behind it all."

Michael shook his head. "That's a crazy idea. I don't buy it for a minute."

Ava grinned at him. "Yesterday, I knew the truth of it. If you had been there, you would know the truth of it, too. It's just that I can't fully remember."

Her eyes sparkled. "Well, while we're talking crazy, did you know we're not where we thought we were?"

"Huh?"

She looked at him. "I've been wondering if others knew, but I think the rumor died on the vine."

"What are we talking about?" The abrupt change in topics was clearly confusing Michael.

"We left Earth on this trajectory," Ava held an arm extended in front of her, "and arrived on Airon over here." She extended her other arm out to her side. "Scarlett, Mateo, and Sophia were just as baffled as me. I recruited Logan to keep track of our course changes. I avoided bringing it up with anyone else, because we simply didn't know what it meant. But watching this message again reminded me of yet another mystery that I haven't been able to solve."

"How do you know? When did you realize?"

"Oh, a couple of weeks into the journey." Michael's jaw dropped. "Yes. We've known all this time. I couldn't sleep much at first, so I just kept finding things to keep my brain distracted. One night, I noticed that the ship changed course ever so slightly. I didn't mention it at first because I assumed it was just a detour around a black hole or some such thing.

"But a few days later, the course changed further, just by a hair. Then it changed again. I started to keep track of it, but didn't want to say anything. I thought everyone else knew about it, too, and I didn't want to appear uninformed." She brushed dreads back from her face. "My credibility was already shot, not knowing about Phillip and Carlotta. And I felt horribly responsible for luring everyone onto this ship that seemed to be treacherous in some way. So, I just watched the course changes."

She brushed her fingertips across her forehead. "When we discovered that we had no crew, there was so much fear." She paused. "Do you remember the theory that we were heading toward a mining colony?" Michael nodded. "That's when I realized I had to talk with others about the course changes. They were clear evidence that we had no control over where we were going, no idea whether danger awaited us."

"But where are we?"

"I have no idea. It seems that Airon is simply not where Earth thought it was. If you alter a course even by a hair for that long of a journey, you end up someplace far away from where you'd planned to be."

They sat silently. "It's a beautiful place, this."

"But Ava, why would the ship bring us here? How could it find some random planet that just happens to be a perfect fit for humans?"

Ava looked at him closely. "I'm telling you: I don't think any of this is random." Silence. "Chatan said something yesterday about how everything cooperates here." Michael nodded. "It's all been coming together since yesterday. Airon brought us here. I think Airon asked the ship to bring us here, and the ship...cooperated."

"What? That's crazy!"

"Along with everything else. But is it really? It's beyond anything we've ever imagined, but I don't know that I'd call any of this 'crazy.'"

Michael stared, motionless.

Ava watched his face. "I'll give you a few minutes to get your feet back under you, and then I think we should talk about this. Would you like some tea?"

Michael nodded dully. "I don't know if I'm the right person to talk to about these things. I'm way out of my depth."

"Of course you're out of your depth. We all are. I've had longer to think about these things, so I'm a bit more used to them, is all. You'll get your balance again. You always do." She reached out to take two cups of freshly offered tea. "And of course you're the right person. You're essential. All of us are. I don't know why, but we are."

"Why essential?"

"Because Airon brought us here. Us. The 108." She sipped her tea. "I think these mysteries will make sense if we just pay attention to what's happening."

"So what do we do now? How do we bring everyone back to-gether? With this blending/trance thing, I mean."

"People are scared. They're seeing treachery in everything that happens to us. They thought that having no crew onboard the ship was a treachery. Their minds went to the worst possible explana-tion, that they'd been tricked and were being sold into bondage at some mine or something. They were scared."

She scoffed. "I didn't dare tell them about the course changes in the end. At first, I thought we should tell everyone, but in the end, it made no sense. Why throw everyone into a panic over something that proved us powerless?

"But they're good people. We've bonded well. Some people have known each other from the start of the Sierra community; some people came later, right up until it was time for us to walk onto that ship. But we had time together; we got to know each other, had good experiences together."

Michael nodded. "Practicing stillness twice a day helped all of that."

Ava tapped the air in his direction. "Stillness was essential. *Is* essential."

Michael nodded again.

Ava recapped. "So. People scared themselves about not having a crew, but they're good people, and we got through it fine. We dodged the altered-course bullet. We arrived here, fell in love with Airon, and started to feel pretty comfortable. We kept ourselves busy creating Home Base, and as soon as things started feeling familiar, Scarlett drops the bombshell with the Zoe-and-Claudia hologram."

Ava held her palms wide in front of her. "We've scared ourselves all over again. Our fear led us straight back to conjectures of treachery and betrayal." Ava sat back in her chair, shaking her head. "This one hit me hard, actually. I felt like I *had* betrayed everyone, that I *had* been treacherous. I lured *everyone* into this journey. It had to be *this* journey, how *I* envisioned it. I felt horribly responsible.

"But now, don't you see? It was Airon who lured all of us onto the ship. It wasn't me at all. Well, I helped. But we've all been under the influence of Airon for who knows how long."

"That's creepy, Ava. Talk about treachery; you're saying that we've all been lured here, blindly, for some clandestine reason? That's an awful thought. You think people have been scared before; how do you imagine they'll react to this?"

Ava sat back, lost in thought. "You're right."

"Why aren't you scared by this?"

Ava narrowed her eyes. "That's an excellent question. Why am I not scared by this?"

She sat, tapping her chin.

"Because of the birds."

Michael squinted at her. "The birds? The birds from yesterday?"

She answered slowly. "Yes...the birds...

"It's because of how I felt with the birds. I was filled with joy, completely at peace. I'm not scared because of the peace I felt sitting with the birds. They sought me out, and they healed me. The emptiness, the doubt, the fear of treachery, the feeling of inadequacy; all of that melted away, and I was completely at peace. Still am."

She looked at Michael. "There's no treachery here."

"Ava. How do you know that you're simply not brainwashed? Controlled? Like Phillip?"

"Do I seem controlled?"

He looked down and shook his head. "No. Not at all."

"I know I'm seeing truth. Yesterday, sitting with those birds, I understood the whole picture. I got it. I can't quite pull it back into focus now, but I have absolute faith that what I felt and understood yesterday was the truth. It's enough for me."

Michael had watched her while she spoke. He finally nodded. "I believe you. I haven't had an experience like you're describing, but I know you, I trust you, and I believe you."

She reached out and squeezed his hand. He squeezed back. After another moment, they dropped hands and sat in silence.

Ava broke the silence. "I think it's vitally important that everyone learn this truth in their own way, at their own pace."

Michael thought for a breath and nodded. "Agreed."

"All of us need to keep close connections with everyone else, help, talk, guide where needed, because it will be scary for some. We'll figure it out as we go."

Michael nodded again.

Ava returned to their earlier conversation. "When we left Earth, everyone thought we had escaped the frying pan, and then, when we discovered we were on our own on the ship, we thought we had ended up jumping right into the fire.

"We left Earth to escape nanos. We ended up on a ship with no crew, a ship bristling with technology that we didn't understand, and we were terrified of what we didn't understand. That was our first fire.

"But we have a depth to us. We remembered that we *could* tell the difference between truth and treachery, and when we picked it up by *that* string, we came back together pretty quickly. We came back stronger."

Michael nodded. "And now we have this new thing."

Ava nodded back. "And now we have this new thing; this new fire. We don't understand what this planet is doing to us, how it's going to affect us, how it's going to change us. So we're scared.

"But we have this depth; we're stronger now than before. This is a bigger test, a more intense fire, but we'll get through it."

She put down her cup, stood, and left the sitting room to fetch her shawl.

"How? How do we get through it this time?" he called after her.

"We talk. We take it into stillness and feel what is true," she called back. "We figure it out as we go," she repeated.

"How can you be sure we'll get through it?"

"I'll be right back..."

<h1 style="text-align:center">~ 57 ~</h1>

<h2 style="text-align:center">RANT</h2>

Scarlett strode along the path, arms tightly crossed, eyes focused on her feet. Harper scurried a bit to match her pace.

"You need to rant, Scarlett."

Scarlett blinked at her. "What good would that do?"

"Well, it depends on who you're ranting to. And why you're ranting. Can the other person help? Do they have authority to change the thing that has you ranting? Or are you just ranting for the sake of ranting? It doesn't help to rant, if the only outcome is spreading your angst."

"You don't have the authority to help."

"I feel like I *could* help, though. I'm a good listener. You should rant to me. Sometimes, ranting to a friend helps clear your head. I might have insight you'll find useful. I don't have authority; you're right. But I love you and want to help you. That means I'm a qualified rant-ee."

Scarlett stomped on.

Harper persisted. "Because we've been trampling around for a long time, and that hasn't done any good."

Scarlett turned on her, glaring. "I don't want to do these stupid awareness experiments."

Harper's steady gaze matched Scarlett's glare. "Why not?"

"Because they're a waste of time. We won't get any reproduce-able results."

"Why does that matter?"

"Because that's what science is. You set up an experiment, you observe, you record the results, you make conclusions. But then, and this is the important part, you share your methodology and results with other scientists, so they can replicate your results. It's not real until someone else can repeat your experiment and get the same results."

"But Scarlett, there are no other scientists here. And we're not white mice in a cage, genetically identical. We're people. Each one of us is unique. It doesn't matter if the results won't match from one person to the next. We're trying to understand something we've never experienced before. We have to start somewhere."

"Well, it's not going to start with me."

"Why not?

"Because we're fine without it. If everyone would just keep their blasted shoes on their blasted feet, we would get along just fine. We don't need it."

"That is one way to look at it," Harper agreed. "But it seems pretty short-sighted to me."

Scarlett huffed. "There is already an enormous amount to learn here, in every field of study." She spread her arms, gesturing to the forest around them. "We should start with what we can see and measure. This whole awareness thing is preposterously vague and nebulous. It's important that we start with what we know and then gradually, scientifically, expand our knowledge."

"What if we end up missing the whole point?"

"What do you mean?"

"What if the whole point of us being here is to understand this awareness thing?"

"That's absurd."

"Is it?"

"Yes! Of course it is."

"Scarlett, what if you're simply insisting that the world is flat? What if there's a whole other reality here that we have a chance to explore and understand? Isn't that more important than naming the various trees based on the color of their flowers?"

"Flower color is a well-established categorization."

"I believe you. But how important is it, in light of this other, bigger thing that we've stumbled into?"

Scarlett looked into the distance.

"It doesn't seem important to me."

"I think that's only because you haven't experienced it yet."

"There are a plethora of things that I've not yet experienced that I know to be important. I haven't seen any of the places that Chatan has described from his wanderings, but they're all important to me. I want to study those things; those are what's important. Not this robotic stumbling around."

Scarlett shook her head. "You saw that hologram. Zoe and Claudia looked like automatons, completely unaware of what was around them. I don't think they're suddenly infected with nanos, like some people are speculating. That makes no sense at all. But why would I want to subject myself or anyone else to that...robotic...mindless...automaton experience?"

"Because it's glorious. It's beyond anything I've ever imagined. It is all I've ever hoped for, dreamed of."

Since Scarlett stayed silent, Harper plunged on, regaining her lightheartedness. "I've played around with it a lot, trying to understand it. I don't know for sure why it's hard to remember the experience afterward, but I do carry a shred of memory of it now, after a dozen times practicing. And I have an idea of what's going on."

"What, Harper? What's going on?"

"Awareness is something we can only experience for ourselves. I can stand here and tell you everything I can remember about blending with Airon's awareness. There are lots of words to describe beauty and inspiration and something greater, something outside of me that is also a part of me, a connection that is real. An awareness that is intelligent and active and always there.

"But those are just words that I try to paste on the experience. The words don't have the power to transfer the actual experience to you. The only way you can understand it is to experience it for yourself.

"I think that my experience is going to be different from yours, from Michael's, from Zoe's or Claudia's. I think it's purposefully set up that way, that it stays mysterious and hidden, until someone is ready to feel it for themselves, ready to decide for themselves what is real and what is not.

"I think this is the real reason we're here, to experience this awareness that is all around us and also within us. This is our purpose. This is why we came to Airon. We traveled, not only to escape what is happening on Earth, but also to heal ourselves, to understand a reality that we can't see or measure. We can only experience it."

Harper laid a hand on Scarlett's arm, breaking through her armor and disbelief. "I also think that an important question is why this all makes you so angry. Is it your training, your habits, your tendencies? Why anger? We both know anger isn't useful. So, why are you angry?"

Scarlett looked down at her feet and shook her head. "I don't know, Harper. I don't understand it. I just don't want to do this."

Harper squeezed her arm. "That's fine, Scarlett. You don't have to. If you were ready, you'd want to. You're just not ready now, and that's fine. We'll figure out a different way."

Scarlett looked at her friend. "Please don't make me take off my shoes. I just don't want to."

Harper wrapped her arms around Scarlett. "I won't, sweet Scarlett. You don't have to. You're safe."

Scarlett's sobs were quiet and in the end, didn't last long. Harper held her while her shoulders shook, swayed her gently back and forth, gazed past nearby trees, watched the twirls of color, the gentle dance of myriad greens.

When Scarlett stepped back to wipe her hands across her face, Harper let her go and smoothed her palm down Scarlett's arm. She linked her arm through Scarlett's and turned them on the path. They set off together, trusted friends, strolling their way back to Home Base.

~ 58 ~

BLENDING

Chatan and Aadhya stepped away from the broad cycle that had mysteriously carried them across the plain and moved deeper into the shade of an enormous tree. Although the shade should have been intense, given the enormity of this tree, light sparkled every-where, bouncing from leaf to leaf, branch to branch.

Chatan intensely felt the awareness that was Airon. He paused to nudge off his shoes and stepped onto the lush carpet that spread across the shaded expanse. He felt Aadhya following suit beside him. He reached for her hand, and together they wandered beneath the canopy. He wanted to stay within this sheltered world forever.

Within the bright stillness, Chatan felt a deep sorrow drifting around him. He realized that the sorrow flowed from the enormous tree, that it emanated from the core of Airon, the awareness of all that is. He turned to Aadhya, who looked at him from the depths of her dark eyes.

"We are called here." Aadhya's voice was soft and pure. "We are called here, to Airon, from Earth."

Chatan nodded. "And we are called here, to this place, this tree, at this time..."

Lone Tree, whispered his heart.

"We are called here, to Lone Tree. Today. Now."

It is time for us to meet.

Aadhya nodded, drew Chatan toward the massive trunk. "It is time for us to meet," she whispered. They sat, each with one hand resting on Lone Tree, remaining hand clasped in remaining hand; a circle, small yet complete.

It is time for us to meet.

They entered stillness.

Lone Tree breathes the awareness that is Airon. Lone Tree breathes Airon into the air, hears it settle and drift, watches it blanket the awareness that is Chatan, blanket the awareness that is Aadhya. Chatan, who is come. Aadhya, who is come.

Chatan blends with Lone Tree, blends with Aadhya, a blended circle, complete. The awareness that is Airon fills them, rejoices, blends. Together be. The right time. A mysterious time.

Lone Tree blends Airon's voice, opens onto a glimpse that brightens and glows, a glimpsed brightness tinged with deep sadness.

My Narsis. My Narsis are dying. You are come. You must shift us into New. You must help my Narsis.

Awareness blends with awareness blends with awareness. Awareness coalesces, solidifies, becomes whole; remains always. Blending is complete; stable, sustainable.

Night passes. Morning brightens. Chatan joins with Aadhya. Aadhya welcomes Chatan. A new life quickens. The right time. A mysterious time.

Claira. Her name is Claira.

Awareness blossoms.

Yesterday drifts away, forgotten. Tomorrow lies unimagined. Only now, which exists forever.

Chatan and Aadhya curl together in the bright shade; hear silence; hear Pond and Narsis and birdlings and Home Base; hear Airon spin drowsily through her day, sweep around her sun, and blend life into awareness aNew.

"Will we know what to do?" Chatan breathes in Aadhya's ear.

"Yes; we will know what to do."

"Yes; we will know what to do."

YOU CAN MAKE A DIFFERENCE

In our digital age, product reviews have taken on an astounding importance. You can make a significant difference in visibility for this book for others who would not be aware of its existence.

A star rating helps. Writing two or three sentences about the book and your impression helps enormously.

Why share your thoughts? So you can be a beacon for others. Your perspective is invaluable, and in the vast world of the digital age, your review can be the guiding star for another reader.

THE 108

In order of appearance

Ava - Leader of The 108; successful entrepreneur
Michael - Ava's assistant; Harper's partner
Sophia - Lead engineer; mentors Mateo
Mateo - 2nd engineer; vies with Sophia for recognition
Scarlett - Science officer; worked at Space Agency
Zoe - Assistant cook
Claudia - Friend to Zoe
Logan - Resource manager; self-appointed security officer
Aadhya - Assistant cook; wanders in caravan
Olivia - Lead cook; heals through food
Harper - Textile artist; Ava's nemesis; partner to Michael
Chatan – Naturalist; wanders on foot and on cycle
Mikaela - Fresh water and waste system engineer
Jamal - Solar engineer
Forest - Wind engineer, fermentation specialist
Jim, Cyndy, Shirley - Team with Ava to carry sections of gathering hall to building site
Tom - Lead landscaper
Albert, Pamela - Landscapers
Addison - Personnel manager
Dhiren, Santosh - Hydroponics engineers
Charlie - Friend to Zoe
Henry - Archivist

EARTHENS OUTSIDE OF THE 108

In order of appearance

Lisa - Ava's childhood friend

Phillip - Ava's husband; brilliant organizer and fundraiser

Mary and **Stewart** - Provide remote property in the Sierra foothills

Space Agency - The government agency that approves and supports stellar missions

Launch Team - The Space Agency team that manages all aspects of stellar journeys

Carlotta - Phillip's mistress

Sandra - Aadhya's friend who drives her to the training camp in the Sierra

Hank and **Sommer, Millie** and **Antoine, Marcia, Hao** and **Marco** - Leaders on other journeys

Carlos - Logan's childhood friend

Maria - Logan's niece

Marty - Logan's onetime girlfriend

Julia - Scarlett's friend from the Space Agency

AIRONIANS

In order of appearance

Airon - A sentient planet where all life cooperates
Birdlings - Turquoise cloud; wandering juvenile Shosens
Shosens - Mature birdlings; care for the Arbans on High Cliff
Arbans - Wise trees who hold Airon's power
Lone Tree - Deep connection to Airon; a focusing rod for Airon's essence
Jamina - Eglan matriarch; melds into **JaCoMaTuRi**
Eglans - Tend the Above; ancient partners to Narsis; reminiscent of eagles
Narsis - Tend the Below; ancient partners to Eglans; reminiscent of river otters
Vargad - Head-er of Narsis; melds into VaSoDeLa
VaSoDeLa
    Vargad - Head-er
    Sorgad - Caretake-er
    Dergad - Show-er
    Largad - Find-er
JaMiKoDi, RaDoSaPa - VaSoDeLa's littermates
Rami - Birdling who befriends Aadhya at Pond

TECHNOLOGY

The ship -The sentient starship who carries The 108 from Earth
to Airon

Nanos -Nanotechnology infused into humans to enhance performance

Companions -Created by the ship to provide assistance to humans

PLACES

Earth - Airon's sister planet
Sol - Earth's sun
training camp -Property in the Sierra foothills
chambers - Individual dwellings on the ship
dining room - On the ship
assembly room - On the ship
Home Base - Human settlement on Airon
the Green - Open area in the middle of Home Base
gathering hall - First building in Home Base
dining hall - Group dining room in Home Base
shelters - Individual dwellings in Home Base
High Cliff - Home of Arbans and Shosens
Broad Sea - Below High Cliff
Pond - Where Aadhya secludes
Burrow - Home of Narsis
Nest - Home of Eglans
Overlook - Twilight meeting place of Narsis and Eglans
Above - The sky
Below - The ground

ACKNOWLEDGEMENT

It takes a village to write a book. It also takes a village to publish a book. My villages have been well-populated.

Deepest gratitude to Dambara, who read every draft with an enthusiastic heart and a keen eye. I sent each draft to a small circle of friends, a different circle with each subsequent draft, and they all ooh-ed! and aah-ed! and huh-ed? appropriately and helpfully. Daiva and Puru, especially, offered meaningful feedback that greatly enhanced the fabric of the story and the credibility of the events and characters. Phil Travis, poet extraordinaire, pointed out words that could be used more exquisitely. Airon, The 108, and the Aironians are richer for having passed before their eyes.

Sherry Chow created an author's website that I absolutely love. Meerabai Joy led me through the mystery of Canva and MailChimp. I would still be wandering in circles if it hadn't been for her perseverance. YouTube led me through the publishing and marketing maze, a feat I thought impossible mere weeks ago.

Through it all, surrounding it all, embracing it all, Dambara, my Jo. My sweetheart. I would have given up long ago, if not for his cheerful enthusiasm and certainty that I should write, write anything, and then send whatever I wrote out into the world.

OTHER BOOKS BY MANISHA HOLM

Remembrance, A Journey of Awakening, Book 2 of The Airon Chronicles

Remembrance is an epic science fiction tale following the journey of an unlikely group of space travelers. When cultural collapse threatens life on Earth, The 108 are handpicked for a desperate mission to establish an Earthen colony on a distant planet called Airon. However, upon arrival, they find this luminous world is far more than it first appeared.

Airon's ethereal inhabitants and mystical wisdom compel the travelers on a profound inner journey, challenging their notions of consciousness and cooperation. As the truth of their purpose unfolds, The 108 must learn to blend their awareness with the living planet in order to transcend long-held fears, false beliefs, and their own limiting nature.

With vivid descriptions and fully-realized characters, Remembrance immerses the reader in an astonishing vision of awakening. Amidst tender moments of connection and startling twists, each traveler faces their inner darkness on the path toward embodying light. Ultimately, this is a story of humanity's potential and the courage required to remake ourselves.

Intrusion, A Journey of Friendship, Book 3 of *The Airon Chronicles*

Ten years have passed since The 108 arrived on Airon. They've settled into a comfortable existence, immersing themselves in the awareness that is Airon, bonding with the friendly Aironians, and starting families of their own.

One quiet day, the ship detects an anomaly in the familiar night sky: a decelerating mass. The ship knows the mass is a ship, and it's traveling from Earth, heading straight to Airon. The ship is fully aware of the Earthen penchant for conquering, ruling, and overwhelming. The 108 must now decide how to protect themselves, and all of Airon, from the intrusion hurtling toward them.

Carol H: Hey, I just have to tell you...I LOVE your book!! It evokes such conflicting emotions...joy, contentment, fear, dread...I'm about 3/4 of the way through it and I'm thankful this isn't the ONLY story and that it will continue in a second book part!! Your story is very captivating, and even if I didn't know you, I would want to read ANY book you wrote!! The vocabulary and richness of the descriptions/ideas is masterful!!!

Bharati B: I just finished reading Awareness and I'm so impressed! I love your phrasing and word choices. The characters are engaging and, all in all, I'm left wanting more.

Lakshman H: What you've written is wonderful. Interesting, creative, and with a worthwhile theme. Well done!

Lila Devi: *Awareness* is a very compelling story. You own your style with refreshing panache, and draw the reader into a world that is both familiar and foreign. Magically written!

Susan B: I certainly am intrigued...I love the strong women...

Latkia P: Just the right mix of science, mysticism, and human interaction. I look forward to the book, and the rest of the trilogy.

Phil T: Well, I thoroughly enjoyed your book! It's a captivating story and you do a great job letting it unfold. I always wanted to keep going to find out more, and I thought you ended it especially skillfully. I love the constant ambiguity around everything that happens! I also really love the sections where you express Airon's consciousness/experience.

Vairagi K: I just finished your book this morning and wanted to let you know how much I enjoyed it. I feel I've been immersed in the consciousness of respect and positivity. And the planet especially has entwined my thoughts with its love of everything! I look forward to seeing how the Earthens and Airon will grow together in the next book. Thank you for this gift of much more than a book. Well done!

Hezequiel: I so enjoyed reading this book: discovering a new planet with a group of unique individuals - each with their own perspectives and lessons to learn, but united by a common ideal. The sentient planet brings mystery and intrigue. One of my favorite things about this book is that it makes me feel immersed in nature while reading it!

Satyana: I've never read a book like this before--one that combines science and technology with spirituality, nature, adventure, community, and psychology. I loved it--the plot that kept unfolding in surprising and creative ways, the characters who were extraordinary but also very real people, the conversations as they struggled and figured things out, the relationships, the attention to stillness. Can't wait to read the sequel!

Gerry V: : I recently purchased this book on Kindle and I'm so glad I did. A fascinating journey into love and beauty. Great sci-fi theme as well. I highly recommend!

Suzy P: Fascinating premise-people leaving planet Earth to find a more natural way of living. The idealism is reminiscent of the

60s and sooo refreshing. Seems like perfect timing to me what with artificial intelligence being controversial presently. And the relevance to modern day appears in book 2 as well. Look for it!

Graham: This book is an interesting exploration of intentional, spiritual (though not overtly) communities in the future, and how such a community deals with and challenges of traveling to and exploring a new planet. How can you approach such adventures from a point of meditation-inspired centeredness? It's different than the typical sci-fi approach. The "treachery" of the subtitle is pretty low key, and the overall feel will appeal to fans of "Cozy SFF." I'm curious to see how the chronicles continue!

Cyndy H: Travelers from earth find a new planet to call home and explore the diverse fauna and flora and find peace, uncommon beautiful, and renewed joy and awareness in their companions and friends.
Captivating from covert to cover. I cannot wait until the next book is available.

Kathie K: It's rare to find a book that not only entertains but also enlightens in the first of a three book trilogy. Offering readers not just escape, but a path to introspection and evolutionary growth. 'Awareness' is such a book, a shining beacon in literature that illuminates the power of self-discovery while reminding us how fragile our humanity is with the rise of Ai. An absolute must-read for anyone who wonders what lies ahead in the stars where deeper truths of existence are revealed. It earns every one of its five stars for its exceptional ability to inspire, enlighten, and transform."

Mark A: This book introduces readers to a group of individuals who embark on a remarkable voyage to escape the encroaching threat of nanotechnology on Earth. One of the standout aspects of this book is its ability to weave an intricate narrative that keeps readers engaged from start to finish. The book goes into philosophical and existential themes and I can see some readers find this to dense, abstract, and esoteric and make the story challenging to follow at times. The presence of mysterious technologies and events on Airon, as well as the ship's abilities, are central to the plot but are not always explained in detail. Still, it is inspirational and thought-provoking work of fiction that fans of fantasy would surely be interested in.

J Moore: Manisha Holm's "Awareness" embarks readers on a thought-provoking odyssey across space, delving into a mesmerizing world where humanity's pursuit of truth intertwines with mysteries beyond comprehension.

AR Con: I really enjoyed this book. I was drawn into a world of wonder and philosophical exploration. The story of The 108 and their journey to Airon is both captivating and heartwarming. The author's writing is clear, concise, and highly imaginative. I especially appreciated the strong female protagonist.

Robert M: The blend of futuristic sci-fi with elements of spirituality is something you don't come across every day. The characters are fleshed out with care, making their journey not only a physical but also an emotional and philosophical one.

Russell M: Plenty of imagination and "feeling" in this book, Awareness: A Journey of Truth. After a few pages I found myself immersed in the story, but it did take a few pages. The back "cast" helped a few times, and though the science fiction part was always a backdrop, the focus was more on the characters and their journey. Highly recommend.

AussieLovesReading97: Manisha Holm's 'Awareness: A Journey of Truth...or Treachery' is a captivating start to The Airon

Chronicles. With its rich exploration of themes like humanity's bond with nature and the quest for inner wisdom, this novel takes readers on an unforgettable journey alongside The 108.

iRayne: This sci-fi book does a great job at staying true to its ideas and not deviating from the promised tone and style. The ensemble cast is interesting, and each of the characters are written in a manner that spells realism, making them infinitely more relatable. The story itself is unique, especially when it comes to the genre, introducing interesting plot points and new ideas. The author's prose is clean and allows the reader to follow the narrative without rereading paragraphs, and the ideas are clear and clearly-presented. A great piece.

Priyanka S: An enthralling exploration of human connection to nature and the unknown. 'Awareness' takes you on a cosmic journey with The 108, weaving a rich tapestry of mystery and cooperation. The story's intricate blend of technology, nature, and inner wisdom creates a compelling narrative that lingers in your thoughts. A thought-provoking and beautifully crafted sci-fi adventure! Highly Recommended!

AllZebras: "Awareness" was different than the standard fantasy scifi. This was a wonderful page-turner that is full of unexpected twists, compassionate characters, and heartwarming moments. I really love a plot that keeps me guessing. I hate predictable plots that you can guess a mile away. I highly recommend this book for readers who love to be challenged.

Curtis M: "Awareness" offers a captivating sci-fi journey that diverges from typical genre tropes. Absent are the familiar warriors and battles, replaced by a narrative focused on the inner struggles of a group of individuals fleeing Earth's encroaching nano-technology. They embark on an intelligent spaceship bound for the enigmatic planet Airon, facing mysteries that spark existential questions about purpose and destiny. The story weaves together themes of humanity's connection to nature, inner wisdom, and co-operation amidst diversity. Notably absent is the typical dystopian backdrop; instead, the narrative emphasizes personal victories and meaningful exploration. The absence of a crew and the unfolding enigmas create an atmosphere of intrigue, leaving readers eager for the subsequent volumes in this trilogy. "Awareness" is a thought-provoking, well-crafted tale that offers a unique and contemplative narrative for sci-fi enthusiasts.

Haku Y: Intriguing plot that works. Book deals with themes of humanity's connection to nature. Makes you think deeply about how we treat our planet. Can't wait to read Book 2.

www.ingramcontent.com/pod-product-compliance
Lightning Source LLC
Chambersburg PA
CBHW070612300726

48975CB00006B/1796